FIRST KILL

Joe made a flying dive at Worthing and grabbed him around the knees just as a bullet whizzed past his head and slammed into the back wall. The two men hit the floor with a grunt as the big man fell backward in surprise.

Mark dropped to the floor below the window, slammed a shell in the rifle and sprang up. Chedos, flattened against the wall, stuck the shotgun barrel out the window and, moving his head around enough to aim, got off a blast at the two Mexicans creeping up to the window.

Mark pushed the sombrero off his head and aimed his rifle at one of the Mexicans trying to reach the cabin from the protection of a small bush in the river. He squeezed the trigger and the Mexican dropped in his tracks, holding the front of his shirt, a look on his face like someone had poured hot water on him.

"Oh, my God," Joe heard Mark say in a sick voice. Joe knew then that the boy had just killed his first man.

ATTENTION: ORGANIZATIONS AND CORPORATIONS

Most HarperPaperbacks are available at special quantity discounts for bulk purchases for sales promotions, premiums, or fund-raising. For information, please call or write:
Special Markets Department, HarperCollins Publishers,
10 East 53rd Street, New York, N.Y. 10022.
Telephone: (212) 207-7528. Fax: (212) 207-7222.

KILLING REVENGE

ERLE ADKINS

HarperPaperbacks
A Division of HarperCollinsPublishers

If you purchased this book without a cover, you should be aware that this book is stolen property. It was reported as "unsold and destroyed" to the publisher and neither the author nor the publisher has received any payment for this "stripped book."

This is a work of fiction. The characters, incidents, and dialogues are products of the author's imagination and are not to be construed as real. Any resemblance to actual events or persons, living or dead, is entirely coincidental.

HarperPaperbacks *A Division of* HarperCollins*Publishers*
10 East 53rd Street, New York, N.Y. 10022

Copyright © 1994 by Erle Adkins
All rights reserved. No part of this book may be used or reproduced in any manner whatsoever without written permission of the publisher, except in the case of brief quotations embodied in critical articles and reviews.
For information address HarperCollins*Publishers*,
10 East 53rd Street, New York, N.Y. 10022.

Cover illustration by Tony Gabriele.

First printing: January 1994

Printed in the United States of America

HarperPaperbacks and colophon are trademarks of HarperCollins*Publishers*

10 9 8 7 6 5 4 3 2 1

1

Autumn had come to the hill country of Texas. The far-reaching and rolling hills and sky-scrapingly high mountains, covered with a sparse amount of grass, but several kinds of trees in different shades of green were embellished in a myriad of colors that would put an artist's palette to shame. Even though the calendar said October, the sun, which had been blazing down on anything that walked, flew and crawled, had lost only a few degrees of heat.

Blooming ocotillo cactus and other flowering plants, which had struggled to add some color to the vastness had finally surrendered the fight to give way and become clumps of dead and dry grass and skeletal branches. The prickly pear cactus changed only a few degrees in its gray-green color from one season to the next. The only thing that seemed unaffected by the changing season was the meandering Limpia Creek and the wind, which never stopped blowing.

The sky was overcast on this particular day. Gray-black clouds hung tenaciously on to the mountain peaks, then turned loose to tease the land with a hint of rain. And from all indications, especially the deep rumbling in the southeast, there just might be a chance for some moisture.

An unusual warm and brisk wind, with the scent of rain in it blew across and caressed the mountains. That and the impending and much-needed rain were the only good things that would happen to the fort and town with the name of Fort Davis, Texas.

Army scout Joe Howard and Colonel Eric McRaney were sitting on the long, wooden bench in the mess hall at Fort Davis. It was a little past noon and the troops who weren't out on patrol had finished eating and had gone about their assigned duties around the sprawling fort that was nestled in a three-quarter circle of granite rocks at the foot of Sleeping Lion Mountain, near Limpia Creek.

The lanky army scout got up, ambled over to the red-hot, potbellied stove, refilled his coffee cup from the much-used black coffeepot, and returned to the table. McRaney shook his head when Joe asked if he wanted a refill.

McRaney stood up and put his hat squarely on his black head. If a ruler had been used to measure the evenness of the placement of the blue campaign hat, embellished with gold braid around the crown, it wouldn't have been off more than a hair. "I think I've reached my limit for the day. I'm beginning to think that coffee makes your hands shake if you drink too much of it."

McRaney held out his long-fingered hands with the nails cut short and even. Joe grinned up at him and shook his head in amusement. The colonel's tanned hands were as steady as a rock. Joe drained his cup, the two men left the mess hall and walked across the dusty parade ground to the colonel's office. Joe hadn't been out on a job in at least a month and knew that his luck wouldn't hold much longer.

"I can't believe how quiet everything has been the past couple of weeks," Joe said, jamming his hands down in his pockets and scuffing his heels in the loose dirt and pebbles as they trudged along.

There hadn't been a wagon train through in almost a month and there hadn't been any trouble with the Indians or Mexican bandits against the stagecoaches coming through. Joe had felt a little guilty, but only a little, when he took his money from the paymaster last Friday. He knew he earned what he made and even more on the other jobs that McRaney always found for him to do.

There wasn't much chance that the sprawling fort would or could ever be overrun since it was surrounded on three sides, south, west, and north with steep, rocky mountains and only open to the east. But he always felt like he was laying his life on the line every time he rode out through the log and rock gate.

"Maybe our luck will hold for a while," McRaney predicted, expelling a long, slow breath and brushing some imaginary dust from the immaculate light blue shirt. Colonel Eric McRaney was probably the only man Joe Howard knew who could stand in the middle of a raging dust storm, and there were certainly more than enough of those in West Texas, and come out with his clothes as clean as they had been when they left the washhouse. His black boots were still shiny even though they'd crossed the dusty parade ground. The crease in the dark blue pants could have been used for a knife. It seemed that dust or dirt were afraid to come near the colonel.

Joe Howard, on the other hand would never pass as a well-dressed man. The well-worn gabardine pants that had been dark brown many years ago were frayed around the cuffs and almost white from so many washings. The tan shirt was soft and comfortable from many wearings and as many washings. No amount of polishing would ever restore the low-heeled boots to anything resembling new. Their only redeeming quality was they felt good on Joe's feet. All in all, Joe Howard looked like he'd been rolling around in the dust or was wearing a dust magnet.

Neither of them knew just how soon what McRaney said would turn out completely opposite.

"I wonder why the Overland Stage is so late?" a big man asked the stage attendant standing beside him in the shade of the porch overhang at Overland Stage Depot in Fort Davis. Irritation was written all over his wide, ruddy, and closely shaved face and in his snapping blue-green eyes. "It should have been here two hours ago. My son is supposed to be on that stage and I have two rooms reserved for us at the Limpia Hotel."

The authoritative tone in his deep voice was supposed to make a difference and it probably would have if he had been in his usual circle of acquaintances. But it didn't make a tinker's rip to Herman Gredes, the stage manager who was leaning lazily against the adobe wall.

Tyler Worthing swatted angrily at the side of his right leg that was the size of a small tree trunk with a shiny, ebony, gold-knobbed walking cane he carried to impress rather than give aid. Good health and a lot of wealth was in his bearing and he was by far the best attired man in front of the stage depot since only he and

Herman Gredes were standing there at that particular moment.

A dark blue gabardine coat and pants fitted the tall, thick body as if they had been made especially for him. The unbuttoned coat revealed a light blue vest with a gold chain looped through one of the buttonholes. A round gold watch hung on one end and a heavy fob on the other.

The man's ruddy complexion was accentuated by a white shirt. A tie tack with a pearl as big as the end of the man's sausage-sized thumb was in the center of a blue-and-white striped tie. A black wool, wide-brimmed hat with a small roll sat on the back of Worthing's head of thick, dark brown hair. He could have shaved in the reflection from his black boots. The way he walked, dressed, and talked shouted money and importance. He was probably used to giving orders and having people jump without any question when he spoke.

As others walked up and began sweating while they waited, his only sign of discomfort was the obvious irritation in the deep frown between his bushy brows and the impatience gleaming in his eyes.

"Oh, anything could've happened, Mr. Worthing," Gredes placated, pushing a wool cap that had been brown a long time ago back on his small head. He squinted an apathetic look up at the big man and sent a thin stream of tobacco juice well away from their feet. He knew that Worthing would jump right down his throat if one drop of the vile-looking stuff hit his boots.

Gredes hooked his skinny thumbs around the green-and-red suspenders holding up his black, baggy pants and shifted the chaw of tobacco that had just about lost its taste several hours ago to the left side of his scraggly, whiskered jaw. He readjusted the cap on his red head, then shifted his washed-out brown eyes away from Worthing, leaned forward from the wall, and looked hard toward the east.

"Art Shives is a good driver," Gredes said, leaning his thin frame back against the wall. "He wouldn't be wasting any time. He'd want to hurry and get here for a drink at the saloon. He must have busted a wheel. That takes a lot of time to fix, you know."

Gredes spat out the wad of tobacco, cut off a fresh plug, put it into his mouth and wallowed it around a few seconds until it was comfortable then began chewing.

"It doesn't take a whole day to change a danged wheel," Worthing argued, wagging his huge head from side to side and pressing his full mouth into a thin line. Contempt was in his gravelly voice. He glanced down at Gredes as if the little man were no more than an ant crawling on the ground and as if he'd just heard the most stupid thing in the world.

"My son is supposed to be on that stage," Worthing continued, a snarl pulling at his mouth. "If anything happens to him, I'm going to hold the stage line directly responsible. It will cost the owners every penny they have!"

Worthing looked around at the small group of people who were listening to see if his threat had impressed any of them. They weren't anymore affected than the stage manager.

Gredes looked down at the sun-baked spot of ground between his scuffed boots as though he'd never seen that particular patch of dirt before. It took a lot of effort for him to hold his thin mouth straight. He wanted to laugh so bad that he had to bite his lower lip to keep from doing it. He knew laughing wouldn't be a good thing to do. The big man had probably never been laughed at in his entire life or at least since he'd reached the two-hundred-pound mark and would no doubt whale the living daylights out of him.

"If Cruz Vega or Benito Juarez are the cause of the delay," Gredes finally said dryly taking a deep breath, then sending a fresh stream of dark brown tobacco juice to the spot between his feet, "you can hold anybody responsible for it that you want to. It would have just about as much effect as me throwing a little, bitty rock out there in the middle of all them boulders." Gredes motioned with his right arm toward the miles and miles of various sized rocks in the vast wasteland.

"I know who Juarez is," Worthing snapped, an angry flush rising from his throat all the way to his hairline. He turned back from looking east and threw Gredes a hard glare. "But who in the devil is Cruz Vega? I've never heard of him."

"Oh, he's just one of them danged greaser bandits who crosses the Rio out of Mexico every now and then when he's broke and comes over here to rob," Gredes replied passively, making a sucking sound with his mouth against his teeth. "As someone of your station in life might know," Gredes went on sarcastically, arching his brows, "there's a lot of wagon trains and stages coming through here from San Antonio and El Paso. The bandits want the money and whatever other valuables are on the travelers. The Indians mostly want the guns and ammunition and really want to drive the whites out. I don't . . ."

Gredes didn't get to finish saying what he didn't want. In a way he was glad when the stillness was broken by the approaching jangle of chains and pounding horses' hooves. Worthing probably wasn't listening to him anyway. Gredes didn't care much for men like Tyler Worthing and was running out of things to say to him. If Worthing's son was on the stage he'd leave soon. But the incoming stage meant that he would have to go to work unloading and then reloading the stage, help the driver change out the horses and help people on the stage.

Gredes forgot all about Tyler Worthing and work as the stage came to a hard, rocking stop in front of them. One of the doors flapped open. Art Shives jumped down from the high seat without bothering to wrap the six reins around the break stick. A wild and terrified expression covered his weathered face.

"Herman, somethin' Godawful has happened!" Shives shouted before his feet hit the ground. Fear was rampant in his blue eyes. Before he could say anything else, Tyler Worthing rushed up to him and grabbed him by the shoulders with his ham-sized fist. Shives was as tall as Worthing's possible six feet two but was at least thirty pounds lighter and looked like a toy in the big man's hands.

"Where's Darius?" Worthing demanded in a roar, his eyes snapping in a combination of rage and worry. "Where's my son? Why are you so late? You should have been here hours ago. It's almost twelve o'clock!"

"Get your damned hands off of me," Shives yelled and glared at Worthing. He put his hands against Worthing's white shirt and shoved roughly out of his grip. "Let go of me, I said!" He winced in pain as he reached up to rub his left shoulder. That's when Gredes saw the red stain all the way down Shives's light brown shirtsleeve.

"What happened to you?" Gredes asked, hurrying over to Shives. "Are you all right? Have you been shot?" He was asking questions so fast that Shives couldn't answer any of them until he slowed down.

"Yeah, I was shot," Shives groaned out in a deep breath. If the pain in his arm hadn't been so excruciating, he would have grinned at the sickening grimace on Gredes's pale face. "But I'll be all right after you dig the bullet out of my arm." He started toward the stage office but Worthing's raging voice stopped him.

"I want to know right now what's happened to my son!" Worthing's eyes were wild and his already huge hands seemed even larger doubled into fists at his side. His mouth was drawn into a tight, white line. "Where is he?"

"Cruz Vega and some of his pepper bellies robbed the stage at about nine o'clock this morning," Shives related before wrinkling up his face in pain. He leaned wearily against the wall, swallowed hard, and pulled in a deep breath. "The only passengers were an old man and a young kid." He stopped and swallowed hard again. He had been going on raw courage and adrenaline and both had just about run out. Just like Worthing's patience. "The old man put up a fight and wouldn't give Vega his watch. Vega killed him. He laughed when he told the old man the time just before he shot him. The old man's body is in the stage. I couldn't bury him by myself."

"Will you stop blubbering about some old dead man, for God's sake," Worthing shouted, his face purple in rage. "What in the devil happened to my son?"

"They took the kid with them," Shives answered simply in a rush of words, then sagged against the adobe wall. His shoulder was hurting too much to be diplomatic.

Worthing's wide face turned almost as white as his shirt at Shives's news and a hard knot worked in both sides of his jaw under thick sideburns. He stared at Shives as though he was something he'd never seen.

"Why did you get shot?" Gredes asked accusingly, switching his gaze from Worthing back to Shives who was obviously in a lot of pain. It was a wonder that Vega hadn't killed him.

"I didn't want to give up the strongbox," Shives answered, running his tongue around his dry lips.

"Did Vega get the strongbox?" Gredes asked, arching his brows.

"Yes," Shives answered meekly, glancing up at Gredes then down at the ground, shaking his head. "They made us stand down on the ground," he finally continued after taking another ragged breath. "I made a mistake in reaching for my gun after they killed the old man. Vega shot me in the shoulder. I guess he thought he'd gotten a better shot and that I was dead when I lay still on the ground. They put the kid on an extra horse. They must have known that someone important was going to be on the stage. Are you Tyler Worthing?"

Shives raised his pain-filled eyes to look at the big man who hadn't taken his gaze from him all the time he'd been explaining what had happened.

"Of course I'm Tyler Worthing," was the big man's sharp reply. Vexation replaced the rage in his blazing eyes under a dark frown. "You should have known who I was when I asked about my son. But why do you want to know who I am?" he barked.

"Just before Vega rode away with the kid," Shives answered, swallowing hard, his legs beginning to sag under him more, "I heard him tell one of his pals that he wished he could see the look on the *mucho rico* gringo's face when he gets the ransom letter."

Without any further comment and without waiting for Worthing to say anything else, Shives stumbled into the stage office and collapsed on a bunk.

Rage, fear, and worry took turns crossing Tyler Worthing's face. He knew he was wasting time trying to get more information out of the wounded man. Actually, if Worthing had been in Shives's worn boots, he would have walked away a lot sooner to get something done about the bullet in his shoulder. Gredes wouldn't be any help either. He had already followed Shives into the office.

"I can see why Geronimo would be on the rampage," Joe Howard said ominously, dropping his lanky frame down on a straight-backed chair in front of McRaney's office and tilting it back against the wall. "He doesn't want outsiders coming through here and messing up his way of life. I know what you're going to say," he hurried on, holding up his right hand, nodding his head forward, hearing McRaney pulling in a short breath and seeing an argument building up on the colonel's lean and clean-shaven face. "I agree that everybody has a right to live where they want but you've got to admit, the Indian has his rights, too. Would you want someone telling you where to live?"

McRaney turned his head slowly to look at Joe. There was an incredulous look in his blue eyes. "Joe, you remind me of a dog I saw in New York about three years ago. It was the ugliest dog I've ever seen." He shook his head remorsefully. "It looked like it had been hit square in the face with a skillet. Its nose was almost flattened under bulging eyes."

Joe knew that McRaney was going to make a point in a roundabout way and that his looks didn't have a thing to do with that point. But he also knew that McRaney would expect an interruption.

Tyler Worthing spun around and swung up on a bay mare with an ease that belied his bulk, pulled her around with a sharp yank on the reins, and turned her down the street toward the sheriff's office.

"This can't be happening to me," he muttered under his breath as he slammed his heels viciously in the horse's side. "I'm Tyler Worthing. I have lots of money and I'm going to buy Butterfield's Overland Stage Line. Things like this just don't happen to people like me."

Sheriff Sam Dusay was sitting in the shade cast by the oblong shadow of the jail, his armchair tilted back against the wall. He never seemed to tire of looking at the magnificent vista that spread out before him, which reached for miles and miles and then some more miles. A wide-brimmed, oval, crowned hat shaded his pale brown eyes from the glare of the sun which had finally broken through the clouds. The land would have to do without rain again. Dusay was using a small knife to clean his fingernails.

Mild curiosity turned his red head when he heard and saw a big, well-dressed man riding a bay mare down the street as fast as the animal could go. People scattered in all directions as the horse thundered past them. The rider hauled roughly back on the reins, pulling the horse to a brutal, hunkering stop before the sheriff.

"I just knew something like this was bound to happen today," Dusay muttered sullenly to the fat, yellow dog dozing on the ground beside his chair. "It's been too quiet for too long." He squinted his eyes, bringing deep wrinkles to the corners and stroked his thick, red, drooping mustache. The dog, disturbed by Dusay's low voice, raised his head long enough to look up at him then go back to sleep without moving another muscle.

There hadn't been any trouble in or around Fort Davis for at least a month. The Indian raids on wagon trains between San Antonio and El Paso had slacked off and the Mexican bandits, usually led by Cruz Vega had left the stagecoaches alone. About the only way that Sheriff Sam Dusay had earned his pay this month was busting up the drunken brawls on Saturday nights down the street at the Desert Rose Saloon.

But from the agitated frown on the big man's sweat-glistening face, Dusay knew that his quiet time had run out. He brought the chair down against the hard-packed ground. The unexpected movement awoke the dog. He jumped up, and tucking his tail between his legs, slunk under the floor.

"Whatever he wants, I'm going to make dang sure he gets it," Dusay decided under his breath. He closed the knife and put it into his pocket. "He's too big to argue with or fight."

Tyler Worthing swung his huge right leg over the horse's back and dismounted. He pounded up the four steps to the plank sidewalk in front of the jail in two long strides. His wild appearance had intensified during the short ride from the stage depot to the jail. In that limited time, a light film of dust had settled over his blue suit and the shine was gone from his black boots.

"I'm Tyler Worthing," he introduced himself without hesitation or an offer to shake hands with Dusay when the sheriff came up on the sidewalk beside him. "I was supposed to meet my son Darius at the stage, which was half a day late. It came in about half an hour ago. Art Shives, the driver, said that my son had been kidnapped by some Mexican bandit named Cruz Vega. I want you to go after him. If you and your deputies had been riding around instead of sitting here in the shade like you had nothing else to do," Worthing rebuked, glaring down at Dusay, "this wouldn't have happened. You should have more control over a situation like this. I thought the sheriff or army was supposed to keep the bandits on the other side of the river."

Dusay watched and listened to Worthing ramble on without comment. He understood all too well why Worthing was upset. But he knew it would be useless and a waste of his time and breath to try and calm this mountain of a man until he ran out of steam and had gotten his anger out of his system. He switched his gaze to the street and then back to Worthing. He'd hoped that the angry man had been a figment of his imagination. But the bulk of wrath was still standing there and glaring down at him. Fire was almost coming out of his eyes and it wouldn't take much for him to blow his stack.

There was a tolerant, almost blank expression on Dusay's lean face as he looked up at Worthing. He would have been all over the man, no matter how big he was if he hadn't mentioned his son being kidnapped somewhere in the insult. He and his wife Lois had lost a two-year-old son to pneumonia three years ago. Having an idea how Worthing was feeling was the only reason that Dusay didn't pop him right in the face. He saw that Worthing's huge hands were doubled into tight fists at his side. But Sam Dusay had a badge pinned to his black shirt. That was probably the only thing holding Worthing in check.

"Mr. Worthing," Dusay finally said politely after he'd batted his eyes a couple of times and taking a long, deep breath, "why don't you calm down, come into my office, and tell me about this. There's no point in us standing out here."

Dusay was mindful of his patronizing tone and would have gotten as mad as a wet cat if someone had used it on him. And from the irate glare in Worthing's blue-green eyes, Dusay knew that he wasn't too crazy about it either. He guessed that the big man hadn't been talked down to in his life or at least since he'd passed the six foot mark and that had happened several years ago.

"Sheriff, apparently you don't have a gnat's idea who I am," Worthing accused snidely, pride and egotism in his deep voice after he had followed Dusay into the jailhouse and the sheriff had closed the door behind them.

"Mr. Worthing, it doesn't matter to me if you're Robert E. Lee's first cousin," Dusay said flatly, cocking his brows and giving Worthing a level look. He sat down in a straight-backed chair behind the desk and breathed a little better with something solid between him and Worthing even if the desk was cluttered. A low, oblong cast-iron stove angled out from the right front corner of the office. Half a dozen sticks of wood were in a box on the floor beside it. A filing cabinet, with the top drawer open and stuffed with papers was in the opposite corner. A gun rack with three rifles and two shotguns was fastened to the wall behind the desk. A door between the filing cabinet and gun rack would open up to six, cramped cells in the back.

Dusay dropped down in the chair. From this vantage point he would be able to see Worthing and the desk would offer a little protection if the big man took a notion to come at him. And it wouldn't take much provocation since the man was so upset and rightly so, over his son's kidnapping. Dusay didn't want to antagonize Worthing, but he wasn't going to be intimidated by him either. He wasn't paid enough for that.

"The only thing that I've heard so far that I consider important," Dusay continued, pursing his lips, "is that your son has been kidnapped. Do you know who did it? Do you know why?"

Tyler Worthing hadn't been talked to in such a rude manner by anyone as insolent and brash as Sam Dusay in a long time. A red-angered hue raced from his thick neck, all over his face and up into his hairline. His eyes flashed and he took a threatening step toward the sheriff who was half his size and about five years younger than his forty-five. He stopped suddenly in his tracks when he realized what that action would get him.

Sam Dusay hadn't been born yesterday and knew exactly what Tyler Worthing was thinking and what the purposeful step meant. "Now, we can be civilized about this, Mr. Worthing," Dusay cautioned, lowering his head but looking straight at Worthing. There was a warning in his voice as he eased back in the chair. "Or it can get nasty. Just remember who's wearing the badge." He tapped the piece of tin on his shirt.

A thick silence hung over the jail as the two men tried to stare the other down. The threatening glare in Worthing's eyes began wavering first and a lot of the tension left his broad shoulders. He realized that Dusay wasn't intimidated by him and that he'd better calm down if he was going to get any help. If he threatened Dusay, the sheriff just might shoot him and he could lawfully do it. Reaching behind him, he pulled the matching armchair nearer the desk and slowly lowered his huge body down into it. The chair actually groaned under his ponderous weight.

Dusay felt a whole lot better when he and Worthing were finally at eye level. If the big man had come at him, he would have had no other choice but to shoot him. There was no way he could have won in a fistfight. He would have been like a rabbit in a wolf's mouth.

"Now, what's all this about your son being kidnapped?" Dusay asked, taking a long breath. He rested his elbows on the arms of the chair, peaked his long fingers, and looked at the angry man who had begun relaxing when he had pointed out who was in charge. "How do you know that he was kidnapped and why would he be kidnapped?" The questions were repetitive but stood a better chance of being answered now.

Tyler Worthing up until now was used to having people jump when he snapped his fingers and gave an order. He was even more irritated at the obviously unimpressed man watching him and was uncertain how to answer the question. He looked around the office to give himself time to calm down. He knew it wouldn't do any good to lose his temper now. He didn't actually see the gun rack behind the desk or the wood-burning stove at the opposite side of the room. An eight-point rack of horns used for a hat rack didn't register on him either.

"Darius was kidnapped because of who I am," Worthing finally said egotistically, throwing Dusay a castigating look. "I'm planning on buying the Overland Stage Line. I wanted to see if keeping this section of it going would be worth my time and money. I wanted Darius to come from Pecos, here to Fort Davis and then go on to El Paso to check it out for me. I've been to Brownsville on business and decided to meet him here for his birthday tomorrow before he went on to El Paso. I can make a lot of money with that stage line, if it's for sale," he continued to the disgruntled look on the sheriff's face. "There's nothing wrong with making money. You could do the same thing if you had the inclination and ambition."

Dusay knew Worthing was right. The big man wasn't the first one since the beginning of time who had heard of a golden opportunity and taken advantage of it. He decided to let Worthing's insult go for now. This conversation wasn't over by a long shot. He'd still get the chance to put Worthing in his place.

"Where and when was your son kidnapped?" Dusay asked, shifting his position in the chair. When he saw a knot standing out under the man's jaw-length sideburns, he knew Worthing wasn't used to being questioned.

"How in the devil would I know where he was kidnapped?" Worthing bellowed, his nostrils flaring, eyes almost wild. His harsh voice bounded off the walls.

Dusay couldn't help cringing.

"According to the stage driver," Worthing continued, breathing hard, "it happened early this morning. If I had been on the stage, by God, it wouldn't have happened." He glared at Dusay. "If you'd had some deputies riding around the way you should, it certainly wouldn't have happened. I'm going to hold you, and the stage line responsible for my son's well-being until he's found."

Sheriff Sam Dusay was positive that if he didn't do something with this man soon, like take the blame for his son's disappearance, or lock him in a cell, that he was going to be forced to shoot him. He'd had all of Tyler Worthing's insults he could tolerate, he wasn't paid nearly enough for this, and his patience had just run out. But there had to be another way to handle the situation and avoid a fight. There was no doubt that he would lose in a fight with the man. One swat of those big hands would have him talking to dead relatives!

"Mr. Worthing," Dusay began candidly, "in the first place, I don't have 'some deputies.' I only have one and Carl Leahey is at home with a busted leg. He got it when a drunk threw a chair at him in the Desert Rose Saloon last week."

Worthing leaned forward, braced his hands on the desk, and stared at Dusay. "How can you get anything done by yourself?" he asked in dismay, a deep frown creasing his wide forehead. He seemed to mellow some. When Dusay only stared placidly at him, Worthing leaned back in the chair.

"I do the best I can," Dusay answered, shrugging his shoulders. He hoped that since a little of Worthing's hostility had abated, he could get a little more information from him. It was worth a try. "Did Shives know who took your son?" Dusay asked quickly. He stood up, walked around to the front of the desk, and sat down on the corner. He felt better being able to look down at the big man.

"Yes," Worthing answered, turning sideways in the chair. "He said it was a Mexican bandit named Cruz Vega. He said they shot him, after they had killed an old man, thought he was dead, and then laughed at how much I would pay to get Darius back. He said he heard the Mexican say that he'd send a ransom note to the sheriff here in Fort Davis in a little while."

Sam Dusay had always wanted a little more money in his pockets than he had right then. But as he sat listening to Tyler Worthing talk, he realized that if he had enough money to buy ammunition for his Colt .38 and Winchester, buy coffee and a good meal when he was hungry and stay in a nice hotel when he and his wife traveled, buy new clothes every now and then, that would be enough.

Dusay's life had been threatened more times than he could remember. But it was because of *what* he was instead of *who* he was and money had nothing to do with it. But it was easy to see that money, and a lot of it was the cause of Tyler Worthing's trouble right now. He didn't envy the big man at all. Chances were, his son was already dead.

Dusay's brows shot up in surprise when Worthing mentioned Cruz Vega. The Mexican was only slightly less known for his thieving ways along both sides of the border than Geronimo was for his raids on wagon trains and stagecoaches throughout the border states.

It was reputed that Vega traveled with no less than ten men and Dusay knew that getting Darius Worthing back would be no easy thing.

"Mr. Worthing," Dusay began dolefully, expelling a long breath, slapping his hands down against his legs, and standing up. He went back around the desk to be well out of the big man's way when he told him what he had to. "Cruz Vega knows this part of the country a lot better than I do. He was born in Lajitas. The only thing I can suggest for you to do is wait until his note arrives and see what he wants you to do. I couldn't go after Vega even if I had the men, without knowing where he is. It would be very foolish," Dusay hurried on when he saw Worthing take a long breath to argue, "to try and find him. Vega could hide anywhere in this country. Even if we found their tracks, with as many men as Vega has, your son could have been taken anywhere."

Dusay knew that Worthing was doing all he could to hold himself in check and that it wouldn't last long. "I know the wait won't be easy," he continued. He was going to try and appeal to Worthing's practical side. "We're not that far from Mexico. I couldn't go over there as a sheriff. I wouldn't have any authority. And, I can't leave town. The soldiers from Fort Davis can't cross the border either if you're thinking about going over there. I . . ." Dusay snapped his mouth shut on the rest he was going to say and a twinkling began in his tired eyes as an idea formed in his head. He shifted his eyes around the small office and finally nodded his head slowly in satisfaction.

"What?" Worthing prompted impatiently, leaning forward in the chair, expectation in his eyes. He gripped the arms of the chair so tightly that his knuckles were white.

"I don't know why I didn't think of this sooner,"

Dusay said, shaking his head in disgust, pulling his mouth to one side. "I know just the man who can help you." A diabolical grin began slowly at the corner of his mouth and was soon a full-blown smile. He stood up and started toward the door, thinking that Worthing would be right on his heels.

"I hope this man isn't as lily-livered and yellow as you've been about going after my son," Worthing said in a heavy, sarcastic voice, heaving his bulk up from the chair.

Dusay was already at the door, his hand on the wooden latch when Worthing's castigation stopped him. He turned slowly around, twin knots standing out in his jaws. He gritted his teeth to give himself a little time to really think about what he wanted to say.

"Mr. Worthing," Dusay's voice was flat and level, "the only thing yellow about me is the piss-stained drawers I wear. Now," he blinked his eyes quickly and allowed the cunning smile to ease across his face, "if you want me to help you, shut up and come on."

Tyler Worthing had never been spoken to by such an insolent man as Sheriff Sam Dusay. Shock was the only thing that kept him from doing bodily harm to the sheriff with his hands. But he knew that wouldn't do because if he started toward him, the sheriff would shoot him!

So, keeping his mouth shut, Worthing followed Dusay out the door and down the plank sidewalk to the Desert Rose Saloon.

Dusay pushed open the bat wings on well-oiled hinges. Worthing was so close on his heels that he almost knocked him over. Beer, smoke, and body scents permeated the air. A mirror that had had a rag passed over it earlier ran the length of the bar. Along the bottom of the bar was a scuffed, brass rail. Rinky-tink music was coming from an upright piano played by a tall, slender young man with plastered-down black hair.

"Well, if it isn't Sheriff Sam Dusay," a woman's drawling voice called out in a friendly greeting. The voice came from a woman sitting on a tall stool at the end of the bar. She was counting money into a green metal box.

"Well, if it isn't Queenie Jeanie Orms," Dusay said in like tone and grinned as he walked across the saloon toward her. Worthing couldn't have been any closer to Dusay if he'd been in tow. Dusay reached out and patted Jeanie's rosy round cheek. "Where's Betty Young?" The two cousins owned the Desert Rose Saloon and always had good beer and whiskey that wasn't watered down and they never let things get out of hand. There had been only a few times when he was called to come and settle things.

"She went down to Billy Leon's Cafe," Jeanie answered, sliding off the stool to go behind the bar. Her bright blue taffeta, calf-length dress swished over several petticoats as she moved. Matching blue ribbons were around her neck and twined in her short, curly red hair. "She's going to bring back lunch. Do you and your friend want a beer?" Her blue eyes twinkled in mischief.

"Yeah," Dusay answered, looking around at Worthing. The big man just nodded. Worthing had been silent all of this time and Dusay knew it was taking a lot of effort for him to do it. If he had been in Worthing's boots he would have been champing at the bit to hurry and get things done. Dusay *was* in a hurry to get Worthing out of his hair. He looked around the saloon and shook his head in disappointment. It was a little past noon and the Desert Rose was almost empty. Jeanie walked to the tap, filled two mugs with beer, and returned to Dusay and Worthing.

KILLING REVENGE / 23

Four men, counting Dusay and Worthing were at the bar. Two men were at a corner table playing a slow game of dominos. One man was playing solitaire at another table and from his disgruntled look, he was losing.

Dusay heard the bat wings slam open against the wall and looked up to see who was coming in. Betty Young had shouldered open one of the bat wings because her hands were filled with two plates covered with red-checked napkins. She hurried forward so the bat wings wouldn't hit her in the backside. "That was close," she said jokingly, throwing a look over her shoulder. She walked to the end of the bar where Jeanie, Dusay, and Worthing were standing.

"Hello, sheriff," she greeted, putting the plates down and removing the napkins. "If I'd known you and your friend were going to be here right now, I would've brought more food." A teasing smile was in her brown eyes. She pushed her wind-blown and short, gray-streaked hair back from her face, then removed a light green cloak from her shoulders, revealing a pink, taffeta dress trimmed in black.

"It does smell good," Dusay said, looking down at meat loaf, mashed potatoes, and corn bread. "Has Bruell Cannon been in here yet?" He drained the beer mug and looked sheepishly at Jeanie for a refill. He still couldn't believe that Tyler Worthing had been so quiet all of this time. The big man had allowed him to do all the talking while he drank his beer. He wondered what Worthing was planning.

"No," Jeanie answered, returning with the beer and shaking her head. She took forks from the box under the bar and handed one to Betty. Jeanie cut off a piece of meat loaf, put it into her mouth, and swallowed before continuing. "He's late today," she finally said, dabbing at her mouth with the napkin. "By this time, he's already had at least two beers and's working on a third."

"That man must have a hollow leg to hold all of the beer he drinks," Betty remarked, rolling her eyes toward the ceiling. She took a bite of corn bread and swallowed. "He's good for business, though. If we had two more customers like him, Jeanie and I would be rich enough to hire someone to run the saloon for us."

Almost as though designed by Providence, the bat wings slammed back against the wall and heavy steps stomped across the wooden floor toward the bar. Sheriff Dusay turned as a man not quite as big as Worthing stopped at the bar next to him.

"Jeanie," the newcomer said, lowering his hands easily down on the bar before him. "I'm behind on my beers and my throat is as dry as the street outside." Around his right hand was a wide, clean, white bandage. The first two fingers on his left hand were wrapped in individual bandages. Pain was evident in his blue eyes.

"Bruell, why are you so late?" Jeanie asked, concern in her eyes and voice when she saw the bandages.

"Oh, he probably got involved with Polly Bullock down at Billy Leon's Cafe," Betty accused, a smile pulling at her full mouth, "and she hit him with a hot pan."

"I wish that was true," Cannon replied, scratching the thick, black beard on his broad face with the little finger of his left hand as he watched Jeanie pull the tap, fill a mug, and set it before him. He picked it up with the heels of both hands and drained it before he continued: "I just come from Dr. Wetherby's. I burned my hands on the anvil at the smithy a while ago." He held up both hands for all of them to see then looked at Dusay. "I came by the stage depot to see if some nails I was expecting had come in." He licked the foam from his mustache. "I heard the stage had been ambushed by that chili belly Cruz Vega." Dislike was in his voice and his blue eyes smouldered. He tapped the empty mug.

"Your turn," Jeanie said, arching her brows and pulling her mouth into a grin when he looked at Betty.

"My pleasure," Betty said smugly, standing up and going behind the bar to refill Cannon's mug. "We're here to serve . . . and serve and serve," she muttered under her breath.

Tyler Worthing shifted his ponderous weight from one foot to the other and Dusay knew that he was getting impatient and thinking they were wasting too much time.

"Sheriff, do we have to stand here and listen to a replay of the morning's happenings?" Worthing asked, tapping Dusay on the shoulder.

"Mr. Worthing," Dusay said, shaking his head and stepping back, "this is Bruell Cannon. I was hoping he would be able to help you. But since his hands are burned, that's going to be impossible."

"What did you want me to do?" Cannon asked, carefully picking up the full beer mug and taking a long swig.

"Cruz Vega kidnapped Mr. Worthing's son," Dusay said and watched Cannon's blue eyes widen. "He was on that stage. I had hoped that you'd be able to go after him."

"Oh, you poor man," Jeanie said sympathetically. "I hope your son's all right. I'd like to get my hands on Vega!" She wrapped her right hand around her left in a tight grip.

"Someone should have killed that worthless piece of border trash a long time ago," Betty said, her eyes sparkling in anger.

"Maybe I should hire you two ladies to go after my son," Worthing suggested, rancor in each word.

"Are you puttin' up a reward fer yer kid?" one of the men standing beside Cannon asked.

"Well, I . . ." Worthing began but Dusay elbowed him in the ribs.

"Mr. Worthing hasn't decided what he's going to do yet," Dusay interrupted, getting a hostile glare from Worthing.

"I wish I could help," Cannon said, shaking his head apologetically. "But I couldn't get much done with these bad hands."

Disappointment was alive in both Dusay and Worthing's eyes. "Thanks anyway, Cannon," Dusay said, taking money from his pocket and putting it down on the bar for his and Worthing's beers. Time was wasting and he knew Worthing was anxious to get something done. He didn't blame him and felt sorry for him. Dusay knew he wouldn't want to be in Worthing's made-to-order boots for all of the whiskey and beer in the Desert Rose.

"Why don't you go over to Fort Davis?" Cannon suggested, resting his arm on the bar as Dusay and Worthing turned to leave. "A patrol could look for the boy as long as he hasn't been taken over into Mexico."

That sounded so simple to everyone who was listening. A patrol *could* search for the boy as long as he *was* on this side of the border. But it would be a waste of time if Vega planned to take him over into Mexico.

"We won't know exactly where Darius is being taken," Worthing said, adjusting the black hat on his head, "until the ransom note comes."

"Let's hurry back to the jail," Dusay suggested, narrowing his eyes thoughtfully and frowning.

"Why?" Worthing asked, giving Dusay a sharp look. He knew the sheriff was stalling so he wouldn't have to get involved. "The stage driver said that a note wouldn't be delivered for a little while."

"That may be just what Vega wants you to believe," Dusay said shrewdly, starting toward the door. "He'll have you so worried that you'll do anything he tells you when the note does come." He caught Worthing by the arm, started walking toward the door. He was surprised when Worthing followed without protest.

"Why did you want me to hush when he asked if I was going to put up a reward?" Worthing asked sharply as soon as they were out on the sidewalk. The bat wings were still flapping.

Dusay couldn't believe that Worthing had asked such a stupid question. Worthing seemed smarter than that.

"Paying a ransom is one thing," Dusay retorted, wanting to slug the imposing man. "Paying a reward is something else. You'd have . . ." he raised his voice when Worthing started to interrupt and probably argue with him. "You'd have every man and his cousin out looking for your son. Somebody, and that includes your son, could end up getting killed."

"I guess you're right," Worthing relented, expelling a deep breath.

Dusay was in a hurry to get away from this sordid mess with Tyler Worthing. He felt bad about the boy's abduction, especially by a worthless bastard like Cruz Vega. But Worthing was going to drive him crazy if he kept arguing with him. If a note had arrived while they'd been gone from the jail, it would get Worthing out of his hair that much sooner.

The two men exchanged only a few words as they walked back to the jail. Fort Davis wasn't all that big and it didn't take long to reach it. It was on the corner up from the saloon and next to the general store.

Clyde Montrose, owner of the Mountain General Mercantile was sitting in front of the store in an armchair tilted back against the wall. His wide-brimmed and oval-crowned hat was pulled low on his narrow forehead, shading his squinted eyes from the brightness but enjoying the sun's warm rays.

"Clyde, is that all you have to do?" Dusay chided good naturedly as he and Worthing approached the man, his arms dangling loosely over the side of the chair.

"Yep," Montrose replied, bringing the chair down with a hard bang against the narrow, plank sidewalk. He pushed the hat back with a thumb under the brim and frowned dubiously up at the two men. He blinked his eyes a couple of times and did a double take when his eyes focused on the big man standing beside the sheriff.

"Are you Tyler Worthing?" Montrose asked, a deep frown pulling between his thin brows.

Dusay's brown eyes widened in surprise and his mouth, under the drooping, red mustache was gaping. How did Montrose know Tyler Worthing? When, and how, had he had time to even hear about Worthing when he'd been with him for at least half an hour.

"Yes, I am," Worthing answered arrogantly, expectation gleaming in his eyes again. "Why do you ask? Have you heard something about my son? Do you know where he is?" His questions were coming so fast that Montrose had to hold up his hand to stop him so he could answer.

"A young Mex kid, wearing enough guns to start a one-man war, put a piece of paper under the jail door," Montrose said, jerking his thumb to the left in the direction of the jail. He squinted a look up at Worthing then glanced at Dusay.

"When did this happen?" Dusay asked, switching a look from Montrose to Worthing and back. Maybe the ransom note or some instructions had arrived from Vega and his part in this would soon be over.

"Oh, about ten minutes ago," Montrose replied, rolling his lips in against his teeth. He crossed his long legs, tilted the chair back against the wall, and looked up at Dusay. "I thought at first that he was going to give me the note. But instead, he just bent over quick, shoved it under the door, said it was for Tyler Worthing, got back on his horse, and rode away like he was on fire."

"Did you see which way he went?" Dusay asked, knowing that his part in this situation *wasn't* going to be over as soon as he'd hoped. If the kid was still in town, Worthing would insist that he look for him.

"Yep," Montrose replied, taking the makings of a cigarette from a pocket on his blue and green checked shirt to roll it. "North," he continued after striking a match with a thumbnail and putting it to the end of the cigarette. "On a roan mare."

"Thanks," Dusay said in a sharp voice. He started toward the jail. Worthing started around Dusay and Dusay had to push ahead of Worthing to beat him opening the door. Bending down, he picked up the twice-folded piece of yellow paper and handed it to Worthing. His name was printed on one side.

Worthing jerked the paper from Dusay's hand. He was in such a hurry to read the note that he tore off a corner of the page. He ran his eyes quickly over the page and his face turned white. He handed it to Dusay to read after muttering a low oath under his breath.

The note, written in a readable hand in pencil and in English was short and to the point:

Worthing: I have your son Darius. Leave thousand American dollars no pesos under rock north side of abandoned cabin in Rio Grande River in Caldelaria.

Four days to do this or son will die. Do not send posse or soldiers.

The note was signed with a large C.V.

"Vega must think you're some kind of a rich man," Dusay said, arching his brows as he looked up from the note.

"I am a rich man," Worthing snapped belligerently. "Look," he said, mellowing a little when Dusay threw him a threatening glare, "we know which direction the boy was riding. We even know what he was riding. All we have to do is follow him. We can find him in a little while. What are you waiting for? Let's go get him!"

Dusay could understand Worthing's concern but he seemed to have more pocket sense than common sense.

"Just because we know which direction the kid went," Dusay said pragmatically, expelling an irritated breath, "doesn't mean we'll know where he'll end up. Having that note doesn't even mean that he was one of Cruz Vega's men. He could have been paid to deliver it. He could still be here in town."

Disappointment, but mostly disgust put a cold look on Worthing's wide face. Dusay really felt sorry for him, but there was nothing he could do.

"Mr. Worthing," Dusay said in a sympathetic voice, "as I told you before, I can't go after your son. Maybe Joe Howard, the army scout at Fort Davis can help you. I hear he's good at his job. I'm very sorry."

A purple hue began creeping up Worthing's face. Dusay thought for a second that he was going to hit him. But Worthing only glared at him for a second.

"You're the sorriest excuse for a sheriff that I've ever seen!" Worthing said in a low voice. His eyes were blazing blue green fire as he stomped out of the jail.

2

"Well, thanks a lot," Joe Howard said in a singsong voice, mock indignation and a twinkle in his brown eyes. He removed the black, flat-crowned hat, pushed his brown hair back from his lean face, and replaced the hat. "I don't believe I've ever had my face compared to a skillet-slapped dog before." Joe pulled down the corners of his mouth and shook his head in desolation. As Joe had expected, McRaney threw back his head and his deep laughter boomed out across the vast wasteland.

"Now that's not what I meant and you know it," McRaney said after regaining his composure. "That dog had hold of an old rag. He wouldn't let go of it until his owner hit him with a stick. That's how you are about the Indians. You won't let go of that idea for anything."

Joe and McRaney had had this same discussion, not argument, about the Indians for as long as Joe had been a scout at Fort Davis. Joe believed that the Indians were being mistreated by being pushed back and forced to give up land that had been theirs since creation. McRaney, along with a host of others, believed that there was enough land for everyone and that the Indians should give a little. Joe kept insisting that the Indians had already given more than most people would have.

"Are you going to hit me in the face with a stick?" Joe asked, wrinkling up his forehead and squinting a look sideways at McRaney. He held up his hands in exaggerated defense.

"No, I'm not going to hit you in the face with a stick," McRaney replied, smirking and shaking his head slowly. "Sometimes I want to kick you in the . . ."

Joe would never know exactly where McRaney wanted to kick him, although he had a pretty good idea. Whatever McRaney was about to say was cut short by a big, well-dressed man riding a bay mare as fast as the long legs would go through the fort's gate.

"What do you suppose is his trouble?" McRaney muttered, standing up and walking in long strides to the top step.

"I don't know," Joe said, shaking his head dismally. "But for God's sake, don't argue with him," he advised in a tight voice. "He's too big for either of us to fight."

Way down in the pit of his stomach, Joe knew that whatever was troubling the big man would end up involving him. It always seemed, especially when everything was going along nicely, something happened to cut into that niceness. McRaney looked down at Joe and grinned.

The big man pulled the horse to a hard, vicious, and hunkering stop before McRaney's office. He swung down and pounded up the four steps in long strides. His obviously expensive clothes were dusty and there was a wild look in his eyes.

"I'm Tyler Worthing," he introduced, impatience in

his voice and without offering to shake hands with McRaney. "Sheriff Dusay in town said that someone here might be able to help me." He switched his frantic gaze from the militarily dressed man over to the plainclothes man still sitting in the chair tilted back against the wall. "You must be Joe Howard."

"You're right," Joe acknowledged, bringing the chair away from the wall and sitting up straight. "But why must I be Joe Howard?"

"Because you aren't dressed like a soldier," Worthing snapped, "and I'd only be wasting my time in talking to him." He jerked his head toward McRaney. "He or the army can't help me."

"I don't know so much about that," McRaney refuted, shaking his head and giving Worthing a stiff glare. "This man is under my command and doesn't do anything unless I tell him. Tell me what's wrong and I'll decide if the army can help you."

Joe wanted to laugh as the two egotistical men tried to impress each other with their positions in life.

"My fifteen-year-old son Darius was kidnapped from a stagecoach this morning by Cruz Vega," Worthing said bluntly, his eyes flashing. "Here's the ransom note." He shoved the yellow paper at McRaney. The colonel took it and looked down at it. A stillness settled over his lean face. "The stage driver was shot pretty bad." Worthing continued, switching his impatient gaze from McRaney to Joe, "and an old man was killed."

Anger shot through Joe like a spring flood through the mountain canyons. He knew he should let McRaney handle this for now but he might as well go on and put in his two cents worth.

"Do you mean to tell me," Joe grated, standing up, "that the sheriff didn't offer to do anything even though he knew someone had been killed?"

"Well, he . . ." Worthing began but stopped when McRaney interrupted.

"Why don't we go into my office and talk about this?" McRaney suggested, handing the note over to Joe. He turned to go inside.

"While we're talking," Worthing shouted, grabbing McRaney's arm and spinning him around, "that Mexican scum could be taking Darius to Mexico."

Oh, my Lord, Joe thought agonizingly to himself. Tyler Worthing doesn't know what he just did. Colonel Eric McRaney might appear to be easygoing but that was only superficial.

"Mr. Worthing," McRaney said in a seemingly calm voice, looking down at the ham-sized, restraining hand on his arm, "I can appreciate your feelings, but if you don't want to spend the next month in the guardhouse, you'd better get your hand off me."

A grin tweaked at Worthing's mouth. He thought McRaney was joking with him. Joe could have told him that McRaney rarely joked. "Colonel, there's no way for you to know who I am," Worthing said obstinately, although he did ease his hand from McRaney's arm.

"Mr. Worthing," McRaney said dryly, "I don't care who you are. The only thing about you that interests me is you said that Cruz Vega had kidnapped your son."

"Why, I . . ." Worthing began, glaring at McRaney.

"All right, you two," Joe interjected, taking the note from McRaney. "This won't get us anywhere."

"You're right," Worthing agreed, glancing from McRaney to Joe and back to McRaney. "I'm sorry." He really wasn't but realized that McRaney was a man he couldn't intimidate with threats or influence.

McRaney gave Worthing an indulgent look and started into his office. Worthing followed without saying anything. Joe read Vega's note as he followed behind Worthing and his heart began pounding faster. He'd been right in assuming that he was about to go somewhere. It was only a matter of time before McRaney told him.

No words passed between the three men until they were in the neatly arranged office. A rebel flag hung on one wall over a safe and an American flag hung on the opposite wall. A wide window gave a view of the Davis Mountains in the distance. A wood-burning stove stood in the far corner and at the opposite end was a four-pronged antler hat rack. Three chairs were in a semicircle in front of the desk and one was by the window.

McRaney walked around the desk and sat down in a wooden, swivel armchair. Worthing sat down in the armchair in front of the oak desk. It actually groaned under his weight. Joe pulled a straight-backed chair over against the wall and sat down. He had a good view of both men without having to turn his head.

"Why did the sheriff tell you to come here?" Joe asked, folding the note and crossing his legs. "Didn't he know anybody in town who would go after your son? Couldn't you hire someone to do it?"

"You can't be serious," Worthing shot back, one argument forgotten as he launched into another one. A deep frown pulled between his thick brows. The corners of his mouth turned down in a snarl. "The sheriff did know a man named Bruell Cannon who he thought would do it. But Cannon had burned his hands at the blacksmith shop and couldn't go. Dusay said he couldn't do anything, especially if Darius has been taken to Mexico. He said his jurisdiction ended at the river. I think he's just too scared to tackle Cruz Vega."

Rage began blazing in Worthing's blue green eyes and he slammed his ham-sized fist down against his thigh. Joe was glad that Worthing wasn't beating on him. If that had been his leg on the receiving end of Worthing's fist he wouldn't be able to walk for a week.

"Sheriff Sam Dusay isn't afraid of anything," McRaney said in the sheriff's defense and watching the big man with hot intensity. "He's a good sheriff but what he said is true. He can't go into Mexico lawfully and he can't leave town unless it's unofficial. The people of Fort Davis are his first priority. The army has no more jurisdiction in Mexico than the sheriff would," McRaney pointed out truthfully. He stood up and walked over to the open window. A warm breeze, with the hint of rain in it came through the opening. It was a good thing that the colonel had put that much extra distance between him and the fire-breathing man who was glaring at him with wild and blazing eyes.

"Are you going to stand there and tell me that you're afraid to go after Darius, too?" Worthing bellowed. He jumped to his feet and started around the opposite side of the desk toward McRaney. Shock raced across McRaney's clean-shaven face. He couldn't believe that Worthing had the guts or nerve to come at him again.

"Hold it right there," Joe called out in a low, level voice, trying to hold his face straight at the strange-sounding name of the man's son. He stood up and rested his hand on the handle of the Colt .45. Worthing turned his head and stopped when he saw intent in Joe's eyes. "You didn't let the colonel finish what he was going to say," Joe cautioned, tilting his head to one side and still holding Worthing's glare.

It was a foregone conclusion that Joe Howard was going to be sent to Candelaria after Tyler Worthing's son. But would that happen before or after Worthing and McRaney got into a fight? Although it wouldn't be an actual fight. Worthing was big enough and strong enough to take McRaney out with one whack. McRaney's only choice would be to shoot him.

"I was going to say that I wouldn't be afraid to walk through hell with the devil," McRaney said in a cold voice, but with gratitude in his eyes when he glanced from Worthing to Joe. "But even though the army can't do anything except follow Cruz Vega to the middle of the river, we can send a civilian over into Mexico and get in contact with the Federalies and hope that they can track Vega down." He looked at Worthing with arched brows.

Uh, oh, Joe thought even before McRaney turned his head slowly back and looked at him with a sly grin in his blue eyes. Here it comes. He's going to tell me that all I have to do is ride down to the Rio Grande River, cross into Mexico, find a regiment of Federalies, and let them take it from there. It never fails! No matter how grim and dangerous a situation might appear, it always sounds so simple when Colonel Eric McRaney explains it. Then when everything fell apart, Joe ended up to his neck in trouble.

Joe knew that he would only be a whiff away from getting killed if he tried to interfere with Cruz Vega's attempt to extort money from Tyler Worthing for the return of his son. In all likelihood, the boy was already dead. What was the boy's name? Darius! Why would parents give their son such a ridiculous name? It should be something simple like Joe.

Joe Howard knew beyond a shadow of doubt that he was going to be the one who would "get in touch" with the Federalies in Mexico. But he wasn't about to volunteer! He knew that McRaney always enjoyed sending him on the little "jaunts" as he sometimes called the jobs that a soldier couldn't do. And Tyler Worthing would enjoy offering him money to go after his son. Men of Worthing's character always got a kick out of waving money at someone.

Joe had never seen Cruz Vega but had heard about him. The Mexican was reputed to be as crafty as a fox in avoiding capture by the U. S. Army or the Mexican Federalies. There wasn't a bounty on him but nobody on either side of the border would be sad if he was dead. Everyone would feel safer.

As Joe and Worthing kicked through the dust toward the corral, Joe wondered how Vega had known that Darius Worthing would be on that particular stage? Obviously it wasn't by accident that the boy had been taken. Joe had read the ransom note. It had been addressed to Tyler Worthing and signed with CV and the son had been mentioned by name. And what a name! Darius Worthing.

Even if Worthing's name hadn't been mentioned, it would have been easy to guess that the boy was the son of a wealthy family by the way he would have been dressed. And undoubtedly someone of Tyler Worthing's bearing would make sure his family dressed befitting his station in life.

"Are you ready, Serge?" Joe asked, swinging the saddle over the gray blanket already on the seal black gelding he'd ridden for almost longer than he could remember. The bridle jangled in his hand as the horse seemed to nod his head in answer to Joe's question. Joe led Serge over to the barracks, went inside, put two changes of clothes, ammunition for the Colt .45 and Henry rifle into one saddlebag, folded a knee-length sheepskin coat into the other bag, and went back outside. He wasn't sure if he would need the coat but at this time of year in the mountainous country of West Texas, anything could happen.

Worthing was waiting impatiently for him at the hitch rail. Joe looked past Worthing toward McRaney's office. He wasn't surprised that McRaney had gone back inside. McRaney had walked with the two men out onto the porch and shook hands with both of them. From past experience, Joe knew there would be no need for him to return to Fort Davis until Darius Worthing was found, no matter how long it might take. But anything could happen, especially when greedy bandits and a lot of money were involved. And a thousand dollars was a lot of money by anyone's way of counting.

"What are you going to do first?" Worthing asked, swinging his log-sized leg over the horse's back and settling his huge body down on the expensive, hand-tooled saddle that was almost lost under him. He was a little more relaxed now that he knew that something was actually going to be done to find his missing son since McRaney had more or less ordered Joe to help him. The intense rage had left his eyes and only natural worry pulled two deep lines between his thick brows.

"I can't do anything until I talk with the stage driver," Joe answered, tying the bedroll behind the saddle. "Art Shives will be able to tell us exactly where your son was taken. There should be some tracks to follow. But since so much time has past, Vega and his men could be anywhere. These mountains are full of easy hiding places and unless we know exactly where Vega wants to meet for the swap, we could be on a fool's errand if we just ride out."

Joe watched Worthing take a deep breath and knew he wanted to argue with him. Worthing would probably want them to ride east of town to where his son had been taken.

Joe and Worthing rode through the fort's gate and out of Limpia Canyon. Joe nodded toward the gray blue, shrouded mountains toward the south. Those mountains had been, and still were hiding places for bandits and sources of wealth as prospectors searched for gold and silver, were refuge for travelers and home for people and animals.

Geronimo also called those very same mountains home especially when the army was hot on the trail for him and his warriors and he had to have places to hide to plot his next raid on wagon trains, stagecoaches, and new settlements. Joe envied the Indian leader and at times felt a kinship to him.

Geronimo went where he pleased and did what he wanted no matter if it wasn't always the right thing. Joe didn't approve of the raids and killings that everyone was quick to credit to Geronimo. He doubted that Geronimo had done all of them.

But Joe knew that if he had been pushed off of land that the Indians believed had been given to them by some kind of spirit, he would also have fought back. There was no way on God's earth that he'd let anyone tell him where to live. No one in their right mind would do a thing like that! Joe believed that every man should be able to live where he wanted or could afford to.

"Where in the devil is Candelaria?" Worthing asked, breaking into Joe's thoughts.

"Oh, it's a border town southwest of here," Joe answered, motioning with a sweep of his right hand toward the towering mountains.

Joe turned a skeptical look at Tyler Worthing and suddenly wanted to slug him. He wondered what the pompously dressed man would do if the tables were turned on him and he always had to be on the move. He knew that Worthing wouldn't like it anymore than he would. Joe felt sorry for him because his son had been kidnapped. But it all came down to the fact that Worthing was a rich man and his son was paying for it. Something about Worthing made Joe's skin crawl.

Joe hoped that Worthing believed what he'd said about riding out without a plan. It wouldn't make much sense and it would certainly be a waste of time and energy for Vega and his men to go so far from Fort Davis only to have to turn around and come back for the ransom. Besides, there wouldn't be enough time. Joe'd never been to Candelaria, but knew where it was.

But then he remembered the note instructing Worthing to take the ransom money to Candelaria. Something was already gnawing way at the back of Joe's mind, trying to push to the front and make sense.

"Do you have a picture of your son?" Joe asked, jerking his head to clear his muddled thoughts. He folded his hands loosely over the saddle horn as they galloped along. It would be a little silly to go out searching for the boy if he didn't know what he looked like.

"Yeah," Worthing answered, nodding and reaching into his coat pocket. He pulled out a cream-colored, leather wallet that probably cost as much as all of the clothes that Joe was wearing and opened it. Pride was evident in the sudden smile that splashed across Worthing's wide and ruddy face as he looked down at the photograph that was almost lost in his massive hand.

"This was made last Christmas just before Virginia died," Worthing said in a soft voice before handing Joe the oblong photograph.

Joe got the shock of his life when he looked at the boy standing in front of Worthing and a tall, very attractive woman with light-colored hair. He had expected to see a little boy even though Worthing had said that Darius was fifteen. Darius! Lord, what a name!

The kid was fat! There was no other appropriate word to describe the boy with light-colored hair who obviously hadn't missed a meal in a long time. He must weigh at least two hundred and fifty pounds! He was almost as tall as his mother but would make nearly two of her.

Tyler Worthing was big boned and carried his weight well. But the kid would no doubt shake when he walked and Joe suddenly got the mental image of a tub of lard with a rope around the middle for handles instead of hands riding a horse and he couldn't stop the smile that shot across his face. The boy's size would put a whole different light on his rescue. Joe knew that Darius Worthing didn't get on a horse willingly and he could see at least four men having to strain and heave to put him on a horse.

"I fail to see anything to laugh at," Worthing snapped, noticing Joe's smile. Joe wasn't aware that the smile was so noticeable. Worthing's deep voice was edged in anger and his eyes blazed. "What's so danged funny?"

"Oh, I was just thinking what a nice looking family you have," Joe answered glibly and shrugging his shoulders. Virginia Worthing was pretty. Her hair was up in a loose bun on top of her head and gave her oval face a regalness.

"Oh," Worthing said, expelling a deep breath. From the doubtful look in his eyes, Joe knew that Worthing didn't believe what he'd just said. If the situation had been reversed, he wouldn't have believed that explanation either. He just thanked God that he wasn't in Worthing's handmade boots.

The two men exchanged only a few more words during the short ride into town. Joe's mind was already racing back and forth as he formed and then discarded plans and ideas. Before Joe realized it, they were at the jail.

"Why are we going there?" Worthing asked when Joe didn't ride on past the jail to the stage office.

"Sheriff Dusay might have heard something else," Joe explained, pulling Serge to a stop before the jail. Joe and Dusay shook hands and Joe didn't waste any time asking if he'd heard anything from Cruz Vega. Joe really wasn't surprised when Dusay shook his head. Vega had what he wanted, had told them what he expected to be done and had set a time limit. Joe did wonder if Vega would really kill the boy if the money wasn't delivered on time.

In all cases, kidnap victims became liabilities the minute they were taken and the kidnapper couldn't be hanged any higher for murder than he could for kidnapping.

"Are you sure there isn't something you can do, sheriff?" Worthing almost pleaded, dropping down on the edge of the straight-backed chair. His eyes bored into the sheriff. He had been quiet while Joe and Dusay had talked. But now he guessed that the show was his since his son and money were still involved. He wasn't too sure about Joe Howard. The army scout had too much of a free-spirit attitude about him.

"As I told you earlier, Mr. Worthing," Dusay said, shaking his head slowly, "I don't have enough men and besides, legally there's nothing I can do. The note made it clear that your son is being held in Mexico. If he was on this side of the border, I would have already been on my way to get him. You can still hire a few men to help you and Joe Howard find your son."

The something that had been trying to get to the front of Joe's head finally clicked into place. This kidnapping had been planned well in advance. It had happened only a few hours ago but already a ransom note had been delivered, telling exactly where the boy would be held.

Vega knew it would be impossible to get the boy all the way to the border before the note was delivered but he was relying on fear and legalities to work in his favor. Even if a posse or soldiers were to come after him, even though the note advised against it, some time would be needed to get men together.

"And a lot of men would end up getting killed for nothing," Joe put in and shook his head when the last word left Dusay's mouth.

"Don't you dare say that my son is nothing!" Worthing bellowed, gripping the chair arms with white-knuckled hands.

"I didn't mean that," Joe placated, wishing that he was back at the fort. "I just meant that even if you took the money to the drop place, there's no guarantee that your son would be there because it's impossible for him to be in Mexico already."

"What are you talking about?" Worthing demanded, a deep frown contorting his features. "The note said that Vega has Darius. It also said for the money to be taken to Candelaria at the Rio Grande River."

Worthing stared at Joe as if he had two heads. He couldn't see what was right before his eyes. Joe knew that Worthing wanted to flaunt his money and power, get a bunch of men together and storm down to the border and get his son. Joe wanted to slug him again.

"I know what the note said," Joe replied, taking a deep breath so he wouldn't slug the big man. "But think about it. A ride to the Rio Grande will take at least four days without pushing a horse. Your son was kidnapped only early this morning. That means he's still somewhere close. Vega might be in Mexico, but your son certainly isn't." Joe cocked a brow and shook his head emphatically.

From the still expression that settled over Worthing's face, Joe knew that his words had been a waste of time. "I think I can do this better alone." What Joe had thought only a few minutes ago was about to become a reality.

Joe realized that he really had wasted his breath by the defiant way Worthing jerked his head up and began shaking it doggedly.

"If you think for one second," Worthing drew the words out, standing up and glaring down at Joe, "that I'm just going to sit here and do nothing while you take a thousand dollars to the sorry bastard who has my son, you're very mistaken. How do I know that you'll even go after him?"

Worthing whirled away from Joe and faced the sheriff, a murderous glare in his eyes. "Dusay, you're the poorest excuse for a sheriff that I've ever seen." Worthing had forgotten that he'd told Dusay that before. "Why can't you do something? He," Worthing jerked his head sideways at Joe, "just wants to take my money. Have you ever had a son kidnapped?"

Dusay compressed his mouth into a thin white line. There was a warning in the glance Dusay threw at Joe.

Without a word, Joe caught hold of Worthing's thick arm and hustled him out of the jail. Worthing's surprise was the only thing that allowed Joe to do it.

"What in the devil do you think you're doing?" Worthing snapped, jerking his arm from Joe's grip as soon as they were outside.

"Sheriff Sam Dusay was just about to eat you for lunch," Joe said through clinched teeth.

"What are you talking about?" Worthing asked, frowning at Joe, pulling his coat together.

"The sheriff and his wife's two-year-old son died three years ago of pneumonia." Joe's voice was flat.

"I didn't know," Worthing muttered, ducking his head and shifting his ponderous size from one foot to the other. "But you must understand my feelings," Worthing continued defiantly.

Joe knew his work was already cut out for him if he tried to convince Tyler Worthing that it would be better if he stayed in Fort Davis and let him handle things by himself. Then out of the far recesses of his mind a solution became clear.

Darius Worthing had been abducted earlier that morning. It had taken longer than usual for the stage to get to town because Art Shives, the driver was wounded. As he'd tried to tell Worthing before, something didn't make sense. It would take at least four days of hard riding to reach the Rio Grande River. This day was already half gone and common sense told Joe that it would be impossible to reach the spot in the allotted time. No horse alive could cover that much ground in so little time.

But, if what Joe was thinking was true, he wouldn't have to worry about going all the way to Candelaria to find the boy. Darius Worthing was a lot closer than Cruz Vega wanted them to think.

Maybe Vega wanted to play some kind of mind or money game with Tyler Worthing. Maybe he just wanted to see the big man sweat. The kid who had delivered the note could be watching the jail right then just to see what Worthing was doing. Maybe Cruz Vega himself was in town.

There were enough Mexicans in Fort Davis for Vega to be lost in the crowd and he was probably getting a kick out of seeing the big man riding up and down the street. Chill bumps raced all over Joe's body and he shivered at the sinister thought that he was being watched at that very minute.

Joe frowned and wondered why Vega would tell Worthing to go one place with that much money if he had the boy at a closer place? Maybe he *was* going to have Worthing on some wild goose chase.

Joe's thoughts took another turn. Maybe Vega hadn't been with the bandits. Maybe the plan had just been his and he let his men carry it out. Vega could be waiting in Mexico for his men to bring the money to him. There was only one way to find out and Joe wanted that way to be without Worthing's help.

"I'm going to talk to Herman Gredes," Joe said, adjusting his hat against the sun's bright rays and starting down the sidewalk to the stage office. He wasn't surprised when Tyler Worthing fell into step beside him. He would have been disappointed if he hadn't.

Art Shives, the driver was still at the stage office when the two men entered. Joe thought that he would have been at home nursing his wound if he had been shot as bad as Worthing had said. Shives was stretched out on a bunk against the wall. A red stained bandage was around his left arm and across his shoulder. Herman Gredes sat at the cluttered desk, his scuffed booted feet crossed on the edge.

"Mr. Worthing," Gredes said, plopping his feet down on the floor, "have you heard anything else about your son?" He sent a stream of dark tobacco juice toward the brass spittoon on the floor by the desk with amazing accuracy.

"Yes," Worthing said, irritation in his voice at the delay he was sure Joe was taking. Vega had already told him where to bring the money. They were wasting precious time talking to Shives and Gredes. If there had been a Gypsy woman, Joe Howard would probably have to talk to her, too. "Cruz Vega left a note at the sheriff's office with explicit instructions on what to do." Maybe that would speed Howard up.

Joe, hearing the urgency in Worthing's voice, knew what he was doing but walked over to the bunk and sat down on the edge by Shives. "Where were you exactly when the stage was stopped?" Joe asked, pushing his hat back and looking down at the man who was in obvious pain.

"We were about ten miles out," Shives said, trying to sit up. But when his face turned ash white with the struggle, he forgot about it. "Almost to Leaning Rock Canyon. They came out of a grove of cedar trees. I could have made it here a lot sooner but the pain in my shoulder wouldn't let me go any faster. I did good to get the old man back into the stage to bring him here for burial. I just couldn't leave him out there for the animals." He made a face at the horrible thought. "Them ten miles was the longest I ever had."

A tight knot pulled in Joe's stomach as he realized that what he had been thinking was true. Darius Worthing was probably only a day's ride from town right now! But getting Tyler Worthing to believe it was going to be almost impossible. Joe wondered why Vega wanted Worthing to take a thousand dollars all the way to Candelaria? He could have settled for any place closer and could have had the money sooner. But there would probably be another note waiting in Candelaria, telling Worthing to go some place else. All the while, Vega would be laughing at him.

"Do you know for sure that Cruz Vega was in the bunch?" Joe asked, narrowing his eyes and looking at Shives.

"Yeah," Shives replied, expelling a deep breath and nodding. "I saw him about a year ago in Laredo. I'd know that tall Mex anywhere. Likes to dress real fancy. Big, black hat and pants with them shiny things down the side and a white shirt. He was the one who done all of the talkin'."

"How did my son look?" Worthing asked before Joe could continue his questioning. A worried frown puckered Worthing's brows as he hovered over the bunk. "Did they beat him. Did he take some clean clothes with him?"

Joe couldn't believe his ears! He'd never heard such stupid questions in all of his twenty-three years. The man's son had been kidnapped and he was worried about him having clean clothes! Good, Lord! If Darius was dead, he wouldn't need clean clothes. But Joe knew the boy was alive. Or he would be until someone in Fort Davis saw Worthing leave for Candelaria with the ransom money.

"Funny you should ask how he looked," Shives said, pulling in a long, ragged breath and licking his dry lips. He tried to sit up again. "He looked sick. From the time he got on the stage in Pecos, until we were stopped, he didn't say very much. In fact, he lay on the seat most of the time. His face was real flushed."

Joe glanced at Worthing when he pulled in a shocked gasp.

"I beg your pardon," Worthing sneered, indignation splashed all over his face. "My son hasn't been sick since he was a baby."

Maybe all of that fat has insulated the boy against illnesses, Joe thought cynically. He pressed his lips tightly together so he wouldn't laugh or smile. He remembered Worthing's reaction when he'd smiled at the family picture.

"Well, I ain't no doctor," Shives shot back, undaunted by Worthing's put-down, "but that boy looked sick to me." He lay back on the pillow.

"Maybe he was just tired," Joe suggested, looking down at the floor, his mind going in a hundred different directions and lacking the patience to hear two grown men argue.

Joe couldn't know if Tyler Worthing would be safe if he took that much money to Mexico alone. But it would be one way to do what he knew he could alone. He knew that he should suggest that Tyler Worthing take a couple of men with him."

"Mr. Worthing," Joe began resolutely, standing up and hooking his thumbs over his belt. "You're not going to believe what I'm about to say and you might not like it, but I don't believe your son will be taken to Mexico. He's a lot closer than we think."

"Where else would he be?" Worthing demanded before Joe could give him a reason for his belief. Worthing's brows shot up and his eyes widened in defiance. "The note said explicitly for the money to be brought to a cabin in the center of the Rio Grande River. That has to be in Mexico, you know."

"The note said only to take *the money* to Candelaria," Joe stressed, closing his eyes, shaking his head and then opening his eyes. "It didn't say anything about where your son was."

"I know he's on his way to Mexico," Worthing said stubbornly, shaking his head.

Joe expelled a long breath and knew it would be impossible to convince this willful and egotistical man frowning angrily down at him that things could be different from the way they seemed.

But this might work out to Joe's advantage after all. Worthing was determined that the money should be delivered to Cruz Vega in Mexico. And, no doubt he wanted to be the one who took it to him. With Worthing on his way to Mexico, with or without bodyguards, and not around to get in his way, Joe could ride out to the place where the kidnapping had taken place and find the boy a lot sooner. He would get a kick out of finding Darius Worthing and intercepting his know-it-all father on his way to Mexico.

"You're absolutely right," Joe relented, letting his shoulders slump in apparent defeat. "So, you go right ahead. Take the money and follow the directions in the note. I'm going to check out an idea of my own. I do think it would be a good idea if you hired a couple of men the sheriff knows to go with you. People have been killed for a lot less than a thousand dollars, you know."

"Just what are you going to do?" Worthing asked, some of his bravado fading a few degrees when he realized that Joe wasn't going along with him. He'd just met one of the few men who had the guts to argue with him. "Colonel McRaney said for you to go with me and help me find my son."

"No, he didn't." Joe shook his head rapidly. "All he told me to do was find your son." Joe was glad that Worthing didn't argue with him. "I'm going to ride out to the place where the stage was stopped," Joe continued, adjusting the Colt .45 around his lean waist and retying the leather thong around his leg. Talking more with Worthing would only delay things. "There should be some tracks that will show exactly where they went." He added the last part to satisfy the skeptical and questioning look on Herman Gredes's wrinkled face.

"How soon will you be back?" Worthing asked, putting a restraining hand on Joe's shoulder as he walked toward the door.

"Just as soon as I find your son," Joe answered simply, afraid that the big man was going to suggest that he'd wait until Joe returned, probably empty-handed and con him into going to Mexico with him.

"How much money do you want?" Worthing asked, moving his huge hand toward his coat pocket.

"We'll take about that when we get back," Joe said, anger boiling up in his stomach. He wanted to reach out and slug Tyler Worthing, even if he had to stand on a box to do it. It was still a matter of dollars to him although he wasn't going to trust him with the thousand dollars.

Shoving his hands deep into his pockets just so he wouldn't strike at Worthing, Joe turned and started toward Billy Leon's Cafe, leaving Worthing to his own devices. He needed to put a grub sack together before he went anywhere. He should have thought about that before he left the fort and let Gipson, the old cook do it for him. It would have saved him money.

Since Art Shives had said that it had taken him longer than usual to reach the stage office in Fort Davis because he was wounded, Joe knew that if a stage had gotten to town in that amount of time with a wounded man at the reins, he could cover that much ground on Serge in half of the time. But since the day was already half gone, he knew he'd have to spend at least one night out in the open even if he got lucky and found any tracks.

Knowing that he might not be able to get a good beer until he returned, Joe walked down the plank sidewalk to the Desert Rose Saloon. That would turn out to be something he shouldn't have done.

Two men were standing at the long bar, each with a full shot glass and a mug of beer before him. Jeanie Orms and Betty Young were behind the bar.

"Hello, you good looking thing," Jeanie greeted, smiling at him, a twinkle in her eyes. "You haven't been in here in a long time."

"It's about time you showed up," Betty said, arching her brows. "Did Colonel McRaney finally turn you loose?"

"Hi, girls," Joe said, smiling at them. "Yeah, he finally turned me loose to go out again." He stopped at the empty space at the center of the bar. "I'll have a beer." He pushed his hat back on his head and rested his foot on the brass rail. Waiting for the beer, Joe looked around the saloon. A slow game of poker was going on at a table in one corner and a drummer was showing a prospective buyer a tin of buttons.

"Jeanie, since you're closer to the keg," Betty said, pursing her lips, "I'm going to let you get this one."

"Thanks a lot," Jeanie said, mock scorn in her eyes. Turning around, she filled a mug and slid it down the bar to Joe.

Joe took a long pull on the beer. It was cold and good. He was about to take another swig when he saw, from the corner of his eye one of the men standing a couple of feet away turn from the bar, pick up the mug of beer in his left hand, hook his right thumb over his belt, and start toward him.

"Frank, don't start anything," the other man cautioned, dread in his hooded, blue eyes.

"Shut up, Hank," Frank growled over his shoulder without taking his eyes from Joe. "I guess you're the one going after that rich man's kid, huh?" Frank stated more than asked, ignoring Hank's warning. His bearded face contorted with a smirk and his gravelly voice was edged with sarcasm.

"If you mean Tyler Worthing's son, yes, I'm going to try and find him," Joe answered complacently, cupping both hands around the mug to make sure that his right hand was well away from the pistol handle. He knew the man's type. He was going to try to goad him into a fight.

"How did you know that I was going after the Worthing boy?" Joe asked, then taking another swallow.

"Oh, I heard Bruell Cannon mention your name," Frank answered, taking a sip of beer. "Do you need some help?" he asked, looking straight at Joe, a challenge in his gray green eyes under arched, black brows.

"No, thanks. I believe I can take care of it by myself," Joe said as calmly as he could, a smile twitching at the corner of his mouth. But he knew that even if honey had been dripping from his mouth, it wouldn't have worked on Frank. There was going to be a fight and he only hoped he could hold his own without having to shoot him.

"Why? Ain't I good 'nuff to ride along with you?" Frank asked. A snarl pulled at the tall and medium-built man's already smirking mouth. His eyes turned sullen.

"Well, it isn't that," Joe hedged, looking up at Frank who was a few inches taller than he, then back down at the almost-full mug of beer. He hoped he'd get to finish it. "I just have my own way of doing . . ."

That was as far as Joe got. Frank slammed the beer mug down on the bar, reached out, caught a handful of Joe's shirt and swung him around to face him. Joe more or less knew what would happen as the man doubled up his fist and aimed it at his face.

Joe turned his head to the right. He could feel the air swoosh past his left cheek as the fist slashed by. Joe didn't have enough time to argue with the man but he still didn't want to shoot him.

Word had traveled fast around town and no doubt the amount of the ransom was already known. Joe knew that Frank was going mostly on liquid courage, mixed with a little greed and wondered how many more "helpful" souls he'd meet before he left Fort Davis.

Joe didn't have any more time to waste. It was getting late. Stepping back and pulling out of Frank's grasp, he jerked his right knee up, and lunging forward, planted it firmly in the man's crotch.

Frank's hold on Joe's shirt was immediately released as he doubled over, clutching the injured part of his body, but leaving his sharp chin jutting out. Joe doubled up his right fist and made contact with it in a brain-rattling blow. Frank's lower teeth cut into his upper lip and blood spurted out of his mouth as he fell backward against the bar and slid to the floor moaning in pain.

Hank must have thought it was time for him to come to Frank's aid. "That will be enough," he said in a low, threatening growl. He surprised Joe by jerking a Remington .38 from a holster at his left side and aiming it directly at Joe.

"I didn't start this, so put the gun away," Joe advised, wiping some of Frank's blood from his hand on a towel that Jeanie had laid on the bar.

"You nearly broke his jaw," Hank accused, glaring at Joe. He thumbed the hammer back on the pistol. From the wild look in Hank's eyes, he was just about to shoot Joe. Frank had regained a little of his wit and was floundering around on the floor like a fish out of water.

Having no choice, because there was murderous intent in Hank's eyes and no amount of talk would change the outcome, Joe jerked the Colt .45 from the holster with a speed that had kept him alive in several other similar circumstances and fired from the hip. The gun exploded, the sound bouncing off the walls. His subconscious heard the drummer's buttons scattering on the floor as Jeannie and Betty screamed.

The bullet tore into the center of Hank's gray shirt.

He froze where he stood, looking at Joe as if he'd told him something he couldn't believe. Hank's knees began sagging under him and blood began oozing from a tiny hole in the shirt. He was dead before he hit the floor.

Frank stayed where he was on the floor, leaning against the bar, blood staining his face, neck and shirt.

Joe holstered the .45 and started toward the door. He didn't want to finish the beer. Sheriff Sam Dusay stopped his leaving by pushing open the bat wings.

"I was wondering how long it would take for you to get into trouble over this," Dusay said flatly, shaking his head wearily.

"It wasn't his fault," Jeanie shouted at Dusay, her eyes blazing.

"That sorry bum on the floor started it," Betty put in, glaring at Dusay. Jeanie walked around to the front of the bar and looked down at Frank who had gotten to his feet.

"Take what's left of your friend," she said snidely, "and get out."

"Don't ever come back in here," Betty cautioned, her hands on her hips as she came up behind Jeanie.

"Ladies, I know who's fault it was," Dusay said, wanting to laugh at the women. "Okay, Howard. Go on. Get out of here."

Joe, regretting that he had just taken a man's life, even though that man had instigated it, and knowing that it had to be one or the other, nodded to Jeanie and Betty, left the saloon, and hurried down the sidewalk to Billy Leon's Cafe. He hoped that he wouldn't get into any trouble on the way. He still had to put a grub sack together.

Polly Bullock was sitting at a table by the kitchen door, a cup of steaming, black coffee before her. It didn't take two guesses from the look on Joe's face for her to know that something was wrong.

"Did you have anything to do with the shot I just heard?" she asked when he dropped down in the chair across the table from her.

"Yeah," he answered, shaking his head disdainfully, "a drunk wouldn't believe that I didn't need any help in going after a rich man's kid. His stupid friend stepped in and I had to shoot him. I want to leave town as soon as possible. Will you fix me a grub sack. I'd like a coffeepot, too."

"Sure," Polly said standing up and smiling down at him, a little pity in her brown eyes. She wouldn't have his job for the world. Shaking her head of curly, blonde hair, she hurried into the kitchen and returned soon with a full, canvas sack. "This should be enough for a couple of days," she said, a soft smile on her lightly rouged cheeks. "There's flour, salt pork, coffee, a coffeepot, and skillet."

"Thanks," Joe said, taking money from his pocket and putting it into her hand.

He hoped to God he could get out of town without having to kill again.

The setting sun would provide only about another half hour of warm rays before sliding down behind the mountains when Joe finally pulled Serge to a stop for the night. He knew it was going to be bone-chillingly cold when darkness finally enveloped the vast mountains and desert. As the shadowy fingers that resembled the purple, shrouded mountains began crawling eastward, Joe began looking around and checking out the possibilities for a warm place to spend the night.

He knew there were hundreds of caves of various sizes in the mountains. He was just hoping that he could find one that wasn't already occupied by human, animal, or insect. He wasn't lucky enough to find one large enough for both him and Serge before his vision was hampered by darkness. The hollow out, about six feet high and five feet deep in the side of a ravine would have to do. He tied Serge to a small cottonwood tree close to the hollow out and was more or less satisfied with his sleeping quarters for the night.

Before spreading out his bedroll and unsaddling Serge, Joe searched carefully inside the hollow out to be sure there were no snakes or scorpions in residence. Of course, not finding anything didn't mean that some crawly, biting, or stinging thing couldn't join him later. But he dismissed that possibility as he kicked out the bedroll, put the saddle at one end of it for a pillow, dropped down, and stretched out.

The inside of the hollow out was warm as the cooling wind began pushing away the day's heat. Joe's sleep would have been peaceful if his dream hadn't been so ludicrous. In it he saw a young boy so fat that he had to ride two horses. The horses, in order to hold the huge body were lashed together just behind the front legs and just in front of the back legs. The saddle wasn't a saddle at all. Instead, a large, leather-wrapped daybed was tied on the horses with thick ropes and the boy sat in the middle of it. Two sets of reins were dangling from the boy's ham-sized hands. Something that looked like thick, brown grease was dripping from the ends of his sausage-sized fingers.

The boy was too big to wear a shirt and pants. A canvas wagon top, with a hole cut in the center was draped over his body. A large yellow dollar sign was painted on the back of it. A black umbrella was serving as a hat. His feet were covered with two cow hides that didn't even resemble shoes or boots.

Joe had no idea where he and Darius were or even

why they were together. The only thing evident was a lot of trees and they were riding toward them. The only problem was that the horses' feet were moving but they weren't gaining any ground.

Suddenly, one of the reins slipped from the boy's hand. The howling wind picked it up and blew it backward at Joe. It wrapped around his neck and began tightening like a vine crawling up a host tree. Joe could feel his breath being choked off and began flailing his arms wildly around to loosen the reins so he could breathe. The boy, hampered by his size couldn't do anything to help and only sat in the middle of the big saddle-bed and watch, a horror-stricken expression on his fat face, his mouth full of food as Joe struggled to free himself.

The next thing Joe knew, he was sitting up straight on the ground in cold sweat, the top blanket wrapped around his neck. Jerking it down, Joe felt foolish as he pulled in a long, deep breath, reached out for the water canteen, and took a long drink. Swallowing, he grinned and wondered if Darius Worthing was anywhere near the size of the boy in his dream. If he was, Joe pitied the poor horse that was carrying him.

Joe hoped and prayed that the boy was all right and that he could find him soon and get him to his father. The only thing bothering Joe was the nagging suspicion that he would be as obnoxious as his father. If that turned out to be true, he'd stuff a rag in the boy's mouth, or better yet, something to eat until he found Tyler Worthing.

Daylight was breaking the hold that darkness had on the land with a thin strip of pink and orange in the east. The fall colors were softened by the early morning haze but would soon be more brilliant as the sun got a better grip on the sky.

Joe wasn't exactly sure how far ahead the place was

where the stage had been stopped and Darius Worthing was taken but he knew he was closer than he had been and chills of anticipation raced up and down his back. With that positive thought in mind, he decided to take enough time to make breakfast. Opening the canvas sack that Polly Bullock had prepared for him yesterday, he was pleased to see six saucer-sized biscuits wrapped in a red napkin. He was glad that he wouldn't have to make bread. He made coffee, cut off four slices of salt pork, and fried it. He remembered Polly saying that the biscuits would do him a couple of meals.

"This will be one of the meals," he said, breaking open one of the brown-topped biscuits that was a lot harder than it had been yesterday. Putting the meat between the bread, he dunked it into the strong black coffee and took a bite. He had tasted better but it would do for now. He'd make fresh bread tonight if he hadn't found Darius Worthing or a trail. When he'd finished eating, he sand-cleaned the skillet, poured water into it and let Serge drink. Maybe he'd find a stream soon and refill the canteen. When everything was cleaned up, he saddled Serge and headed east.

3

Art Shives had said that Cruz Vega and his men had been waiting in a grove of cedar trees when he was almost to Leaning Rock Canyon and where the land stretched out for about a mile south. When Joe reached the place where a rock was leaning almost precariously over the trail and with a deep drop-off to the left, he felt as though he'd already been there since Shives had described it so well.

Something made him pull the Henry rifle from the scabbard and put a shell in the chamber as he approached the large clump of cedar trees. Apprehension caused the hair to stand out straight on the back of his neck and he shivered even though it was already comfortably warm from the sun finally pushing through the haze. He felt like twenty pairs of eyes were watching him.

Evidence from human and horse told Joe that several men had indeed been waiting for someone to come along this way. Joe wondered from the amount of cigarette butts and horse droppings on the ground how long at least ten men had waited there with the soul intent of kidnapping Darius Worthing? Did they have any idea how fat the boy was? But when that much money was up for grabs, size was probably a small matter. Joe wished though that he could have seen the look on Cruz Vega's face when he saw the size of his victim.

Suddenly, like a bolt of lightning out of a blue summer sky, a thought eased a stillness over Joe's tanned face. Someone, and it had to be Cruz Vega, knew exactly that Darius Worthing was going to be on that particular stage. They hadn't taken just anyone because an old man had been killed because he wouldn't give up his watch. Darius Worthing's name had been on the ransom note that was soon delivered. Did Tyler Worthing know about the obvious plot?

Nah, Joe told himself, shaking his head in deep thought. The big man's worry seemed to be sincere.

Joe rode out of the trees and made a wide half circle away from the area. Tracks, probably made from the stage were still visible. Trampled grass, loose ground, and small rocks told Joe that a lot of activity had taken place right here not long ago. The tracks started south across the wide-open stretch of land and he felt like an actor on a stage for everyone to see. Had Cruz Vega posted some of his men out there to see if Tyler Worthing or the sheriff would come looking around? Joe's skin crawled and he was almost certain that he was being watched.

Had Cruz Vega been smart enough to send someone into Fort Davis to watch and see who would head south with the money? That was one of the things that kept gnawing at Joe. Why did Cruz Vega want the money taken so far when he and the boy were so close? Joe knew he was wasting time. He could sit there all day on Serge and never come up with an answer.

It was even possible that Geronimo and some of his Apache braves were watching him and he'd really have to think about that. Geronimo divided his time and place of residence between the mountains of Northern Mexico, Texas, New Mexico, and Arizona Territory. Of course, it would be just as bad if bandits other than Vega's men were his observers. He could end up just as dead!

Knowing that he couldn't waste anymore time if he was going to accomplish anything today, Joe pulled Serge around and began following the tracks that angled southeast. He was only mildly surprised when the tracks headed in that direction instead of southwest that would have ended up at the Rio Grande in Candelaria.

If Tyler Worthing had been along, Joe would have said "I told you so" and would have enjoyed the look on the big man's face.

The body-jarring ride was taking Joe through a mountain range he'd never been in, and he'd traveled just about every mile of this vast land. Granite mountains with tops that could tickle the white clouds with their saw-jagged edges spread out for miles before him. The land was too inhospitable for humans to call home and was used by those crossing the river for any number of reasons. It was well south of the area where wagon trains and stagecoaches normally traveled between San Antonio and El Paso and Joe knew without much thought, that Tyler Worthing was wasting his time and money if he wanted to extend a stage line this far unless he hired out stages for private use such as on hunting trips for mountain lions and black bear. That would take a lot of extra money on the passenger's part.

He was still following the visible trail, which he

hoped belonged to Cruz Vega and his men. He smiled when the image of last night's dream flashed in his mind and he laughed out loud when he remembered Art Shives saying that Darius Worthing looked sick. It could have been something the boy had eaten. From the picture that Tyler Worthing had shown him, it was evident that the boy hadn't missed many meals.

Joe was puzzled when the tracks he was following wound down into a narrow trail through a canyon that opened up on the south side into a wide valley. Inside the valley and protected on three sides by the canyon walls were a group of adobe buildings too small to be called a town but too large for a settlement. Village would be a better description. Joe's heart skipped a beat, then leaped up into his throat.

He knew this was where he would find Cruz Vega and his captive, Darius Worthing in only a matter of minutes. He wondered, as he angled Serge down the steep trail, who would be waiting for Tyler Worthing when he crossed the river at Candelaria with the ransom money? Joe wondered how far Worthing had gotten.

Not having any way of knowing how many gringos, if any, would be in the village, Joe knew that he would have to come up with some plausible reason for passing through this remote part of the country. Then his brain went into gear. He could rely on the rumor that a lot of gold and silver were being taken out of the mountains in Mexico and he was on his way to get his share of the wealth.

If this village was like the others he'd been in, the cantina would be the best place to get information. But what kind of information? He couldn't just come plain out and ask if Cruz Vega was in town with a kidnapped gringo kid! Joe grinned at the stupid thought. His throat was so dry that he could probably rake sand off of his tongue with a knife and knew that a beer would be just the thing for an excuse to go into the cantina.

Curious, dark eyes in brown faces followed him as he rode down the narrow, dusty street. Two small white-clad Mexican boys were playing with a black-and-white cat, stopping when he pulled Serge to a halt beside them. Children were more apt to answer his questions than grown-ups.

"Niños, donde está cantina, por favor?" he asked, grinning down at the boys and licking his dry lips.

At the prospect of getting some money from this thirsty gringo, the boys looked slyly at each other, nodded, and smiled shyly up at Joe. Without saying anything, they both pointed their brown arms down the street.

Knowing what they expected, Joe fished two pecos from his pocket and dropped them down into the dirty brown hands. The boys, one with the cat dangling under his arm, hurried off in the opposite direction, talking in their native tongue probably about the candy they could buy.

Still grinning, Joe kneed Serge into a deliberately slow and steady pace down the street past a mission with a cemetery about a hundred yards behind it, a blacksmith shop that probably served as an undertakers, several buildings that gave no indication as to what they were and finally the cantina with four hearts painted over the door. Lively music from an accordion, trumpet, and guitar poured from a wide window on either side of the door of the Quatro Corazones Cantina.

Joe's heart was in his throat and beating like a hammer when he dismounted and tied Serge loosely to the hitch rail in front of the cantina. Trying to act as nonchalant as possible, Joe caused quite a stir and every head in the place turned in his direction as he walked in toward the bar.

Four Mexicans were standing at the bar, each wearing a long-barreled pistol tied low.

God, please, Joe prayed under his breath, don't let me get killed in such a small place.

"One beer, *por favor*," Joe said, holding up his index finger and expelling a fake, dog-tired breath. He leaned his arms wearily against the edge of the bar so he would not appear too threatening. But that could be a mistake if he was jumped. But that was a chance he'd have to take.

"No beer, señor," the tall, thin barkeep said, shaking his head of thick, black hair. There was no apology in the deep, accented voice, just an explanation. The man watched Joe with steady, black eyes.

Joe thought the man was refusing to serve him a beer because he was the only gringo in the cantina. He felt the hairs stand up on the back of his neck and let his right hand move slowly from the bar and down to the handle of the Colt .45. Quickly realizing that the move could be a mistake and could get him killed, Joe held the Mexican's steady gaze and hoped he could bluff his way through.

"No trouble, señor," the barkeep said, an edge in his voice although he placed his hands palms down on the bar. "There is no beer." He shrugged his thin shoulders. "There is only tequila or pulque." His thin, straight, black brows arched over his eyes. He closed his eyes slowly and opened them while Joe made up his mind which of the two drinks he wanted.

"Tequila," Joe finally said, rolling his lips in against his teeth and making a sucking sound. He knew he could handle the tequila much easier than the milky, liquid mess made out of rotten cactus juice. He shivered at the thought and felt his stomach turn over.

Joe noticed that the music had slowed as he looked around the crowded cantina. He brought his hand back up to the bar but turned his body so that his hand was right over the pistol handle. Everyone seemed to be waiting to see what his next move would be.

A breathtakingly beautiful, black-haired girl, wearing a skintight, red, taffeta dress that flared out around the knees made her way, walking like a lazy cat, the same greedy look in her dark, velvetlike brown eyes that the small boys had had. She knew that he would be good for at least one drink.

"Why are you here, señor?" she asked in a blunt but sultry voice and fluttered her thick, long, black lashes up at him. "Are you just passing through and knew that Quita was thirsty?" Her voice trailed off and she wiped her hand across her heart-shaped face that would have been the color of lightly creamed coffee if it hadn't been so flushed.

Joe leaned over and looked closer at her, not because of her sultry beauty or the obvious invitation in her eyes, although either of them would have been enough to get his attention if he hadn't had other things on his mind. She was one of the most beautiful women he'd ever seen. She tried to sound and look provocative, but she just didn't quite make it. He saw sweat beaded on her upper lip and even in the dim light he saw some sort of blotches on her otherwise smooth skin. She began swaying and before he could catch her, the enticing beauty hit the floor at his feet in a crumple of red dress and black hair.

A surprised gasp erupted from the cantina's patrons.

"Que pasa?" the barkeep asked, his previously oblique eyes flying wide open as he peered over the bar

for a closer look at the girl lying on the floor. "What did you do to her?" Accusation snapped in his eyes.

"I didn't do anything to her," Joe said, dropping down on one knee by the girl. Placing a thumb and finger against her throat, he could feel her heart pounding. Noticing how warm her throat was, he laid his hand on her forehead. The crowded cantina was warm, but not enough for her to feel like that. She was burning up with fever!

A crowd had gathered around them, all muttering in a language in which he knew just enough to get by. Joe started to pick her up but felt a restraining hand on his shoulder. He turned around and looked up to see a brown-skinned boy about sixteen years old standing there with a threatening glare in his dark eyes.

"What are you going to do with her?" the boy asked in broken English.

"I'm going to get her up off of the dirty floor for one thing," Joe snapped, looking down at the boy's hand on his shoulder, "and take her over to that table, so get your hands off of me."

"You are not going to touch her again," the boy informed protectively, drawing up his medium-sized body to try to look much larger. Joe, realizing that more time, time he didn't have to spare was going to be wasted by some more liquid-fed courage, didn't say anything to the boy. He reached out, grabbed the boy by the arm and swung out as hard as he could. The boy, caught off guard, went flying across the cantina and landed up against a wooden shelf filled with earthen bottles and jugs. Those that were filled, spilled their contents and shattered along with the empty ones when the boy bounced away and hit the floor with a thud as the shelf crashed around him. Joe didn't waste any extra time to see what the boy would do even if he was able to get out from under all of the rubble.

Doing as he had started, because it was apparent that no one else was going to, Joe bent down, picked the girl up, and carried her over to a table near the window. The two card players jumped up and swept the cards and money out of the way.

Joe got another shock when the light showed him a better view of the girl's face. The blotches turned out to be small blisters and were scattered all over her face. His heart skipped a beat and he felt cold in spite of the warmth in the cantina. Joe Howard had seen this once before and had been lucky enough to survive a case of smallpox!

"What is going on here?" An authoritative and accented voice asked from behind Joe.

The army scout whirled around and looked into the blazing, black eyes of the man he knew instantly had to be Cruz Vega. There was a mixture of expressions in the deep-set, black eyes under peaked black brows. By anyone's standard the tall and muscular man, dressed as Art Shives had described in a white shirt and black pants with conchos down the side of the flared legs was handsome. Black jaw-length sideburns accentuated a narrow face and thin nose. "What is wrong with *mi hermana?* My sister?"

"It doesn't matter who I am," Joe answered, hurrying back to the bar to pick up a full earthen pitcher of water. Returning to the table, he took a bandanna from his pocket, poured some water over it, and dabbed it over the girl's face. "If I'm not mistaken," he went on and looking up at Vega, "this girl has smallpox. You could be in for a lot of trouble."

An immediate hush replaced the murmuring voices and the crowd of curious spectators moved quickly away.

Some even left the cantina, crossing themselves in their haste to leave.

At the touch of the water on Quita's face, her eyes fluttered open. She caught hold of Joe's arm and tried to sit up. Joe put his arm under her shoulders and raised her to a sitting position on the table.

"Cruz, what is the matter with me?" she asked, surprisingly in English in a weak voice, glancing from Joe to Vega and held out her hand to the man who had stepped back, well away from the table.

Vega shifted his fear-filled, black eyes from the girl to Joe and back to her again.

"This gringo says that you have smallpox," Vega answered in a grave voice, a deep frown pulling between his eyes. "But it is probably only the heat that is giving you that rash. You will be all right in the fresh air."

Joe knew that the heat couldn't be the case because the weather had been so cool the past few weeks.

"Have you felt sick very long?" Joe asked, moving his hand in a circular motion over his stomach and touching his head.

"It's just been since . . ." Quita began but got no further than that.

"*Silencio*," Vega snapped in a cold, warning voice, his eyes boring into hers. He shook his head rapidly. "It is just since you have been working so hard dancing here in the cantina. All you need is a little rest."

"What should I do?" Quita asked, a wild expression in her fear-filled eyes. Joe grabbed her arm when she raised her hand and started to scratch one of the blisters on her face.

"Don't scratch those places," Joe warned in a gentle voice, shaking his head slowly when Vega shrugged his shoulders negatively. "Go home. Get into bed and take whatever you have for fever. Whatever you do, don't scratch your face. It will only spread the infection."

Quita slid off the table and on unsteady legs walked out the door. She'd barely gotten outside when a Mexican man about Joe's age and size came hurrying into the cantina. Fear was rampant all over the dark, bearded face. "Cruz, you had better come quick," he said urgently. He was breathing hard and his eyes were wild. "Something is terribly wrong with Alberto and that gringo kid."

Joe watched some of the color drain from Vega's brown face and his gut feeling told him that he'd been correct in his assumption that Darius Worthing was here, and remembering what Art Shives had said about the boy being sick, knew that he was the carrier of smallpox!

Oh, my God! Joe thought miserably. I wish I was back at the fort or about to lead a wagon train through Apache country!

Without hesitation or trying to stop Joe from following him, Cruz Vega hurried out the door, swung up on a solid white mare tied next to Serge, and followed the other man down the narrow, dusty street.

Knowing that he was about to find Tyler Worthing's fat son, Joe leaped into the saddle and caught up with Vega in only a matter of seconds as Serge's long legs ate up the distance. Joe wondered again why Vega had sent Worthing on such a long ride with the ransom money when he and the boy were right under his nose? But Joe knew he was right in his assumption that Vega was going to have Worthing do a lot of unnecessary riding. Would that ride end right where they were? More than likely.

Joe suddenly felt sorry for Darius Worthing. Not only was the fat kid the son of a pompous ass like Tyler Worthing. That, in itself was bad enough. To compound matters, he had been kidnapped by a man renowned for his ruthlessness on both sides of the Rio Grande, but now he had smallpox! Joe wondered how many of the villagers had been exposed?

The short ride took them to a small, adobe cabin at the edge of the village where three horses were tied under a cottonwood tree. Uncertainty pulled a frown over Vega's face. Joe knew the Mexican was trying to decide whether or not to go into the cabin. Without pushing his presence on the man, Joe, with a knot that felt like the size of his fist bunched up in his stomach, followed close behind Vega when he finally went cautiously into the cabin.

If indeed the boy was inside and sick Joe and everyone who had been in contact with him since he'd been brought to the cabin would have to be quarantined and in normal circumstances would be at least a week before he could be moved. But in this instance, necessity would overrule precaution and he would do everything he could to get the boy out of the village. For a split second Joe wondered how he could get word to Tyler Worthing and especially Art Shives. The stage driver should know that he had been exposed to smallpox!

The cabin interior was dim and it took a few seconds for everyone's eyes to adjust to the shadows. When Joe was finally able to see, he got the shock of his entire life!

Lying on a bunk in the left corner of the cabin and moaning was an older Mexican man. But that wasn't what had gotten Joe's attention and made his heart leap up into his throat in a choking knot.

In the opposite corner, on another bunk was a young boy who could have been fifteen years old. That was the only thing that this boy and Darius Worthing would ever have in common! Even under the red blanket, Joe could tell that this boy was much shorter than even him, and he stood five feet seven, and would weigh only about a hundred and ten pounds if he weighed an ounce! Tyler Worthing had said that the photo of his family had been made last year just before Christmas. It might have been possible for someone to lose that much weight in that length of time. But it would be absolutely impossible for Darius Worthing to shrink in height that much.

Who was the boy, wrapped in the red blanket, lying on the bunk? Did Cruz Vega know that he'd been tricked?

Joe hurried over to the bunk for a closer look at the boy as Vega eased over to the other bunk where the old man lay. Just as Joe had expected, the boy's slender face was covered with blisters that were on the verge of bursting. He placed his hand on the boy's forehead and it felt like fire.

"What are we going to do?" Vega asked over his shoulder to the man who had come to the cantina to get him only a few minutes ago. "If what this gringo said," he jerked his thumb over his shoulder toward Joe, "is true, we could have a disaster on our hands. If I had known that the boy was sick, I would not have taken him." He nodded toward the boy on the bunk then shook his head regretfully. Fear and worry were evident in his voice and rapidly blinking, black eyes.

If the tracks hadn't led from Leaning Rock Canyon straight to the village and if Cruz Vega hadn't been called by name at least twice, Joe would have tried to convince himself that he was in the wrong place.

But he knew that couldn't be when Vega said he wouldn't have taken the boy if he'd known he was sick. It was apparent that Vega didn't know who he had kidnapped.

This didn't make any sense at all!

The cabin was small enough for Joe to hear what Vega said but he pretended not to notice as he bent over the boy. Whoever he was definitely had the smallpox! Joe stood up and walked over to the door and stood in the warm sunlight.

"How long has that boy been here?" he asked, a concerned frown between his brows as he rested his hand on the Colt .45's handle. He was surprised that Cruz Vega hadn't disarmed him. He wondered why Vega hadn't stopped him before he reached the cabin and certainly before he went into the cabin. If he had been in charge of something like this and holding a gringo kid for that much ransom, there would have been no way that a stranger, who just happened to be a pushy gringo, would have been standing there asking questions.

Maybe things weren't as bad as they seemed. Joe knew the boy had had smallpox for at least three days for the blisters on his face to be so pronounced. The boy's face was thin, almost emaciated. Joe wished again there was some way to get word to Art Shives in Fort Davis. He had been exposed to the disease and could infest those in town and that could set off an epidemic! But most of all, he wished he could get word to Tyler Worthing and let him know that he didn't have to go all the way to Candelaria. Worthing shouldn't have been so stubborn and come along with him.

Joe really wished that Tyler Worthing *had* been there right then. He would have actually given a month's pay to see what kind of look the big man would have on his wide face.

"Who is he?" Joe asked, turning away from the door and starting back toward the bunk in the corner. He knew Vega was scared. If he could convince him that the boy was seriously ill, maybe they could just leave. "How long has he been here?" Before Vega could answer, a bigger and more staggering question popped into his brain.

Where was the real Darius Worthing? Why had this boy been on the stage in which the fat kid, who would have put a thousand dollars into Vega's pocket, should have been riding? Maybe there had been a mistake in the date that Worthing and his son were supposed to meet in El Paso.

But that didn't make sense either. Worthing said that he was meeting Darius in Fort Davis as a surprise for his birthday. He already had rooms rented at the Limpia Hotel. How had Cruz Vega known that Tyler Worthing was going to be in Fort Davis on that particular day? Someone must have followed him from Brownsville. That same person had to have been in on the plot with someone in Pecos.

"His name is Darius Worthing and it is none of your concern how long he has been here," Vega's accented answer was angry and snappish. Worry, agitation, and disgust took turns replacing expressions on his brown face. If he had any knowledge about the illness, he knew that his plan wasn't going too well.

"It is my concern," Joe said contritely, taking a deep breath. "If he's been here over two days, he's probably in the most contagious stage of smallpox right now. I don't want to be stuck in here with him if you quarantine the entire village. How long has that man been sick?" He jerked his head toward the opposite corner where the man was moaning.

Joe watched Vega's lean face as reality hit him. He must have known that his plan was in deep trouble. But then a cunning, almost a weasel-like smile cut across Vega's face. Joe felt his heart sink down to the pit of his stomach. He knew that another plan was taking shape in

Vega's mind and he didn't even want to think what that plan might be.

"Who are you?" Vega asked again, lowering his head and giving Joe a level look with skepticism in his black eyes that were crinkling at the corners. "What are you doing here?"

"I told you before," Joe answered, shifting his weight from one foot to the other, wondering how he was going to fit into Vega's plan. He knew that if he was in the Mexican's black boots, believing that the boy who was tossing and turning restlessly on the bunk was Darius Worthing, he'd still go through with his plan. He wouldn't let a thousand dollars slip through his fingers so easily.

"I'm Joe Howard," he continued. "I heard there was a lot of gold and silver in those mountains." He inclined his head toward the mountains that seemed so near but were really several days' ride away. "I decided to come down, try my luck, and get rich quick." He smiled and wiggled his brows up and down. "It would sure beat the heck out of working for almost nothing."

A sly smile pulled at the corner of Vega's thin mouth and his eyes twinkled. "Gringo, there are even easier ways of getting rich than digging the ground. As you said, it beats the heck out of working."

Joe pretended to let the remark slide when he glanced over at the boy on the bunk. Kidnapping did beat the heck out of working, so long as the ransom was paid and you weren't caught. Joe turned around and ambled over to the bunk. He was surprised again when Vega didn't try to stop him or at least take his gun. Joe felt the boy's forehead. It still felt like fire.

An earthen pitcher of water was on the floor by the bunk. Joe dipped the corner of the red blanket in the water and bathed around the blotches on the boy's face, then his neck and arms. The boy calmed down a little.

Joe knew that a doctor wouldn't be able to do anymore for the villagers who were going to be sick than he was doing for the boy at the moment but he decided to try something anyway. It just might work. He knew that Vega wouldn't allow him to leave but he was going to suggest it.

"These people," he began, nodding at the boy and then to the man in the opposite corner, "need a doctor." He stood up with purpose and faced the brown-skinned bandit. "The boy could die. So could that man. Fort Davis isn't too far from here. If I leave right now, I could get there late tonight and could be back here, with a doctor, by noon tomorrow."

With real intention, that he knew wasn't going to work, Joe started toward the door. But, just as he expected, Vega pulled a walnut-handled Remington .38 from a smooth holster and aimed it at him.

"Hold on, gringo," Vega said in a velvet-smooth voice and shook his head slowly. "You are not going anywhere. You happened by here at the wrong time and the right time. You seem to be the only one who knows what this disease is and what to do. You have to keep this boy alive. If you don't," he shrugged his shoulders lazily. "Who knows?"

Joe knew that Vega really believed that the sick boy on the bunk was Darius Worthing. He could almost see dollar signs dancing in Vega's eyes. Vega was probably already counting the ransom money.

"Just the boy?" Joe prompted, watching the expression change in Vega's eyes. "How about the others? They're just as sick, or will be if they've been in contact with him. And that even includes you."

Maybe, if he could appeal to Vega's practical or humane side, he'd let him take the boy away from the village if he thought he was a health risk. But Joe was to learn that money, or the prospect of a lot of it, would overshadow practicality or compassion.

"Are you going to have someone take care of Quita and him?" Joe asked, motioning to the man on the opposite bunk. He could see a flush on the man's face and knew that he was in the first stages of smallpox. A flushed face usually indicated a high fever that precedes the disease. If Vega wouldn't do anything for the man, surely he'd have enough sympathy to do something for his sister and the boy who was worth some money to him.

"Do not worry yourself about them, gringo," Vega advised, wrinkling his forehead. "The boy is your main concern. Tell me what you want and I will see that you get it."

Joe offered no objection when Vega walked over to him and removed the Colt .45 from the holster. There wasn't a heck of a lot that he could do about it. He felt naked from the absent weight on his right side. It was at times like this that he wished he carried a hideaway.

Joe knew Vega was getting nervous and was in a hurry to get out of the cabin. He wondered if Vega would have the sick man taken some place else and he also wondered if he would post a guard at the door to be sure that he didn't try to leave with the boy or just leave?

Joe knew it wouldn't make any difference to Vega if he tried telling him that the boy on the bunk wasn't Darius Worthing. He wished now that he'd brought the picture with him. But Vega would only think that he was just trying to confuse him to help the boy get away.

Joe's questions were soon answered when Vega said something in rapid Spanish to the man he called Resta and who had summoned him from the cantina. Resta looked happy that he was being sent away and left at a fast run. Joe and Vega were quiet until Resta returned with two burly Mexicans. Resta waited outside the cabin. The two men didn't look too happy about being there but Joe knew that when Vega told them to jump they didn't hesitate by asking how high.

Joe remembered them being in the cantina earlier and knew that they'd heard him say that Quita had smallpox. Evidently they'd heard about the disease and knew that it was contagious and deadly. Not only had they been exposed by Quita, they were about to get another dose of it.

Joe watched in dismay as Vega ordered the two men to come into the cabin, pick up the sick man and take him out. Vega had moved outside and stood waiting at the door all of this time with Resta.

"If you need anything," Vega said, swinging up on the white horse, "tell Resta."

Joe hurried over to the window. Vega was already out of sight down the street. Resta had picked up an armchair, walked about fifty feet from the cabin, probably thinking that it was a safe distance and sat down in the shade of a juniper tree. Across his fat, protruding belly was a Winchester rifle and in his waistband was Joe's Colt .45. Joe knew he had to get his pistol back some way if he and the boy were going to get out of their predicament.

Joe rushed back to the boy when he heard him sit up on the bunk and ask for a drink of water.

"Who are you?" Joe asked, handing him a tin cup of water. "Don't waste my time and your energy by saying you're Darius Worthing," Joe cautioned, shaking his head rapidly to emphasize his words. "Because I know you're not. Tyler Worthing showed me a picture of his family and there's no way in the world that you could be Darius Worthing."

The boy drained the cup, licked his thin lips, then lay back on the rough blanket. He took a deep breath and closed his eyes. Joe had never seen such a sick-looking human being in all of his life. He remembered the time he'd had the pox and knew exactly how the boy was feeling and felt sorry for him. Not only for being sick, but for being in this sorry mess, no matter how he'd gotten into it.

"I'm Mark Humphrey," the boy finally answered weakly, expelling the breath and opening his fever-dimmed brown eyes. He raised his hand toward his face, but Joe stopped him.

"Do you know Darius Worthing?" Joe asked, an odd feeling building up in his stomach. Why was Mark Humphrey here? Why did Cruz Vega think he had Darius Worthing? But he'd have to wait until Humphrey answered his question before he said what he was thinking.

"I met him this one time in Pecos," the boy answered in a desolate voice. "He said he was supposed to meet his father in El Paso at the end of the week. He was supposed to ride the stage because his father wanted a report on how the Overland Stage Line operated between Pecos, Fort Davis, and El Paso." Mark shook his head, took and expelled a long breath.

"He said his father was thinking about buying the line," Mark continued, "and starting a run down this way. Darius said he didn't want to waste the time on a long and dusty stage ride and wanted to go by train and wait in El Paso. He paid me twenty dollars to take his place on the stage. I was supposed to meet him there and tell him about the ride. Then he'd tell his father what I said and Worthing would make his decision from that." There was no shame or guilt in Mark's voice as it trailed off. He was just answering Joe's questions. Joe realized again what a loud voice money had.

Like Quita had started to do, Mark reached up again and almost scratched his face.

"Don't do that," Joe said. "It'll spread the infection." He shook his head, not so much at the boy, but more at the disgust he felt for the two Worthings. Both of them thought that money could get them anything they wanted. One Worthing's selfishness could end up getting Joe and Mark killed. The other Worthing's stubbornness could also end up getting them killed.

"Did you try telling Vega that you aren't Darius Worthing?" Joe asked, pulling the blanket up over the boy's slender shoulders.

"Sure, but he wouldn't believe me," Mark answered in a hollow voice. "I guess I wouldn't either if I had kidnapped someone for a lot of money and they were trying to get away." He started to grin but the movement caused his skin to itch again. He raised his hand but fought down the urge to scratch his face.

Joe thought that sounded logical. The only thing bothering him right then was how was he going to get away with a sick boy and go after Tyler Worthing? He wondered what Worthing would do when he found out what his son had done?

The sudden image of Tyler Worthing's ruddy and wide face popped into Joe's imagination. He would give a month's pay to see the look when he saw sick and thin Mark Humphrey instead of his fat kid. Joe couldn't stop the laugh bursting from his mouth.

Mark Humphrey, unaware that something funny had happened, stared up at Joe.

"Cruz Vega is asking a thousand dollars from Tyler Worthing for the return of his son," Joe told Mark in glib amusement. The boy's light brown eyes flew wide open and his mouth gaped. His face was already flushed with fever but a deeper red colored it even more. Despite him feeling so rotten, Mark laughed until his eyes smarted after he recovered from the shock.

"That's really funny," Mark said around the laugh. "That sorry Mexican thinks I'm worth a thousand dollars. A man thinks his fat and spoiled son is worth a thousand dollars and is on his way to pay it to get him back. I've never had that much money in my life! Did you bring any of it with you?" His eyes gleamed in excited expectation and he raised up on his elbow. "I've never seen a thousand dollars. I'd like to see what it looks like." He grinned up at Joe.

"No," Joe answered, shaking his head. He felt sorry for the boy who was caught in the middle of this. For a malicious second he told himself that Darius Worthing should be the one lying on the rough, red blanket and sweating like a hog with sores all over his fat face. But no one deserved to be as sick as Joe knew Mark Humphrey was.

"What are you going to do?" Mark asked, touching one of the many puss-filled places lightly with the end of his finger. "If I'm being held for a ransom, and if you don't have it, someone has to take it somewhere. Who has it? Where is he going?"

For a sick boy, he sure could ask a lot of questions, Joe thought. Did a lot of money have that effect on people? To Joe, it was make a dollar, spend a dollar.

In as few words as possible, because his brain was spinning around, trying to think of a way out of this complicated situation, Joe explained to Mark who watched and listened with rapt attention. Every now and then he licked his dry lips.

"How long have you been here?" Joe asked, one

plan finally taking shape in his mind. He narrowed his eyes as he looked at Mark. "How long had you been sick before you got on the stage?"

Judging from some of the scabs which had already formed on Mark's face and remembering his own bout with the disease, Joe knew he should be well enough to travel soon. But he also knew that that soon wouldn't be soon enough. Tyler Worthing was on his way to Candelaria with a thousand dollars right then. Joe wondered if Cruz Vega had left to try to intercept Worthing before he reached the designated spot or let him reach Candelaria only to find a note sending him somewhere else, maybe back to this very spot.

Joe suddenly realized that what had started out to be a simple job of taking some money to Mexico and bringing back Darius Worthing would no doubt end up taking him all the way to El Paso. It had all sounded so simple when Colonel Eric McRaney had assured him how easy it would be. Someday, I'm going to take McRaney with me on one of these "simple" jobs, Joe promised himself with a sadistic grin.

Joe knew that Mark had been with Cruz Vega at least two days. But what really interested him now was how long had he been ill before the spots appeared on his face.

"I began feeling awful about two days before I met Worthing," Mark answered, arching his brows in thought. The movement of his skin must have set the abscesses to itching again because, without thinking, he slapped his hands against his face and pressed against it as hard as he could. Drawing in a ragged breath, he lowered his hands and a shiver consumed his entire body. He gritted his teeth so hard that knots bunched in his jaws.

Joe felt defeated with Mark's answer. He had the

vague recollection of being kept in the house for at least a week. But he'd thought that his mother was being overly protective. He'd known that he should've been out playing in a couple of days.

But there was more than just smallpox involved here. He didn't know what Vega would do when he found out that the boy he had kidnapped two days ago wasn't his ticket to a thousand dollars.

Joe knew that he had to get to Tyler Worthing before he reached Candelaria. It was just possible that some of Vega's cronies could be waiting there to take the money instead of sending him some place else. Worthing already had an early start on Vega who was still in the village. Three men, maybe four, counting the one in Pecos who had plotted with Vega on the kidnapping, must be burning up the telegraph wires!

But no matter how many plans Joe thought up, he couldn't do anything without a gun. He could see his Colt .45 in Resta's waistband and a helplessness washed over him.

"Have you been putting anything on your face when it itches?" Joe asked, another plan taking hold and beginning to grow in his mind.

"Yeah," Mark said, sitting up on the bunk. "This stuff really helps." He reached down and picked up a thick, pale, green stem from the floor and squeezed out a drop of clean liquid, then dabbed it on a red place at the end of his nose.

Joe took the stem from Mark and smelled it. There was no odor. When he rubbed a drop between his fingers, it was cool and soothing.

Joe jumped up and hurried over to the window. Leaning over the adobe sill, he saw a cactuslike plant about ten feet from the cabin. "Who gave you this?" he asked, turning away from the window.

"I mentioned to the girl in the red dress, when she brought me supper last night, that my face itched," Mark answered. "She went outside, then came back with that stem and said that it was good for stings and bites and that it might do me some good. It has helped some, but these places sure do itch."

Joe turned back to the window. "Hey, Resta!" he yelled out. The guard had slumped down in the chair but jerked up straight and shoved his black sombrero back on his curly, black head. "I need a new stem from that plant for the boy's face. It's itching him like the devil."

Joe hoped that Resta would bring the stem into the cabin instead of pitching it through the window as he would've done if he knew there was a contagious disease inside.

Joe's hope, or maybe it was an unconscious prayer, came true. Resta plodded over to the cactus, switched the Winchester to his left hand and broke off one large, thick stem. With the stem between his fingers, he opened the door with his right hand.

Resta, being right-handed worked to Joe's advantage. Joe flattened his back against the rough, adobe wall to his left of the door. The three-plank door opened back to the left. Resta stopped after coming only a few inches into the cabin. Maybe it was to adjust his eyes to the dimness or maybe he was afraid to come any further into the cabin because he suspected there might be a trap or he was afraid of being exposed to the smallpox.

Resta never knew when Joe caught him by his right arm and swung him further into the cabin. The motion took the Mexican around in a half circle and his black-bearded face was smashed when Joe slammed him hard against the wall. Joe heard the cartilage crack in the man's thin nose and bright red blood began dripping down into the black mustache above Resta's thick lips.

The surprise attack loosened Resta's hands on the rifle and cactus stem. The rifle made a thudding sound on the dirt floor. With a swiftness that denied his illness, Mark leaped from the bunk, hurried across the short distance, and jerked up the rifle. Joe swung the guard back around and gave him a hard jab in the middle of his bulging stomach. Resta doubled over, leaving his already jutting chin sticking further out. Joe let go of Resta's arm, laced his long fingers together and, swinging hard from the left, let his doubled fist connect with Resta's chin. With no other sound than a soft grunt, the guard hit the floor on his back, with his arms sprawled out at Joe's feet.

Without wasting time, Joe jerked his Colt .45 from Resta's waistband and returned it to his own holster. He felt complete with the familiar weight on his side. He unbuckled Resta's gunbelt and pitched it over to Mark. He grinned when he buckled it around his own waist. Mark had to use the last notch in the belt and there was so much left over that he had to roll it up and stuff it into his pocket so it wouldn't get in the way. Mark tied the holster to his leg so it wouldn't flop.

Joe ripped off a piece of the thick red blanket and stuffed it into Resta's mouth. Then he tore a longer strip from the blanket and wrapped it around the guard's face and tied it in the back. Jerking the leather chin strap from the sombrero, he rolled the guard over on his stomach and tied his hands behind him. Tearing a longer strip from the blanket, Joe tied Resta's feet together and, with Mark helping him, rolled him across the floor and pushed him under the bunk.

Joe stood up, wiped the blood from his hand and took a long breath. The entire incident had taken only a few minutes, if not seconds, but it seemed to go on and on. He used a little time to take a drink of water from the pitcher on the floor.

It would have been ridiculous for Joe to try and take Resta's place under the tree until dark. He was nowhere near Resta's size. That would be like trying to pass Mark off for Darius Worthing. Joe looked up at the clear, blue sky, judging from the position of the sun, he figured it was only about ten o'clock. Cruz Vega would no doubt make another check on the cabin before long. He and Mark would have to try to get away before then. In fact, they were going to have to leave in only a matter of minutes.

Joe didn't know how successful he'd be in getting Mark away from the village. He wouldn't have been so worried if the boy hadn't been sick. But he knew the outside exposure to Mark wouldn't be any worse than it had been the past few days, first on the stagecoach and now in the drafty cabin.

Joe felt a little better knowing that it was going to be much easier helping Mark get away than it would have been if Darius Worthing had been the one standing there, watching him with expectation in his eyes. Mark only had the smallpox working against him. Darius Worthing had all of that fat. Joe shook his head in disgust.

No horse, carrying such heavy weight, would be able to move fast enough or long enough to get far enough away from Cruz Vega and they would be sitting ducks.

Knowing that Darius Worthing was no doubt safe in El Paso and probably sitting down at a table full of everything from the kitchen except the stove, shoveling it in with both hands, Joe gave a silent prayer of thanks. He would be able to move a lot faster with Mark.

But just thinking about that fat kid caused an anger to boil up in Joe that he'd never experienced before against a man younger than he. When he found Tyler Worthing, he was going to make it his business to tell him exactly what his spoiled son had done.

Joe was amazed at the thought because he'd just made up his mind that he was going to accompany Worthing all the way to El Paso to meet that kid and give him a thrashing he'd never forget.

But for a man of Joe's height of five feet and seven inches, weighing only a hundred and twenty pounds, to give a boy of Darius Worthing's size a thrashing would be like an ant tying into a dog.

". . . to do?" The last of Mark's question broke into Joe's thoughts and he jerked his head around to look at him. Joe wanted to laugh at the comical picture Mark presented. He was wrapped in the remaining black wool blanket, his brown hair hanging down in his blotched face.

"What did you say?" Joe asked, blinking his eyes several times as the smile pulled at the corner of his mouth.

"I asked what we were going to do?" Mark repeated, a puzzled frown puckering between his eyes. He was standing beside the bunk, the guard's rifle clutched in his right hand.

"I know it's too soon for you to be out of bed," Joe said in a soft voice and smiled apologetically at Mark, "but, we've got to leave soon. You can't be any worse off out in the open than being here in this drafty cabin. Cruz Vega could come back any minute or someone could miss the guard if he's gone too long from under that tree. I'm surprised someone hasn't already come to check. Did you bring any clothes?"

"I did, but they're on the stage," Mark replied,

shaking his head disappointedly. Joe took and expelled a weary breath. Mark should be kept as warm as possible. But the only things available were the wool blanket that Mark already had wrapped around him and the clothes on the unconscious guard. Resta's clothes wouldn't fit either Mark or Joe, so there was no need to take any of them.

"Put that stem in your pocket," Joe said, glancing quickly from one side of the cabin to the other as his mind began racing again. "Get those other two blankets from that bunk and put on that hat." He nodded toward the bunk in the opposite corner.

"How are we going to get away?" Mark asked, a look in his brown eyes that told Joe he was beginning to question his sanity. There were two of them and only one horse, Serge, outside.

"I don't know what Cruz Vega was thinking when he left here," Joe said, a sneaky smile easing across his face, "but my horse is still out front. Vega should have taken him. But maybe he was in too much of a hurry to leave." Joe eased over to the window and looked up and down the street.

"All we have to do," he began, looking around at Mark, "is ride east a little way, then turn back southwest. There's no need to go back to Fort Davis to find Tyler Worthing. He's already on his way to the border with the ransom money." Joe pulled in a lung full of air. "Are you ready?"

If Mark Humphrey had been forced to walk, wrapped as he was in the blanket, carrying the two blankets and the guard's rifle, he never would have made it. He could barely move as it was and Joe was doubly thankful that it wasn't Darius Worthing struggling toward the door. He definitely wouldn't have made it.

Another thought struck Joe and he wanted to laugh

again. He didn't know how much time Mark had spent with Darius Worthing, but if Mark was carrying the smallpox then, that meant that the fat kid had been exposed to them.

A new picture of Worthing, sitting at the table, changed in Joe's mind. Now he could see the fat kid shoving food into his mouth with one hand and scratching the pussy blotches on his face with the other. Joe couldn't stop the laugh and got a questioning look from Mark.

"I guess I'm as ready as I'll ever be," Mark answered dubiously. As he passed Resta's sombrero on the floor, he managed to bend down and pick it up. "I've always wondered how one of these things would feel," he said, jamming it down on his head. His ears were the only thing that kept the hat from covering his eyes.

Joe stuck his head out the door just enough to look up and down the street again to make sure that no one was coming before stepping out of the cabin. The sun was so bright that he squinted his eyes against the stabbing glare.

Motioning for Mark to follow him, Joe grabbed him around the waist, swung him up on the back of the saddle, then swung up himself. He kneed Serge in the side and it didn't take long for the village to be engulfed in the rocky canyons and mountains as Serge's long and strong legs ate up the miles.

As they galloped along, Joe wondered and worried about their getaway. It had been much too easy. But maybe Cruz Vega was thinking that no attempt to escape would be made so soon since the boy was so sick. Vega couldn't know that there was any connection between Joe and Tyler Worthing. Joe wondered again why Vega hadn't taken Serge with him.

But that thought soon dissipated when they topped

a small mesa and Joe looked back toward the village. A dust cloud, kicked up by at least six horses was coming at a fast pace behind them. Serge was a strong horse and could cover a lot of ground as long as he was carrying single. But now, extra weight, slight as it was, was slowing him down. Joe knew they would have to either find a hiding place or stop and make a stand. And, six against two wasn't very good odds; especially if Cruz Vega thought that Joe had just snatched a thousand dollars worth of boy from his hands.

Joe had never been in this particular part of the country before but could tell that it was pretty much like that around the fort. Mountains. Gullies. Ravines. Hills. Any of them a potential hiding place. And any of them a potential place for an ambush.

With the odds against them, because Cruz Vega probably knew the country as well as he knew the back of his hand, Joe didn't feel very protective or protected even though Mark was wearing Resta's gun belt around his thin waist and still holding the rifle.

"How good are you with a pistol?" Joe asked, looking over his right shoulder at Mark who was holding tightly onto his waist with his left arm.

"I'm better with a rifle than a pistol," was Mark's simple answer.

Joe heard confidence, no bragging in Mark's voice and he believed him. But he had to be sure. Two against Cruz Vega and his men didn't make Joe Howard feel very comfortable.

"Just how good is that?" Joe pressed, feeling a smile on his mouth. He was good with a pistol but was just as good with the Winchester at long range. It was a sad thing to be thinking about how good a man was with a firearm in order to take another man's life. But that's the way it was in the game of life, especially if greed was dealing the hand.

"Well, not to be bragging," Mark said, drawing out the words, "but I can knock a squirrel out of a tree at a hundred yards." Joe could tell that Mark wasn't bragging. He was just answering Joe's question.

"Can you knock a Mexican out of a saddle a quarter of a mile away?" Joe asked glibly, pulling Serge down into an arroyo that at one time, maybe thousands of years ago, before man had set foot on the land, had been a bubbling river.

Joe knew they couldn't stay there very long or they'd be like two rabbits chased by half a dozen hounds. They followed the arroyo until it dropped down into a gully deep enough to hide a man riding a horse.

"I don't know," Mark answered in a tight voice. "I've never had to kill anyone."

"Maybe it won't come to that," Joe said, trying to sound reassuring.

"Have you ever killed anyone?" Mark asked, spacing out the words.

Joe knew Mark's question had to be answered and he wished that he didn't have to tell him the truth. But a lie would be much worse on him.

"Yeah," Joe answered, nodding slowly, "at Chickamauga." He didn't see any need to tell Mark about having to kill men during the time he rode for Wells Fargo and even more recently as army scout at Fort Davis. That wouldn't help matters.

The gully of red clay and rocks was about fifty feet high. The ground was a mesh of rocks, pebbles, and loose sand. It ran smoothly for a hundred yards, made a sharp left, and continued on.

Joe could tell that Serge was getting tired from carrying double for such a long time and at such a fast pace and was having trouble keeping his footing on the loose rocks.

"I hope we can find a place to hide soon," Joe said. He glanced over his shoulder at Mark. The boy's flushed and blotched face was almost obscured by the blanket and sombrero. Joe pulled Serge to a stop and dismounted. "I'm going to walk for a while. That might help."

Mark probably knew it wouldn't do any good for him to offer to walk. He knew he wouldn't be able to get ten feet, so he didn't say anything. He just nodded and wished instantly that he hadn't. His head began pounding and he thought, for a second, that he was going to puke. He wished he could get his hands on Darius Worthing at that very minute! No matter how big he might be, Mark knew that he would jump on him with both feet. Right then, twenty dollars just didn't seem to be enough for what he was going through.

4

As Joe Howard walked along, leading the seal black horse, he would give the last cent he had in his pocket right then to get his hands on Colonel Eric McRaney, Tyler Worthing, and most of all Darius Worthing. He'd take great pleasure in choking all three of them. He wondered how Darius's fat neck would feel in his hands?

Colonel McRaney would get his for making this job sound so easy. When the colonel explained anything, it sounded as if he were explaining to a child how a four-piece puzzle would always fall into place. But a puzzle was one thing. Only pieces of cardboard or paper. But when human beings got involved, that was something entirely different.

No matter how difficult or dangerous any particular job might be that McRaney was talking about, Joe always got the feeling that he just couldn't wait to jump right into the middle of it. McRaney was so good at simplifying things that he could probably entice Joe into plunging butt naked into a bed of prickly pear cactus and have him end up thinking that the idea had been his all along.

Tyler Worthing would get what was coming to him for being so hardheaded and not coming with Joe or at least for not listening to what he had to tell him. If he had done that he could've told at once that Mark Humphrey wasn't his spoiled, fat kid. They would have known that Darius had paid Mark to take his place on the stage and they could've gone back to the fort and waited for the next stage or train to El Paso.

Joe knew full well that if Darius Worthing should somehow materialize in front of him right then, that he would tear into the pampered and probably obnoxious brat with everything he had and mad as he was getting just thinking about him, that would be a lot!

But then he gave the kid the benefit of the doubt. Maybe he was misjudging him. Tyler Worthing was obviously a very rich man and was probably used to getting what he wanted. That trait had carried over to his son.

"It must be nice having money and money does have a loud voice," Joe muttered to himself as he plodded along. Something was trying to make its way to the front of his mind again but it just wouldn't surface. But something about the entire thing just didn't make any sense. Maybe it would all come together before too long.

How did Cruz Vega know that Darius Worthing would be on that particular stage? That was simple. Someone told him. Did Tyler Worthing have a thousand dollars on him? The answer to that was simple also. Only a stupid man would be riding around the country alone with that much money on him. Tyler Worthing might be a lot of things but he wasn't stupid. But he hadn't mentioned anything to Joe about going to the bank in Fort Davis to get any money. He would have to have a letter of credit from a bank in Pecos stating that he had money there if he tried to write a check.

Joe had been with him from the time they had left the fort until they left the sheriff's office and he'd gone to Billy Leon's Cafe. Of course, Worthing could have gone to the bank after Joe left Fort Davis. Joe hadn't noticed any bulging satchels or odd look about Worthing's saddlebags to indicate that he was carrying anything out of the ordinary. But then, he wouldn't have been carrying a sign telling how much money he had.

For one heart-stopping second Joe Howard was hit with a thought that made his blood run as cold as ice water in his veins.

Could Tyler Worthing, the man who seemed so concerned about his son, have set him up to be kidnapped? Or worse yet, killed?

If what Joe was thinking was true, it wouldn't be the first instance since time began that one member of a family had turned against another. He had even fought in a war where brother had killed brother and each one had believed that his side had been right.

This can't be true, Joe argued with himself, shaking his head. What would Tyler Worthing gain by having his son killed? Money could be an important part of it and it was obvious that he wasn't poor. His one suit would probably cost more than all of the clothes Joe owned!

But that was another thing that didn't make sense to Joe. If Worthing wanted his son dead, he could have gotten someone to do it in Pecos and for a heck of a lot less than a thousand dollars!

No, Joe told himself again and shook his head doggedly. Darius Worthing had been kidnapped by Cruz Vega just for money. But the same question reared its ugly head. Who had told Cruz Vega that Worthing would be on that stage? Who was the setup man in Pecos?

Joe had been walking for about ten minutes when he saw exactly what he was looking for. In the left side of the gully was a cave that would suit their needs for a while. It wouldn't be long before dark and Mark Humphrey should be in as warm a place as possible for the night. He would probably be just as warm inside the cave as he'd been in the adobe cabin and Joe felt good about finding the cave when he did. If Vega and his men were still following them, they couldn't be picked off because the gully was too tight for someone to stand on the opposite side and fire down on them. On the other hand, they would have a good view of the upper ledge. If someone tried to come in from either side, Joe would be able to hear them.

Once again, things were too simple. Something had to go wrong!

Joe wondered why it was taking Cruz Vega and his men so long to catch up with them. For a second, he put himself in Vega's boots. Joe had only told Vega his name. But Vega, knowing that Mark, who he believed to be Darius Worthing would tell Joe that he'd been kidnapped and they would be on their way to Candelaria to find Tyler Worthing. If Vega wasn't following too closely on their trail, Joe knew he was hoping to intercept them before they reached Candelaria.

The cave was wider than it was deep and Joe would have a good view of each end of the gully. No one could come into either end of it without him knowing. They couldn't be picked off from this angle and he knew that he and Mark would be safe for the night. That is, if Vega or one of his men didn't already know about the place and was waiting for them.

Joe reached up to help Mark slide down from the saddle and it didn't take two looks to see that the boy had gone just about as far as he could that day. The pus-filled blisters stood out more on his pale and drawn face. If he hadn't had the blanket high up around his neck, his chin would have been touching his chest. His eyes were almost closed.

God, please, don't let this kid die on me, Joe prayed silently. He doesn't deserve to be in this mess as sick as he is. But then, nobody deserved to be kidnapped. He eased Mark from the saddle and set him down on the ground just inside the cave entrance. Mark slumped against the wall and expelled a long, slow breath.

"Would you like some coffee?" Joe asked, before thinking. Not only was Mark tired and sick, he was probably hungry. Joe knew he was hungry. He hadn't eaten since early that morning.

Just before making a huge mistake, Joe caught himself. "Uh, oh," he said, shaking his head regretfully. "I'm afraid the coffee will have to wait. Vega could smell or see the smoke from a fire. I should have thought about that before asking. I do have some fried salt pork and biscuits."

"That'll be okay," Mark said in a weak voice. "I'm not much on coffee anyway. Do you have any water?"

Joe took the grub sack from the saddle horn and squatted down on the ground by Mark. He handed him one of the biscuits, a piece of cold meat, and poured water into a tin cup. Suddenly the question that had been trying to make its way to the front of his mind finally made it and he put words to it.

"Mark," he began, breaking off a piece of biscuit that was almost hard enough to drive nails, "how did Cruz Vega know that Darius Worthing was going to be on that particular stage?" Joe put the bread into his mouth and worked it around until enough saliva had saturated it to make it easy to chew.

Mark was about to take a bite of meat but paused

with it halfway to his mouth. He stared at Joe for a second, shifted his eyes down to a rock between his feet then back up to Joe's questioning gaze.

"I don't know," he finally answered in a puzzled voice, shaking his head. A deep frown pulled lines between his brows. "I was feeling so bad that it really didn't dawn on me that Worthing's name had actually been mentioned until I tried telling Vega that I was someone else."

Joe chewed thoughtfully on the biscuit for a while. Darius Worthing wouldn't have known that Cruz Vega would try to kidnap him. Joe didn't believe the fat kid would be in on any conspiracy or scheme to stage his kidnapping. He just hadn't wanted to endure the long stage ride from Pecos, down to Fort Davis and finally on out to El Paso. A train ride would be more comfortable and better and more food would be available.

Darius Worthing had probably seen his father use his money to buy and maybe even bribe to get what he wanted and saw no reason why he couldn't do the same thing. All he was interested in was getting to El Paso before his father in the easiest way possible. Darius had no way of knowing that his father would surprise him on his birthday in Fort Davis.

Someone in Pecos must be working with Cruz Vega and had heard Tyler Worthing say that his son was going to be on the stage or maybe even Darius himself had said that he was going to be on it. Then Joe thought of another angle.

"Did Art Shives, the stage driver and Vega seem to know each other?" Joe asked, washing the biscuit down with a swallow of water from the canteen. Some coffee would really taste good right now, he thought dismally.

Shives would be an unlikely candidate in all of this since he'd been shot. But a share in a lot of money, and a thousand dollars *was* a lot of money, would dull the pain of a bullet wound and Joe knew that things more strange than this had happened before and all for the want of money.

In thinking about Shives's wound a little more, it really hadn't seemed all that bad.

"Since you mentioned it," Mark said, nodding his head slowly, "the driver didn't seem very surprised when the stage was stopped. And I remember hearing him call Vega by name."

But just because Art Shives had called Vega by name, and Joe remembered Shives telling him and Herman Gredes that Cruz Vega had stopped the stage, didn't necessarily mean that he actually knew him. But that wasn't so. Shives had said that he'd seen Vega once in Laredo.

Joe had heard enough about the Mexican bandit that he probably would have called him by name if he'd seen him. In fact, he'd known immediately who Vega was the minute he'd come into the cantina earlier that day because Shives had described him so well.

This new revelation sort of blew a hole in Joe's theory about a conspiracy between Shives and Vega. But somebody somewhere had to know that Darius Worthing was going to be on that stage! That somebody had to live in Pecos.

Joe could just hear Colonel Eric McRaney telling him how simple it would be for him to go to Pecos and find out who that person was. That was no doubt what he'd have to do when he returned from El Paso. He shook his head dismally at the thought.

That thought brought up another question. Why hadn't that person in Pecos made sure that Darius Worthing had gotten on the stage? A boy that big would be awfully hard to miss!

Joe was so engrossed in his thoughts, about to ask Mark what had happened in Pecos for the two boys to change places that he had dropped his guard and didn't know that someone had entered the gully until the quiet was broken by a noise that would rattle the mountains around them.

"Come on here, you goldang, lazy, worthless, old mule ass," a voice bellowed out amid the clatter and clanging of pots and pans. "I don't know why in the sam hill I keep you around. All you want to do is kick and sit. I could get more use out of a stinkin' goat. At least, I could eat the goat. Come on here."

Joe leaped to his feet, his heart stopping in his chest, and jerked the Colt .45 from the holster, aiming it directly at a grizzled, old prospector just coming around the longest part of the bend in the gully. The old man was riding one of the most beautiful bay mares that Joe had ever seen. The mare's coat and four brown stockings gleamed in the sun and was evidence that the old man spent a lot of time brushing her. The long, flowing mane and tail were free of cockles and burrs. The old man was leading the object of his verbal abuse, a mule on a long rope. Joe was soon to realize that the insults to the mule were out of affection and not annoyance. The fat mule was so smoke gray that he looked almost silver and walked with a gait that did his species proud.

"Hold it right there," Joe said, thumbing the hammer back. "Keep your hands where I can see them."

"Whoa, Thimble," the old man said, pulling back sharply on the reins. His black brows, with a lot of gray in them arched in a little fear and a lot of surprise.

" 'Pears we'uns gonna be sharin' our abode with others tonight," he said, holding Joe's gaze intently. With an agility that was uncharacteristic of his obvious old age (or maybe he just looked old because he was so dirty), the old man swung his right leg over Thimble's head, removed his left foot from the stirrup, turned sideways on the saddle, and slid to the ground.

"Keep your hands where I can see them," Joe reminded when he thought the old man was going to make a move for a Remington .38 at his side. Joe really didn't think that he and Mark were in any danger from the old man unless he might talk them to death. "Who are you? What are you doing here?"

"Well, now, boy, I could ask ye the very same thing," the bowlegged man answered shrewdly, levity in his gravelly voice as he tugged on the rope to bring the mule closer. "But since it's ye who's holdin' a persuader on me, I guess I'd better tell ye that I'm Buford Chedos. I been comin' to this here particular cave fer the past two years to rest a spell after spendin' a little time in my digs across the river. Now, would ye mind tellin' me what ye're doin here?"

Still holding Joe's gaze, he reached up and removed a nondescript hat that hadn't been black in a long time from gray-streaked dark brown hair. Joe wondered why he hadn't spent as much time on his own appearance as he did the bay and mule?

But Chedos probably thought that he needed a healthy horse for riding and a healthy mule for packing more than he did clean clothes and well-groomed hair and beard. Who would see or smell him out here in these mountains anyway?

Chedos's green-and-red checked flannel shirt was faded from much wearing and maybe a little washing and the black-wool pants, held up by suspenders had holes in the knees, revealing red underwear.

Joe was embarrassed when he realized that he was holding his breath against some invading odor and was shocked when there was none when he exhaled and took a deep breath. He saw a knowing twinkle in the old man's pale blue eyes.

"Iffen ye ain't gonna shoot me," Chedos said, wrinkling up his forehead, "will ye lower that hammer and let me put my shotgun down?"

"Sure," Joe said, lowering the hammer and returning the pistol to the holster. From the knots on Chedos's gnarled hands, Joe knew there was no threat to him and Mark.

Without mincing words Joe explained part of his and Mark's reason for being in the cave. Chedos seemed more concerned than surprised when Joe hesitantly told him that Mark had smallpox. He left out the part about Mark being worth a thousand dollars to Cruz Vega.

"I had them pox when I was jest a tad," Chedos said, rolling his mouth in against short, yellow teeth. "Iffen it weren't fer this scraggly old beard of mine," he reached up and ran a dirty-nailed hand over his matted beard, "ye could see what them things done to me. Some of the pits are so deep I could almost wash my clothes in 'um."

Joe and Mark laughed at Chedos's exaggeration and Joe wondered why he used that particular comparison. Joe believed he was right in his assumption about Chedos being no threat to him and Mark. He felt safe for the time being anyway. All of that might change if Joe told him about the ransom money on Mark.

"Does Cruz Vega know that you come through here very often," Joe asked, hoping Chedos wouldn't ask why he wanted to know.

"Yep," Chedos answered, nodding and leaning back against the bay. He hooked his thumbs around the suspenders. "He thinks I'm crazy, wanderin' 'round in these here mountains by my lone self. But he don't bother me and I don't bother him."

Joe hoped that if Cruz Vega saw Chedos's animals in the gully he wouldn't bother them and maybe he and Mark could get a good night's sleep. Their work was still cut out for them if they reached Tyler Worthing before he reached the drop place in Candelaria with the thousand dollars in ransom money for his son.

But he knew that wasn't going to happen when he heard horses coming at a fast pace, or as fast as the ground would allow. Joe shifted a quick look from Chedos, to the approaching sound and back to Chedos. His heart jumped up in his throat and he gripped the pistol handle.

"I ain't been here very long," Buford Chedos said, almost spitting the words out and pulling the animals closer to the cave, "and we'uns ain't had much time to talk, but I think there's somethin' ye ain't tellin' me by the funny way ye're actin'."

Joe was amazed at the old man's astuteness at figuring out so quickly that something was wrong. Maybe him mentioning Cruz Vega so soon had something to do with it.

Joe was sure that the horses coming down the gully were ridden by Cruz Vega and his men and he thought it was ironic that everybody was arriving at the same place at the same time. He just wondered why they hadn't caught up with him and Mark by now? The only one missing in the scenario was Tyler Worthing. An idea took shape in his mind and he hoped he would have time to make it work.

"I'll tell you all about it later," he said, reholstering the .45. "I'm sure that's Cruz Vega and his men coming now." He jerked his head in the direction of the noise. "They're after us." He nodded toward Mark. "I hate to ask you to lie, but would you tell them that you haven't seen us. I'm sure he'll ask you."

Joe gave himself enough time to swat Serge across the rump and send him down the west end of the gully. The big horse would come back when he was called and Joe wasn't worried about him running too far away. He had just enough time after Serge had disappeared around the bend in the gully to help Mark stand up and move further back into the cave when he heard the horses stop at the opening.

Joe Howard had never felt so inadequate and scared in all of his life as he did at that very minute as he and Mark stood silently in the back of the cave and listened. He'd never hidden from anything in his life, but knowing that they were outnumbered, he had to think about Mark Humphrey. And he couldn't take a chance on getting Buford Chedos hurt.

If he had stayed out in the open with Chedos, Vega would probably think that Chedos was mixed up with him. Vega would know that Mark was in the cave, would kill Joe and Chedos and go on with his plan to extort a thousand dollars from Tyler Worthing.

If Buford Chedos didn't phrase his words just right, he could be in as much trouble as Joe and Mark.

Oh, my God! Joe was suddenly hit by a thought that almost caused his knees to buckle and at least ten small knots formed into one large one. He had just met Buford Chedos! The old man had admitted being on speaking terms with Cruz Vega. How much on speaking terms he thought? Would Chedos tell Vega that they were in the cave? Self-preservation made Joe ease the .45 from the holster. He shouldn't have holstered it in the first place. There was only one thing he could do if Vega came into the cave.

But Joe didn't want to kill Cruz Vega. He just wanted to beat him to Tyler Worthing and see the look the big man would have on his face when he heard what his son had done.

Joe's heart jumped up into his throat when he saw Mark, standing in the shadows, let the blanket fall from his shoulders and bring the rifle up to waist level. Joe put his finger against his mouth and pursed his lips. He felt a little better when he realized that another advantage seemed to be swinging their way. He and Mark were in the shadows and had no trouble seeing out. Vega had the light in his eyes.

Joe knew he could handle the situation, but any number of small things could still end up getting all three of them killed if Vega believed that they stood between him and a thousand dollars. Joe was aware again of how loudly money could talk.

Joe wished right then that he was still sitting on the porch in front of Colonel McRaney's neatly arranged office at Fort Davis and arguing with McRaney about what he would do if he had a lot of land. At the present time, he was worried if he was going to get out of a small cave alive!

"*Buenas tardes, Señor* Buford Chedos," Cruz Vega's low, smooth voice greeted. "How have you been since I saw you last? Have you been as successful in the mountains this time as you were before?"

Joe removed his hat, dropped it on the ground and flattened himself as much as he could against the cave wall. It seemed to take forever to inch his way to the front of it. He was on the west side of the cave and the shadows would still help hide him and he would still be able to see and hear Vega and Chedos.

"Successful? Ha!" Chedos scoffed, disgust in his raspy voice. He slapped the reins absently against his left hand. "That dadblamed, cantankerous old mule ass decided he didn't want to go up as high in the mountains this time as we went before. But I got 'nuf out of the other place to tide me over fer a spell." Joe saw him pat the pocket of his dirty green-and-red checked shirt. "We'uns is gonna spend the night here in the cave like we generally do, build a nice warm fire, eat somethin', then light out first thing in the mornin'. What 're ye'uns doin' this far from yer place?" Chedos squinted a look up at Vega, his blue eyes almost lost in the wrinkles around them.

"Oh, we are just out for a ride," Vega answered, evasiveness in his voice. He shook his head slowly and looked around the sun-baked vastness.

Joe hoped that Serge was far enough away and that Vega wouldn't see him. Vega would probably remember seeing the black horse in the village and would know instantly that Joe, and Mark were somewhere close.

"Did you happen to see a gringo and a boy riding a black horse?" Vega was trying to sound and act nonchalant but Joe saw an intenseness in his black eyes. Joe held his breath, having no idea how the old prospector would answer. Joe knew that if he was wearing Chedos's run-down boots and could end up getting killed, he'd tell Vega the truth without hesitation.

"Another 'Merican?" Chedos asked, reaching up and scratching his head. Believable shock widened his eyes and wrinkled his forehead. "Nah. If I had, I'd still be talkin' his ears off. I ain't seen anuther white human bein' in such a long time that I've almost plum fergot what one looks like. Why do ye ask? Why in the world would two men be ridin' double out here in this kinda country?" He indicated the mountains and desert with a sweeping motion of his right arm.

A cunning look, bordering on a snarl, eased across Vega's brown face. If Joe had been in Cruz Vega's place, he wouldn't have believed a word Chedos said. Vega had been right on their heels when they'd left the village. He and Mark had been riding double in unfamiliar country. Vega, on the other hand, was riding single in country he'd been raised in and he no doubt suspected that this old man was giving him a lot of double-talk.

"Well, the boy is ill," Vega answered, shrugging his thin shoulders, benevolence in his voice, "and I want to find him before he gets worse. And I might as well tell you this. The boy is worth a thousand American dollars to me."

Once again, Joe knew that if he was in Chedos's place, he would have made Cruz Vega a deal right then to split that much money with him and tell him where he and Mark were. But then the old prospector could be thinking why should he split the money with Vega when he more or less had Joe and Mark all to himself? He already knew that Mark was sick and probably couldn't put up much of a fight. Maybe he could get the drop on Joe and all of the ransom money would be his.

Joe was conscious of a long pause and a nervous knot bunched up in his stomach. He knew that Buford Chedos must be considering his options. With that much money up for grabs, it would be a hard thing to turn down. Especially since Chedos had known Vega much longer than he'd known Joe Howard and Mark Humphrey. If Vega found out later that Chedos had lied to him, he would probably kill him.

But Joe Howard was about to have his faith in his fellow man restored. Up to a point anyway.

"A thousand dollars ye say?" Chedos said morosely, smacking his lips together. "I wish I was worth a thousand dollars to sumbody." He shook his head sadly and expelled a long, deep sigh. "I ain't never seen a thousand dollars in all of my born days. Have you?"

Joe hadn't had time to tell the old man all of the

details and he knew from the calculating expression on his face and the way he shifted his weight from one foot to the other that he was going to have a lot of explaining to do. He wished Vega would hurry and leave. He was getting tired of standing in this cramped position by the cave entrance.

Joe threw a quick glance back at Mark Humphrey. He was still standing in the corner, the rifle now at hip level. But he didn't look so good. Even in the dim shadows, his face appeared even more flushed and Joe knew that his fever was coming up. Joe could only hope that he would remain quiet for a little longer.

Joe's patience and nerves were on the verge of wearing out when Vega removed the big sombrero, absently wiped the sweatband, looked at Chedos narrowly, then replaced the sombrero. The Mexican reigned the white horse around, kneed him in the side, and let him take a few steps away before pulling him to a stop.

"Maybe I should leave one of my men here with you just in case that gringo and boy should come this way. The gringo could be dangerous if he thinks you might try to help the boy escape." He arched his black brows questioningly. "What do you think?"

Joe could feel his heart literally stop beating in his chest and a cold sweat popped out all over him. His lungs felt like they were on fire as he held his breath. It was a good idea on Vega's part, but was the last thing that Joe needed. If Vega did insist on leaving one of his men behind, Joe knew that he would no doubt have to kill him in order to escape. He wasn't sure just how many riders Vega had with him now. He thought he'd counted six when he saw them leaving the village. More could have joined Vega or some could have dropped back. He eased the hammer back on the pistol with his thumb.

"Ye kin do whatever ye want," Buford Chedos said

apathetically, pulling his mouth down at the corner. "But if ye do leave sumbody, tell 'em not to bother me. I'm only gonna be here long enough to fix a bite to eat. My belly's rumblin' like thunder. Kin ye hear it?" He patted his middle and squinted a pitiful look up at Vega. "Then I'm gonna sleep till mornin', get up early, and start out again. Ye probably already know it, but these mountains is fulla caves. Them two could be hidin' in anyone of 'um."

Joe suddenly realized that Vega had been bluffing Chedos. If the old man had protested too much about Vega leaving someone behind, that would have been a dead giveaway that he knew more than he was telling about him and Mark. There wouldn't have been any need to leave anyone there. They would have just stormed the cave and that would have been it for all three of them.

"Perhaps you are right, *Viejo*," Vega said, expelling a long breath and pulling the sombrero low over his forehead to shield his eyes from the rays of the setting sun. "I do not have time to search every one of them."

Joe breathed a little easier when he counted six men ride past the cave opening. He waited a few more seconds before stepping out even though Chedos had gone about the business of gathering limbs and twigs and begun building a fire. Vega was no doubt crafty enough to send one of his men back to check on things.

"I think it's safe to come out now," Chedos said without looking up as he poured water from a canteen into a battered and blackened coffeepot and set it on a small circle of rocks under which he'd built a fire. He dropped down on a large rock with a grunt, stretched out his legs, then turned his full attention on Joe Howard. From his fixed expression, Joe knew that it was time for him to begin explaining and that Chedos would sit right there until he did it to his satisfaction. Joe was correct in his guess.

"Now, what in the devil did Vega mean," Chedos began, tilting his head back then lowering it to give Joe a level gaze, "when he said that kid was worth a thousand dollars to him? I ain't goin' nowheres and I'd like to hear all 'bout it."

"Couldn't we have a cup of coffee first?" Joe asked, turning his attention to the boiling pot. The coffee was giving off a tantalizing aroma and despite what McRaney had said about coffee making his hands shake, Joe knew he'd feel much better after he'd had a cup. But first he had to get Serge back and stood up.

Joe didn't know how good Chedos was with his Remington .38 or the Winchester. But something told him that Chedos had needed and used more than luck in staying alive in these mountains all of these years. But he placated himself with the knowledge that he could rely on his youth and speed if things got out of hand and Chedos threatened him.

"I'll tell you all about it in a minute," Joe said, stepping further out into the gully. Using the small, jutting-out branches of a juniper tree and rocks for footholds, he climbd up on the bank and looked around, expecting to see Cruz Vega, or one of his men standing there, waiting for him. He wouldn't have been the least surprised to see one or all of them waiting, their guns aimed at him.

He was a little disappointed that the top of the bank was as desolate and empty as the rest of the country. He wasn't worried when he didn't see Serge anywhere. Putting his thumb and forefinger between his teeth, he whistled and could hear the reverberating echos across the canyon. He had just enough time to jump back down into the gully when he heard the pounding hoofbeats of a horse coming and knew that it would be the seal black horse.

"How did ye know that yer horse wouldn't run away?" Chedos asked, a mystified frown drawing his unruly brows together, when Serge trotted up to Joe and nuzzled his shoulder. He'd forgotten his previous question.

"Oh, Serge and I have been together for a long time," Joe said, smiling softly. "We sort of understand each other." He rubbed between Serge's big, brown eyes before taking the grub sack from the saddle horn. He cut off several thick slices of salt pork and hurried to make flat bread. Since Vega knew that Chedos was there and was going to make a fire, now would be a good time to make a hot meal.

When everything was ready, he put the meat and bread on a tin plate, poured the strong and wonderful-smelling, black coffee into a tin cup, and took it into the cave for Mark. The boy had leaned the rifle against the wall, sat down, and pulled the blanket up around him. He had been dozing but awoke and ate when Joe touched him on the shoulder.

Joe went back to the mouth of the cave, fixed a similar sandwich, then dropped down on the ground by Chedos and filled a tin cup with coffee. The first sip had been well worth waiting for.

Knowing that the old man was being eaten alive with curiosity about his and Mark's presence in the area and especially Mark being worth a thousand dollars to Cruz Vega, Joe went into more details this time. He particularly liked Chedos's reaction when he told him about Darius Worthing's plot to deceive his father.

"Why, that low-down, spoiled-assed brat," Chedos said with fire edging his words and spitting in his eyes when Joe finished telling him everything. The words exploded from his bearded mouth. "That boy needs his fat butt paddled good. Does his pappy know what he's done?" He cocked his head sideways and gave Joe a skeptical look.

"Not yet," Joe answered derisively, shaking his head and arching his brows. He drained the coffee cup, poured out the dregs and grinned. "But he will as soon as I can find him. As big as that kid's butt is, it will take a boat oar to paddle it."

Chedos's laughter at Joe's remark bounced off the cave walls and Joe smiled. It was the first time in a couple of days that the army scout had had a good reason to laugh.

"Wouldn't ye like to see it happen?" Chedos asked, blinking his eyes when he'd finally regained his composure.

"Yeah," Joe replied, refilling his cup.

Night began settling over the mountains like a soft, velvet blanket and the sounds that only the dwellers of the area could make wafted across the vastness. A dove cooed to its young or mate. The wind, the never-ending wind, whispered over and touched the land with a gentle, loverlike caress. A sound, like a woman in pain, which could only have been made by a cougar, sent chills up and down Joe's back and he shivered although it was still warm in the cave. Birds, crickets, and coyotes added their own distinctive sounds of trills, chirps, and bays. Joe knew he'd never heard anything that sounded so good.

"What do ye suppose Worthing will do when he sees this boy?" Chedos asked, pouring out the remains of his cold coffee. He stood up, stretched, and looked around at Mark Humphrey who had dropped off to sleep again. His splotched face was nestled in the blankets around his neck and he was already snoring. He had put more of the cactus liquid on his face and it looked a little better.

"I don't know," Joe replied, swallowing a mouthful of coffee, "but I wouldn't miss it for the world. He'll be able to tell with one glance that Mark isn't his son," Joe continued candidly. He stood up, untied his bedroll, and kicked it out.

"From the short time that I was with Tyler Worthing," Joe went on, "he didn't seem to be the type of man who would appreciate someone playing a trick like this on him, even his own son, especially where his money is concerned."

Joe dropped down on the blanket, stretched out, leaned his head against the saddle, pulled his sheepskin coat over him, and closed his eyes.

A sinister laugh from Buford Chedos popped Joe's eyes wide open and he raised up. He could see Buford Chedos's grinning, bearded face in the dying light of the crackling fire.

"You nearly scared me half to death," Joe snapped, leaning back on his elbow. "What's so funny?"

"Oh, I was jest thinkin'," Chedos answered around the laugh, "that I ain't never seen nobody who was worth a thousand dollars." He glanced over at Mark, coughed, and cleared his throat. "In fact, I ain't never seen nobody who even had a thousand dollars."

"Well, don't feel so alone in that," Joe rebuffed after he'd yawned, "neither have I. But what's so funny about that?" He failed to see anything funny or even a little amusing in what Chedos was talking about.

"I was also thinkin' that when Cruz Vega has had time to look around," Chedos went on, leaning back against the jagged cave wall and stretching his short legs out, "ye're goin' to need an extra gun. Ye can use me." He held an imaginary rifle up to his shoulder and said "pow" as he pulled the trigger with a gnarled finger. "I ain't got nothin' else to do and I want to go along with ye anyway. I want to see Tyler Worthing's face when he finds out what his kid's done."

Joe took a little time to give some extra thought to Buford Chedos's offer. There was a lot of merit to it. Cruz Vega would probably know that he had been tricked no later than noon tomorrow, if not sooner when he hadn't crossed any fresh tracks. There had been only six men including Vega but the odds were still against Joe since he would have a sick boy with him no matter how good Mark had said he was with a rifle. Chedos just might come in handy.

"You're absolutely right," Joe agreed, lying back down on his blanket and pulling up the coat, "and you've got a deal. I could probably make it by myself. But Mark will need some help." A soft smile touched his face as he glanced over at the sleeping boy. "Do you think there's any need for one of us to stand watch?"

"Nah," Chedos answered, wiggling his hips in the soft dirt for a more comfortable place then pulling his blanket around him. "I sleep light. I'll hear anything if it comes up."

The crackling fire was soon the only sound except the long and deep breathing of the three men heard in the cave. Outside, the wind was still blowing across the land as it had done from the beginning of time and it picked up the dove's soft cooing and the coyote's lonely cry.

Joe Howard would swear that he'd been asleep for only a few seconds when he heard Serge nickering low in his throat. Joe knew there had to be something other than night creatures around the cave for the black horse to act that way. He and Serge had camped out so much that he was used to all of the night sounds.

Getting up quietly, Joe adjusted the gun belt around his waist and eased to the front of the cave. He had to step over Buford Chedos who was snoring almost loud enough to cover the unmistakable sounds of footsteps.

"Some light sleeper," Joe muttered, with a snort under his breath.

Stopping at the mouth of the cave, Joe listened, and wondered if Cruz Vega had actually decided to send one of his men back to keep an eye on Chedos after all. That's what Joe would have done if the situation had been reversed. In fact, he would have insisted on leaving someone at the cave in the first place.

But whoever was approaching the cave could be anyone, not necessarily one of Vega's men. An Indian could have seen them, decided to wait until after dark, kill all three of them, and steal the horses. Or it could be some nefarious character on the run, looking for some easy pickings.

Joe wanted to believe that it wasn't any of Cruz Vega's men because he didn't hear any jangling spurs and he remembered seeing spurs on all of the Mexicans. But spurs could be removed. And he really didn't think that it was an Indian. Indians didn't like being out at night. If something happened to them, their spirits couldn't find the way in the dark to wherever they were supposed to go.

The footsteps were coming from the east side of the gully. Whoever it was would have to come around a corner before actually reaching the cave and Joe would have enough time to do whatever he needed.

Joe flattened himself against the west side of the cave and peeped out. Serge nickered low in his throat when he saw Joe. The crunching steps on the pebbles stopped for a second. Even though Joe was holding his breath, he was sure that the night walker could hear his pounding heart. The sound roared in Joe's ears and his lungs were on fire. He parted his lips a little and slowly pulled in a breath. He stuck his head out just a fraction and could see the long shadow cast by the light of the rising, yellow moon as a man began moving again.

Hoping that he would have enough time to get out of the cave before the intruder reached it, Joe inched his way against the wall, bent down low, and hurried as fast as the position would allow, out the west side of the cave. He was glad he hadn't put on his hat and didn't wear spurs.

Turning quickly back to his left, Joe eased up the sloping side of the gully and felt good when he was able to climb up on the top without any trouble.

Standing up, but back far enough so that the moon's silver light wouldn't throw his shadow, he was able to look down on the gully below. He had been right in his first assumption that Cruz Vega had sent one of his men back to the cave to keep an eye on Buford Chedos when he saw the shadowy outline of a sombrero.

But what good would one man do? Joe asked himself as he squatted and watched the Mexican easing his way toward the cave. Vega should have sent at least two men back. There was the chance that one man could be overpowered just as Joe was about to do to the man below. This wasn't very good planning on Vega's part.

Then Joe had another thought. Maybe the man had just been sent back to see if Joe and Mark were actually there. Then he would return to Vega and they would take care of the three gringos in the morning.

Joe was suddenly presented with the problem of what he was going to do with the Mexican. In the far recesses of his mind, he knew how it was going to end but didn't really want to think about it or admit what he knew what was going to happen.

He had already killed one man, the one in the Desert Rose Saloon in Fort Davis. He didn't want to admit it, but deep down in his gut, he knew that some others would end up getting killed before all of this was over. Probably himself.

Joe didn't want to shoot the man. That would be murder although he was sure that Vega's man wasn't there to sit down and play a game of checkers with him.

Joe couldn't know how close Vega and the rest of his men were and a shot could carry a long way in this night-shrouded country. He couldn't afford to tie him up and leave him. The Mexican could probably get free in a matter of minutes and find Vega. Joe couldn't see leaving the man tied up inside a cave. The very thought of that caused Joe's breath to catch in his throat and he thought he'd smother. There was only one alternative, but he would worry about that later.

The Mexican was directly below Joe now and in the bright moonlight Joe saw a long-barreled pistol gripped in the man's hand. That might simplify things. Joe waited until the Mexican moved forward a little more before he jumped. He just hoped to God that he wouldn't miss, slip, or fall.

Joe had the element of surprise on his side and it worked! He caught the Mexican around the neck in the crook of his arm as he catapulted from the top of the cave. Both men landed with a grunt and what Joe guessed was a curse in Spanish from the Mexican on the rocks and pebbles almost at the cave opening. He recognized "Dios" but nothing more.

Joe's unexpected attack knocked the big, gray sombrero from the Mexican's mat of curly, black hair. Joe had hoped that he would lose the pistol instead. But things don't always work out the way they should.

The Mexican was the first to get to his feet and he came up in a swift crouch, aiming the pistol at Joe. If the light had been better he would probably have been able to get off a good shot. But he took too long in aiming the pistol and that gave Joe an advantage. Joe couldn't let him fire the pistol! That would alert Vega!

Joe rolled to his knees, jumped up, and made a flying dive at the Mexican, grabbing him around the knees, his head ramming into his stomach.

The impact took the Mexican backward, knocking the pistol from his hand to land on the ground, well out of his reach. Joe landed on top of him, came up on his knees, leaned back, doubled his fist, and swung as hard as he could at the man's chin.

Joe's aim in the dark was no better than the Mexican's had been with the pistol and he only succeeded in grazing his chin. Joe lost his balance and fell sideways. The Mexican drew up his right knee, pushed it against Joe's stomach, and shoved. Joe went flying backward and it was all that he could do not to fall flat on the ground.

The Mexican wasted no time in getting to his feet and starting at Joe, muttering in such rapid Spanish that Joe couldn't catch a single word. But, judging from the vicious, raging tone in the man's voice, Joe guessed that it wasn't anything good.

The Mexican bent sideways and when he straightened up, a long-bladed knife, that had been in a sheath on his belt was now gripped tightly in his right hand, gleaming in the moonlight. Joe's only expertise with a knife was at mealtime and his blood ran cold when he saw it! He was beginning to doubt who the winner of this fight would be.

God up in Heaven would have His hands full helping Joe Howard come out of this situation alive!

Joe scrambled up into a low crouch in order not to present such a big target and sidestepped the furious Mexican rushing at him. Taking just part of a second to glance past the Mexican, Joe saw Buford Chedos standing outside the cave. He hoped that Chedos wouldn't take it upon himself to try to shoot the Mexican. In the darkness, the old man's eyesight might not be all that good and he could end up shooting him instead. Joe hoped also that Chedos would know that Cruz Vega would hear the shot and wouldn't do it.

Joe almost pressed his luck too far in taking his eyes off the Mexican. The bandit was advancing menacingly toward him. As he lunged at Joe, the knife shimmering in the moonlight, Joe reached out and grabbed his arm. Joe doubled up his right fist, put all of his life-preserving strength behind it, and plowed it into the man's lean midsection as hard as he could. The air swooshed out of the man's mouth as he folded over. But he didn't lose the knife as Joe had hoped!

"You are going to die, gringo," the Mexican promised in halting English and in a ragged breath. He straightened up to pull some air into his lungs and lunged at Joe again.

"I don't think so," Joe refuted, breathing hard. As the Mexican came at him again, the knife still gripped in his hand, Joe reached across with his right hand, caught the knife hand, and spun the Mexican around, his back against Joe's chest and pushed the knife hard against the center of the Mexican's light blue shirt.

Joe hated to do it, but there was no other way. Wrapping his left arm around the struggling man's neck, Joe gave one more sudden, hard push. Joe felt the Mexican stiffen against him, removed his arm from his neck, and clamped his hand over his mouth so he couldn't scream out.

Joe felt the man go limp in his grasp and dropped both hands at the same time. The Mexican crumpled to the ground in a lifeless heap. In the illuminating moonlight, Joe could see that the knife was imbedded to the hilt in the man's chest.

"It dang sure took ye long 'nuf," Buford Chedos criticized, hurrying over to Joe who was still looking down at the dead man. "Why in the devil didn't ye jest shoot him?"

If Joe hadn't been so tired, out of breath, and disgusted that he had just killed a man, he would have tied into the old man for his lack of common sense. But instead, he just pulled in a long breath so he wouldn't before answering.

"A shot would have carried too far," Joe finally said, shaking his head and swallowing hard. The Mexican wasn't the first man he'd killed but each time wasn't any less awful. "If Vega doesn't hear anything for a long time, I hope he'll think that he," he nodded toward the still, crumpled body on the ground, "is just waiting to follow you in the morning or is waiting to see if Mark and I show up later tonight."

He saw Chedos finally nodding in agreement, although it didn't help or hinder what had already happened.

"We've got to get him buried," Joe said, bending down and pulling the knife out of the Mexican's bloody shirt. He cleaned the blood from the blade by running it up and down in the sand, then pitched it over in front of the cave. He was surprised to see Mark standing there with the blanket wrapped tightly around him. The boy's eyes were as wide as they would ever be. Joe wondered how long he and Chedos had been awake?

"These shells might come in handy," Joe said, unbuckling the gun belt around the Mexican's waist and pulling it out from under him. Walking over to the pistol on the ground, he picked it up and put it into the holster. He turned back around and was horrified to see Buford Chedos going through the dead man's pockets! The old man probably hadn't had any sense of morality in a long time.

"Don't say nuthin' agin it," Chedos cautioned in a snapping tone when he stood up and saw Joe frowning objectionably down at him as he dropped some coins into his pocket. "He woulda killed ye in a spittin' second. 'Sides, it ain't no worse'n takin' his guns and shells."

"I guess you're right," Joe relented, seeing the logic in what Chedos said. A dead man couldn't spend money any better than he could shoot a gun.

Without saying anything else, the two men caught the dead Mexican by the arms and legs and carried him a few yards down the gully and piled enough rocks around the body so no animal would be able to get to it for a long time, or at least until they left tomorrow morning.

Maybe, if Vega came back to check on the cave, he would see the grave and take it back to the village for a proper burial in the cemetery behind the church.

But, Joe thought sadly as he placed the last rock on top of the rest, this grave will still be right in this same place if I come back through here in ten years.

When the gruesome task was completed, Joe and Chedos walked slowly back to the cave and sat down.

"Do you think there is anyone else out there?" Mark asked, sitting down between Joe and Chedos in the opening of the cave. He reached out slowly, picked up the knife, and put it in his waistband.

"I wouldn't think so," Joe answered, leaning over

against the side of the cave. He was totally exhausted, but knew he wouldn't be able to sleep for a little while yet. He knew that Mark was scared and this was probably the first time in his young life that he had ever seen anybody killed right before his eyes. "If there were, we wouldn't be sitting here right now and talking about it. We would be as dead as that Mexican."

Nothing else was said and even though Joe had fully intended to stay awake, because he couldn't trust Chedos to do it, he never knew when he slumped over on the cave floor and Mark gently pulled the sheepskin coat over him.

5

The next thing Joe Howard knew, he was being awakened by Buford Chedos shaking him roughly by the shoulder the next morning. He would have sworn that he had dozed off for a few minutes only a short time ago.

But that couldn't be because the entire eastern sky was already awash in pink, pearl, and orange with the first light of morning as day made a new claim on the land.

Joe knew that it wouldn't be long before the sun would crawl up from its hiding place behind the mountains and Cruz Vega would more than likely come looking for them when his man didn't return.

Joe had to will his eyes open and it took a lot of convincing for his sore body to sit up and then finally stand up. He had been telling himself for a long time that he was getting too old, even though he was only twenty-three, to be sleeping on the ground like this and the fight with the Mexican last night made him realize it even more. In fact, it had made him even more aware of what his body had been through in the last few years. He could have made the fight a lot shorter last night by just shooting the Mexican. But if he'd done that, he wouldn't be sitting here right now, thinking about what could have been.

Joe *was* only twenty-three but being an army scout had taken its toll on his body from falls, fistfights, and actually being shot. Camping out in all kinds of weather and riding long distances on some of Colonel McRaney's "simple" jobs hadn't helped much either.

Joe had told himself each time that he returned from a job with all of his bones more or less in place, that that was his last job. But then, something would come up and Eric McRaney would describe it in such glorified simplicity that he couldn't wait to be gone again.

Maybe after this one!

Buford Chedos had already made coffee and the tantalizing aroma set Joe's mouth to actually watering. He stood up, started to stretch his arms over his head to relieve the stiffness, and was made acutely aware of his aching bones from sleeping on the ground when the shoulder he had landed on last night tackling the Mexican rebelled at the movement. He paused long enough to rub the spot then bent down to roll his blankets together and glance over at Mark Humphrey.

The boy was awake and in the pale light forcing its way into the cave Joe thought he looked a little better. Some of the scabs had dried up and fallen off. He must have slept as well as Joe had last night no matter how short the time had seemed. The fact that he had killed a man hadn't kept Joe awake at all. Was he getting that complacent about his work? Had he reached the point in his life when he didn't care?

No, he told himself, shaking his head realistically.

It's all part of the job! Part of survival. Live or die. Kill or get killed. He hoped he'd never get to the point in his life where he'd kill just for the fun of it.

"I'm so hungry I could eat this hat," Mark called out from the back of the cave, breaking into Joe's thoughts. He picked up the big sombrero and hung it around his neck. He stood up and joined Joe and Chedos at the front of the cave.

"Don't you think some coffee, meat, and bread would taste a lot better?" Joe asked, grinning up at Mark as the boy nodding left the cave to answer nature's call.

"I looked around for that Mexican's horse," Mark said when he returned, "but I didn't see anything."

"That's too bad," Joe said, draining his second cup of coffee and standing up. "We could have used it for you to ride. We've got to hurry and get out of here. Cruz Vega could come looking for us at any time. He'll know something is wrong when his man doesn't come back." He looked over at Buford Chedos who was draining his coffee cup, a morbid thought narrowing his eyes. "I'd hate like the devil to be in your boots if Cruz Vega ever sees you again."

"Why?" Chedos asked, glancing up at Joe as he dropped the battered tin cup into a grimy canvas bag, lack of concern in his blue eyes.

"Cruz Vega sent that man back to this particular cave for the sole purpose of seeing if Mark and I were here," Joe answered, looking the old man straight in the eye and wondering why he was ignoring the obvious. "When that man doesn't return to Vega soon, Vega will come back here to see what happened to him. Vega knows you wouldn't have any reason to kill him and that will leave only one alternative."

"What in the sam hill are ye talkin' 'bout?" Chedos

asked, staring in a frown up at Joe as he got slowly to his feet.

"You were the last one to see any of them," Joe explained, pulling the cinch tighter on Serge. "When Vega finds that grave, he'll wonder why you killed him."

Joe was amazed at how simple his explanation sounded and was shocked when Chedos didn't seem too concerned about it.

"Anythin' coulda happened to that Mex," Chedos pointed out in a tone of voice someone would use on a child. "He coulda even been attacked by Indians. Or bandits coulda done away with 'im."

Joe dropped his head, raised his eyes, and gave Chedos a skeptical look. But Chedos's explanation was as simple as Joe's and he let it go. It made sense, but would Vega believe it?

It didn't take very long to put everything away after breakfast. In fact, they ate in such a hurry that they hardly tasted the food. Not that it was all that good.

The sun had already released its grip on the mountain peaks in the east and the warm rays were beginning to feel good. It would probably be another nice day in Southwest Texas as far as the weather was concerned. The animals wouldn't get so hot and they could really cover a lot of ground in getting to Tyler Worthing before Cruz Vega did.

Joe paused, his foot in the stirrup. Would Tyler Worthing give Vega the thousand dollars if his son wasn't with him? Joe knew the answer to that was no. Not willingly anyway.

Of course, there wouldn't be much of an argument, or even a fight over the money. A thousand dollars wasn't something to be given up so easily. But all Vega would have to do is just shoot Worthing on sight and take the money. Everything would be over.

"I'm gonna ride along with ye'uns," Buford told Mark, a gleam in his twinkling blue eyes. He laughed when Mark arched his brows in surprise. "I wouldn't miss seein' the look on Worthing's face for anythin' when he see ye. And so's we'uns can make some good time, I'm even gonna let ye ride old Smoke."

Joe swung his right leg over the saddle, made himself comfortable, but jerked around at Chedos's unexpected offer. From the way the old man had been cussing the gray mule yesterday, Joe didn't think that the animal would be fit for anyone to ride and was just used to pack.

"What's that look fer?" Chedos asked, noticing Joe's surprised expression. He frowned and waited for Joe's answer.

"Oh, I just thought from the way you were bad mouthing him yesterday," Joe said in a level tone, although a grin was beginning at his mouth, "that that poor excuse for a mule was just something you brought along to vent your bad feelings on."

"Oh, but no," Chedos refuted, shaking his grizzled head rapidly, the frown deepening between his brows. "I wouldn't take a gold monkey fer old Smoke. I jest fuss at the old mule ass 'cause he don't pay me no mind." His robust laughter burst out as he rubbed the mule's wide forehead.

The mule's long ears looked like pieces of gray silk as they wiggled up and down at Chedos's touch. A loud bray erupted from Smoke's teeth-filled mouth that could probably be heard for miles. Joe worried if Vega and the rest of his men were close enough to hear it. He prayed to God that they weren't as chill bumps played chase up and down his spine.

"Are we going to stand here all morning talking about a danged old mule?" Mark asked, irritation flashing in his eyes. "Somebody could shoot us while we're standing here."

Joe noticed, in the better light that Mark's face was a lot clearer. Joe had seen him dabbing the liquid from the green stem on the sores. That and time had helped heal the scabs and he felt like griping. That was a good sign. Joe felt a little better about the situation.

"No, we're going to leave right now," Joe answered, shaking his head. "The sooner we leave, the sooner we can find Tyler Worthing and this crappy job will be finished. Why don't you ride Serge?" he offered, dismounting and holding the reins out to Mark. "You might be able to handle him a little easier than that mule. I'll ride old Smoke."

"You might be right," Mark agreed, throwing a skeptical and sideways look at the austere-looking mule. "I've never ridden a mule before."

Joe hadn't been on a mule in a long time either. In fact, the last time he remembered riding a mule was on his folks' farm in Tennessee and that was long before he'd fought in the Civil War. He was doubting the merit of his offer as he untied his bedroll. He took out one of the blankets, retied the other blanket and his sheepskin coat, and lay the blanket across the gray mule's wide and smooth back.

"This gray bag of bones won't bite me, will he?" Joe asked, gathering up the reins and a handful of gray mane before swinging up.

"Bite?" Chedos repeated in mock dismay. "That old mule ass!" He frowned so he wouldn't laugh at Joe. "He won't bite nuthin' 'cept grass."

"I'm taking your word for it," Joe said, gripping the mule's sides with his knees. Old Smoke stiffened under the unfamiliar hands, shook his head, flattened his long ears back against his head, and took a couple of pounding steps on the loose gravel.

"If you throw me," Joe threatened in a cold voice that sounded just like Buford Chedos, "I'll kick you so hard you won't be able to walk for a week." He knew that his body would really be rebellious tomorrow. Before he led the way out of the gully, Joe glanced back over his shoulder at Mark and Serge. He could almost swear there was a forsaken look in Serge's eyes. But that was impossible. Could animals have feelings? He couldn't worry about that right now. There were too many other things for him to worry about.

They started out of the gully with Joe in the lead. When they had some solid ground under them, the rocks and pebbles left behind, Joe was amazed at how easy the mule was to ride. But he didn't want to ride him all the way to Candelaria. The insides of his thighs were already getting sore. Maybe they could find or buy a horse somewhere before long for Mark to ride. It was too bad that they couldn't find the dead Mexican's horse. But there was no use in thinking about that now.

They rode until the sun was directly overhead and decided then would be a good time for lunch and let the horses and mule rest.

Secure in the knowledge that Vega and his men weren't actually breathing down their necks, the three men ate a relaxed meal of meat, bread, and four small potatoes Chedos surprised Joe and Mark by frying. They tasted wonderful cooked in the salt-pork grease.

After spending as much time as they thought they could safely spare, everything was picked up, cleaned up, and packed up.

They had ridden no more than a mile and discovered that they were on a mesa which gave a panoramic view for miles to the southeast, south, and southwest.

Five hundred yards directly to the south as the mesa sloped down into a valley, was a small whitewashed frame house.

Whoever had built the house hadn't given much thought to planning as Joe would have. The house had to have been built much later than the dense grove of oak trees had been standing to the east side of it. Joe would have put the house a lot closer to the trees, if not in among them for the shade. The house was directly out in the open. Their approach would have been seen without them being able to find some cover if they hadn't ridden up on the mesa first.

From their vantage point they saw a corral at the west side of the house. Joe counted at least ten horses in the corral but that didn't give him any clue as to how many people were in the house. Maybe they could buy one of the horses.

Joe knew that one of them would have to go down to the house and see how the odds were stacked against them and check out the possibility of getting a horse. It didn't take but one guess to figure out who that one would be. Him! Something in the back of his mind told Joe that it wouldn't be a good idea for all three of them to ride down.

Mark Humphrey was out because he was still wrapped in the blanket and from the pale hue now very evident on his thin and splotched face, he had gone just about as far as he could that day. Even riding Serge hadn't helped all that much.

Buford Chedos couldn't go down because he was too old and couldn't move fast enough if he happened to get into trouble. He would probably have been seen before he got ten yards down the mesa.

Joe wished now that he had accepted some money when Tyler Worthing offered it. They could buy a horse now. Joe had money in his pocket and would use it if necessary, but he was on business for Worthing even though he didn't have Darius with him. Darius! What a name.

Joe dismounted and eased over to the edge of the mesa. He dropped to the ground on his belly so as not to be outlined against the sky. He was unsure what he was going to do about going down to the house. If it belonged to Cruz Vega or some of his people and they knew about Darius Worthing's abduction, Joe could be walking into a trap!

But, as luck would have it, things were a lot better in one way for Joe, Mark, and Chedos than they appeared. He finally decided to walk the distance, and if things were on his side, say that he had lost his horse and had left a sick boy, with a mule, on top of the mesa and wanted to buy one of the horses in the corral. He decided not to mention Chedos in case something went wrong. But in order to get a horse, he'd have to get to the house.

Joe walked over to the sloping south edge of the mesa and started down. He felt totally alone since Mark and Chedos had dropped back and there was no sign of human life at the house.

Joe was surprised and pleased at the same time to see that the grass was much higher than it looked from high up on the mesa. If he squatted down, the grass would hide him until he was almost to the house.

Joe's knees began screaming from being in the crouched position for so long when he was only half way to the house and he knew he couldn't continue the rest of the way like that. Knowing that he would have to crawl the rest of the way, he dropped down on his stomach, and began the arduous task of inching forward.

He'd only gained a little ground when he was

KILLING REVENGE / 133

stopped abruptly by the chilling and unmistakable rattling sound! His blood ran cold and his breath literally stopped in his throat! His heart began pounding, the sound roaring in his ears.

The sound seemed to be coming from all directions at the same time. He had no choice but to lie there on the ground and try to determine where it was actually coming from before he could do anything about it.

God, I wish Darius Worthing was here instead of me.

Taking a chance, Joe raised his head to look directly ahead of him. He couldn't believe his eyes! Not ten feet away, but well within striking distance before him was one of the biggest and ugliest reddish brown diamondback rattlesnakes he'd ever seen. The head was as wide as Joe's flattened hand and the body seemed to be as thick as his arm. That snake probably had enough poison to kill him, Mark Humphrey, Buford Chedos, and the three animals. Sweat began oozing from every pore in his body, as the snake's long, black, forked tongue whipped in and out of its slit mouth.

If the situation had been different and if he'd had time, Joe would have backed up and gone around it. The snake was only trying to protect itself. But he didn't have the time to waste. He decided to try something and prayed that it would work.

Easing his right arm out, he found a flat rock that fitted his hand well and gripped his fingers around it. In the awkward position that he was in, he managed to pull his arm back, hoping that he had enough power behind it, and threw the rock. He saw the snake strike out at it with sharp fangs that was fear magnified into looking like gleaming curved daggers, and then, still giving off its warning signal, the snake slithered away in the tall grass.

Taking a deep breath and wiping the stinging sweat

from his face and eyes on his shirtsleeve, Joe, hoping that there were no more scaly obstacles in his way, began crawling toward the house again.

Although it took Joe only about twenty minutes, even with the interruption by the snake to cover the distance between the mesa and house, it seemed like a lifetime had passed when he finally reached the back of the house.

Joe stood up and listened carefully at the back window. When he didn't hear anything, he moved easily around toward the front. He removed his hat, peered around the edge of the house, and got one of the biggest surprises of his life. Only the surprise of finding out that Mark Humphrey wasn't Darius Worthing was greater.

Sitting in a rocking chair, her head lolled back against a pillow and sound asleep was one of the oldest and most wrinkled women that Joe Howard had ever seen. There were enough wrinkles on her long face to plant a bumper crop. She would be a perfect match for Buford Chedos. Her mouse-colored, brown hair, that had been up in a bun about a month ago was hanging down around her dirty face in matted strings. A baggy, red sweater, with holes in the elbows was unbuttoned over a long, blue dress that hadn't had a hem in it for a long time. The skirt was pulled up over her knees, covered with thick, black stockings. On her feet were old, brown, unlaced brogans. Her mouth sagged open and she was snoring loudly enough to drown out just about any sound around. Joe probably wouldn't have heard the rattling snake if she'd been with him.

Joe stood listening and when he didn't hear any other sounds, guessed that she was the only one at the house. He started to take a step up on the porch as he replaced his hat.

"Forget whatever you've got in mind, lad." Her

sudden warning shocked him. Joe froze in his tracks when he found himself staring at the business end of an S&W .44. "Don't make old Alice Manning have to shoot you."

Old Alice had brought the pistol up in her right hand that had been dangling over the arm of the chair with a speed that could have almost matched Joe's.

Joe never felt so stupid in his life! In the past three days, he'd outwitted a notorious Mexican bandit, had been exposed to smallpox, had killed a man in a saloon in Fort Davis, and had killed a Mexican last night in the moonlight with a knife he'd taken away from the man. He had even gotten away from a deadly rattlesnake. All of those accomplishments should have been enough to make a man feel good about himself. He would have, too if he hadn't had a pistol aimed at his midsection by this dirty, old woman who had gotten the drop on him. That sort of took the wind out of his sails.

Joe had had guns aimed at him countless times. But never by a woman. Not to mention a dirty and wrinkled, old woman. He didn't know whether Alice Manning could even be called a woman. To him, she looked like an old, dirty bag of rags, sitting there in a rocking chair, holding a gun on him.

But Joe Howard had just been taken in by an old woman who probably hadn't chewed solid food in a long time, judging from her toothless gums.

"I don't mean you any harm, ma'am," Joe said and was embarrassed to hear his voice actually shaking. He kept his right hand well away from his Colt .45. Something in her green and deep-set eyes told Joe that she wouldn't hesitate in shooting him. "All I need is a horse. I'll buy anyone of those you have in the corral for a reasonable price."

If Joe hadn't known better and recognized his own

voice, he would have sworn that Colonel Eric McRaney was standing there on the front porch in his clothes and explaining in a few simple words what he needed. But something in the old woman's washed-out eyes let him know that he wasn't going to be as persuasive as McRaney would've been in getting what he wanted.

"You want a what?" Old Alice asked, lowering her head and turning her eyes up at him. "How in the world did you get so far out here without a horse in the first place?"

Joe was amazed that one more wrinkle could find a place on her narrow forehead as her thick brows shot up in surprise. But he got a good feeling that she was at least willing to listen to his reason, or excuse for being there.

"Ma'am, you'd really help me out of a bad situation if you'd let me tell you exactly why I'm out here."

Joe felt like a ton had been lifted from his shoulders when Old Alice nodded, pushed her stringy hair back out of her dirty, wrinkled face, and smiled up at him.

If Joe Howard knew what lay in store for him, he would have run as fast as he could back through the knee-high grass, kicked any rattlesnake out of the way, and gotten back to the mesa as fast as he could.

Dirty, wrinkled, toothless, and old Alice Manning turned out to be a sympathetic listener, or so Joe thought when he finally convinced her that he wasn't going to hurt her. Of course, there wasn't much chance of that happening since she was holding a gun on him.

Something had told him not to go into exact details as to why he happened to be standing on her front porch needing a horse. He only told her about Mark being sick and that he had given him his horse so that Mark could handle him better than a mule. Joe kept emphasizing how ill Mark was and hoped that it would work on her maternal instinct.

But from looking closer at the woman, that instinct was well hidden by all of the grime and wrinkles and Joe couldn't stop the shivers. If she had always looked as disgusting as she did right then, no man would want to get close enough to her, unless he was falling-down drunk, to make her a mother.

But she had something that Joe Howard needed and it wasn't companionship. He needed a horse for Mark and he would kiss her foot, nothing else, to get it.

Oh, no, I wouldn't, he changed his mind quickly, mentally shaking his head in disgust as he looked down at her dirty, high-topped shoes. I'd carry Mark Humphrey all the way to Candelaria on my back before I'd touch anything on that woman! Not as long as I've got a dollar in my pocket. There was no telling what kind of little critters were living on her shoes and dirty stockings. I don't even think I'd even wish her off on Buford Chedos! The old man wasn't half as dirty as she was.

"Do you mean to stand there and tell me," she reprimanded, drawing her brows together, sitting up straight in the chair, and glaring at him, "that you left a sick boy up there?" She jerked her head backward toward the mesa where Mark and Chedos were waiting.

"Well, it isn't as if he were alone," Joe continued, suddenly feeling like an abusive parent. "He's with a . . ."

Whatever had been taking care of Joe Howard all of these years stepped in again and made him bite off the rest he was going to say about Buford Chedos being up on the mesa with Mark. "He's been riding my horse, but with him being sick, it really has taken a lot out of him. You know how it is to do anything when you don't feel well. We really do need to buy another horse for me to ride."

"Don't tell me you've been walking all of this

time," Alice said suspiciously, her eyes boring into his. Then an odd expression brought a couple more wrinkles to the corners of her eyes as she narrowed them.

Joe took a long, uneasy breath and thought he'd just figured out why she was out here alone in the middle of this no-man's-land. She would talk a person to death or drive them crazy with questions.

"No, I haven't been walking," he answered candidly and shaking his head wearily. "I've been riding a mule." He pulled in a long, exasperated breath and let it escape through clenched teeth. "We haven't been able to make much time because of that worthless hay burner. You know how contrary they can be."

Joe was still hoping to play on her sympathies.

A stillness settled over Old Alice's dirty face and she continued looking at Joe. She dropped her gaze down to the porch for a few seconds. Then she threw back her head and peals of crackling laughter burst from her mouth. She sounded like a hen laying an egg.

"Now, that's the dangest thing I ever heard," she finally said when she regained her composure. She wiped the back of her hand across her watery eyes, then blinked them several times. "Somehow I just can't picture in my mind, a handsome stud of a man like you," she moved her eyes almost lustfully up and down his lanky body, "riding a mule! Ha! A stallion maybe. But a mule?" She arched her brows, pursed her lips, and shook her head slowly. Her eyes twinkled.

Joe had never been called a stud, and for some reason, he felt like all of his clothes had just been ripped from his body by her look.

Old Alice's look scared Joe half to death. He hoped she wouldn't try to attack him. He'd just have to shoot her. That was all. "Well, the boy *is* riding my horse," Joe said lamely in self-defense. "He doesn't look too bad." Joe felt his face turning redder at her relentless gaze.

Another grin slid across Alice's face and her eyes twinkled. "Which doesn't look too bad? The boy or the horse?"

Joe wanted to vomit when she licked her lips! Did she think she was flirting with him? If she did, she missed by a mile! She reminded him of an over-the-hill hussy.

He watched Old Alice in exasperation, irritation, and disgust. He'd come across a few women in his young life; both young and old women. But he'd never met one like Alice Manning. She could probably have blown him right off the porch with the S&W lying in her lap. It was apparent that she wasn't afraid of him, or anyone else for that matter, because she was way out here in the middle of nowhere alone. That was something in her favor because as far as he could see, the only thing she had of value were the ten horses in the corral. He wondered why she had so many? He didn't know what she had in the house and was certainly in no hurry to find out. Only God knew what would happen to him if he went into the house with the woman!

"The black gelding looks good," Joe finally answered, his face still red but with pride swelling out his chest. He still felt like a first-class fool. "It's the boy who doesn't look so good."

Old Alice's attitude and questions had Joe's head spinning round and round and he was annoyed with himself for wasting so much time. He should have already had the horse and been gone.

"Why don't you motion for the boy to come on down here?" Alice finally asked, a serious look replacing the lecherous smile. "Will he be able to make it and bring the horse and mule with him?"

"Yeah," Joe said, nodding with relief that things were beginning to move, and in his favor.

Joe, still without asking why she was out in this particular part of the country alone or actually seeing if she was alone, walked over to the edge of the porch. He was just about to step out into the yard when a movement at an oak tree about a hundred feet from the house caught his eye. Joe cursed himself for being so slack in his observance of what was going on around him. Some deep, gut feeling told him that someone was holding a gun on him.

Had he walked into a trap or was someone just protecting the old woman, house, and horses?

Pretending not to be aware that they, or most probably just he was being watched, Joe stepped off the porch and under the guise of stumbling on a rock, took several steps backward. The subterfuge put him more in front of the house. Supposedly struggling to regain his balance, Joe took a quick look at the two windows, one on either side of the front door. He knew someone else was watching him when he saw the curtain moving at the window to the right of the door. There wasn't enough breeze to stir the curtain and besides, the window was closed!

Joe, knowing that he was in the middle of a trap, gave himself a little time to wonder how well-armed the people were who were behind the oak tree and window? He also wondered how many people were watching him from those two places?

He had seen only one movement behind the tree but that didn't mean that others weren't hiding further back in the trees. No telling how many were in the house, just laughing at how stupid he'd been.

Joe Howard, army scout from Fort Davis, Texas, knew that he had actually walked into a trap! Old Alice was going to insist that he bring Mark Humphrey, Serge, and old Smoke, that mule ass as Chedos affectionately called him, down from the mesa into that trap!

If I could get my foot around far enough, he thought angrily to himself for not being more careful, I'd kick myself in the butt! He should have tried to see how many people were in the house before going up on the porch. But that could have gotten him killed. As if this couldn't!

Judging from the ten horses in the corral, the movement by the tree, the moving curtain, and Alice Manning, there could be at least seven more people hiding somewhere. He knew that the odds were stacking up against him and he didn't see any way out. Unless . . .

If he called just for Mark to come down from the mesa, that would leave Buford Chedos up there to bring some kind of help. If Mark didn't come down, Old Alice would send someone to the mesa and find Mark and Buford Chedos.

"What are you waiting for, lad?" Alice asked in an almost motherly voice. "Why don't you call that poor, sick boy down here? There's no need for him to wait up there alone in this heat." She wiped her hand across her forehead. Joe was amused at her act. A cool breeze was blowing and it wasn't all that hot.

Suddenly Joe was aware that she was talking only about Mark Humphrey. He was glad now that he hadn't mentioned Chedos. Maybe something good could come out of this mess after all!

Joe took a deep breath and hoped that he could pull this off. "Hey, Mark," he yelled out, cupping his hands around his mouth so his voice would carry better. "Come on down. Bring Serge and the mule with you."

Joe heard his echoing words reverberating against the canyon walls and out across the miles and miles of dry wasteland. The unexpected sound startled the horses in the corral.

Thinking that maybe he hadn't called out loud enough for Mark to hear him and that being the reason why he didn't answer right away, Joe repeated his call.

Joe Howard had believed in God for as long as he could remember. He'd had more than one prayer answered over the years and hoped the one he was now sending upward would make it to God's busy ear in time.

When Mark finally stood up, waved to him and Joe saw him take up the reins of the mule and Serge, Joe knew that another of his prayers had been answered. He just hoped that Buford Chedos would stay hidden until he figured out what Old Alice was doing out here and why he was being watched by one person in the house and another behind the tree.

Alice Manning was armed, and if the other two had guns, there wasn't much he could do to extricate himself and Mark from this situation.

Darius Worthing, just you wait!

Joe watched Mark swing up on Serge and begin leading the gray mule down the sloping side of the mesa. The boy and the two animals were more than halfway to the house when Joe heard the unmistakable sound of a hammer being cocked back on a pistol to his right. Whoever had been hiding behind the tree had finally decided to let his presence be known.

Joe knew that he was covered from the right and left and made no attempt to reach for the Colt .45 at his right side. He also knew that any help was out from Mark even though he was armed to the teeth with a rifle and two pistols. But both of his hands were full: one holding the blanket around him and guiding Serge and the other leading the mule.

"Well, Aunt Alice," a slow drawl said behind Joe,

"will you look at what's comin'. I never thought we'd get somethin' like this. That black horse should bring at least fifty dollars." Excitement took over in the youthful sounding voice.

Joe was sure, or hoped so anyway, that as long as he didn't make a move for the .45 that he wasn't in any real danger. With that in mind, he turned slowly to his left to see who had come out from behind the tree calling Alice "aunt," who was now standing at the edge of the porch with her S&W aimed directly at him, and who had come up behind him.

Joe would have bet all of the money in his pocket, which was about twenty-five dollars, and all of the money that Tyler Worthing was supposed to be carrying, and that was at least a thousand dollars, that the man who had sidestepped toward the house but was still holding a pistol on him would be a male copy of the dirty haglike woman who was smiling at him like a cunning fox.

It was a good thing that Joe didn't have a chance to bet his money or that no one was there to call the bet. He would have lost every penny.

Standing there was a neatly dressed young man who was only a couple of inches shorter than Joe's five feet seven, but a lot thinner than Joe. Joe would guess that they were the same age. Joe couldn't help doing a double take at the boy's appearance.

His gray shirt was clean and pressed. The dark blue pants were also clean with a sharp crease that would have cut bread. The lean, angular, and tanned face was framed with a neatly trimmed beard and pencil-line mustache the same color as the curly, light brown, trimmed hair. Joe couldn't believe it, but there was a twinkle in the pale blue eyes.

"Louis, I can see you riding a mule," Old Alice said

candidly, nodding her head which was probably a breeding ground for all kinds of crawly things. Joe couldn't stop the shiver.

"Now, Aunt Alice, you know very well that I wasn't talkin' about that mule," Louis argued grimly, although a grin spread across his face. "I was talkin' about that big black horse the kid's ridin'. Don't you think I'd look grand on him?"

Joe was suddenly hit with the question about the ten horses in the corral and he wondered what Louis meant when he'd said that Serge would bring at least fifty dollars? Were these people stealing horses from travelers? If they were, where were the people who had owned the horses? Were they dead? Where were the bodies?

Discarding bodies wouldn't be any problem. There were enough gullies, ravines, and canyons to take care of that.

Oh, my God, Joe thought as fear spread through his body, pulling a tight knot in his stomach. Were he and Mark going to end up in one of those places?

No, he comforted himself, forcing a deep breath into his lungs. Not as long as Buford Chedos was still up on the mesa.

Joe couldn't stop another shiver from consuming his body and got sick in his stomach and hoped that he was just letting his imagination run wild with him. His morbid thoughts were interrupted when he heard the approaching animals and turned back around to see what Mark would do when he became aware of what he was riding into.

Joe wasn't sure how good Mark would be with a gun even if he would be able to free his hands from the blanket and two sets of reins. Mark had told him in the cabin at Vega's village that he could knock a squirrel out of a tree at a hundred yards. But this was a whole different situation. These were people who could shoot back.

Even though Mark was wearing a gun belt and pistol and had a knife, Joe didn't try to give him any signal that someone was in the house or that Alice Manning was standing on the porch with the S&W in her hand.

Joe knew Mark could see Louis standing behind him with a pistol and hoped that he wouldn't do anything heroic or stupid. Joe had done enough stupid things already. He knew that unless something miraculous happened and he was able to get the drop on Louis, and that was highly unlikely, their only chance of getting out of this mess would have to come from Buford Chedos.

Joe looked past Mark toward the mesa. As far as he, or anyone, could tell, no one was up on the flat ground. He was glad that Chedos had figured out that something was wrong at the house when he had called out for only Mark to come down with Serge and the mule. Joe just hoped that he would have a chance to call for Chedos's help.

Mark Humphrey had been clever enough to ascertain that something was wrong when Joe called out twice for only him to come down from the mesa with the horse and mule. Buford had suspected the same thing and strongly cautioned him to be careful and not try to do anything until Joe told him what to do.

"Wonder why he wants you to bring old Smoke?" Chedos asked, a bewildered frown between his brows as he patted the former object of his derision. Concern was deep in his eyes.

"I don't know," Mark replied, shaking his head, gathering up Serge's reins, and swinging up. "Something has to be wrong. That was the only way he had to tell you to come in later and get us out of a mess."

The worried look eased away from Chedos's eyes, he took a furtive breath and nodded.

"Can ye see anythin' down there?" Chedos asked, halting in a step toward the edge of the mesa. He put his gnarled hands up and shaded his eyes. "These old peepers of mine ain't what they used to be."

Mark looked down at the house and started to shake his head, but shading and squinting his eyes against the sun's glare, peered closer.

"Yeah," he answered, his voice strained, reining Serge around. "A man just came out from behind a tree and has a gun on Joe. Something *is* wrong and just calling for me *is* his way of telling us that. You'll probably be able to work your way down when it gets darker. I just hope we're still alive by then."

From the thoughtful look clouding the old man's wrinkled face, Mark knew that several plans were already taking shape in his mind. He just hoped that none of them would end up getting them killed.

Mark still wanted to see the expression on Tyler Worthing's face when he showed up in Candelaria and he sure wanted to go along with him and Joe to El Paso. He was going to hit Darius Worthing hard enough to take at least twenty pounds off of him. That would be a dollar a pound. The same amount that Worthing had paid him to take his place on the stage. Somehow it still just didn't equal out. Not when it was his life that was on the line! He wondered what the fat kid would be doing if he was there?

Mark could still remember, because it hadn't been that long ago, not even a week, when the fat kid had approached him while he was sitting on the wooden bench in front of the stage office in Pecos, hoping to earn a few dollars unloading and loading the stage.

Darius Worthing, his fat body waddling with every step, had looked down at him, really looked down at him, a cunning smile on his thick-lipped mouth and in his hazel eyes. Mark could still hear the petulant tone in his voice like he was talking to someone beneath him.

"You look like you could use twenty dollars." The pompous tub of guts had stood with his arms folded across his flabby chest, or folded as much as the bulk would allow. One brow had been arched haughtily and Mark thought he saw Worthing's nose twitch.

Mark hadn't felt well for a couple of days and really didn't have the inclination to work. But he was just about down to his last dime. If Dawson McInnis wouldn't let him work that day at the stage depot, he'd have to wash dishes at the Mountain View Cafe for a meal. He was too proud to take a handout meal.

The words illegal or immoral didn't fit into his vocabulary right then, but he knew that whatever the fat kid leering down at him had in mind would end up being one of the two. But twenty dollars was a lot of money and would help take away any pangs of conscience that he would get later on.

After Worthing finished his explanation of why he wanted Mark to ride the stage to Fort Davis from Pecos and then to El Paso and make notes about the accommodations along the way while Worthing took the train, then give him the detailed report for his father after he arrived later in El Paso, Mark didn't think the plan was all that bad, especially after he'd given it some consideration and Worthing had dropped twenty dollars into his hand. Mark noticed that Worthing made sure not to touch him. Mark knew that everybody would get what they could use. He would make twenty easy dollars.

Darius Worthing would have a soft train ride to El Paso and Tyler Worthing would get the report he wanted on the stage line.

Of course, Mark hadn't planned on coming down with smallpox or ending up being kidnapped by a Mexican bandit named Cruz Vega! He wondered how Joe Howard would have handled the situation if Darius Worthing had really been the one he had rescued from the adobe cabin in the village? He would make it a point to ask him later.

But right now, he was sitting on a seal black horse, holding the reins to a gray mule, and about to ride down from a safe place on a mesa probably right into a trap! All of this because he wanted to earn a fast twenty dollars! He had spent only a little of the twenty and had felt good while he was doing it. He didn't feel so good now!

A chilly, fall wind had replaced the warm breeze blowing across the mesa and Mark was glad he had the blanket wrapped around him. He wished now that he'd taken the buckskin jacket from the dead Mexican at the cave before Joe and Chedos buried him last night. The worms were probably already chewing holes in it. He shivered at the sickening thought.

As he rode down from the mesa and approached Joe and the man standing behind him, he caught the minute shake of Joe's head. It wouldn't be any trouble to ease his right hand holding the blanket together inside to the pistol at his hip. He was close enough and he knew he'd be accurate enough to get the man holding a Remington .38 on Joe. But when he saw Joe shift his eyes quickly back and forth a couple of times toward the house, he knew that someone else had Joe, and probably now him, covered.

* * *

Joe wondered what was taking Mark so long to ride down from the mesa. Then he realized that he and Buford Chedos were probably trying to figure out why he had called for only Mark to come down.

A knowing look was in Mark's eyes and Joe saw an expression there that almost scared the life out of him! Since Mark had no way of knowing that Old Alice was on the porch and armed, he knew that the boy was going to try and take Louis.

Furtively, Joe glanced toward the house, back to Mark, to the house and finally back to Mark. He was about to get dizzy. He felt the slight frown on his face and hoped that Mark understood it. Relief, so great that his knees wanted to buckle under him washed over Joe as Mark relaxed in the saddle. Mark had realized what his look meant just in time.

"You're right about that horse, Louis," Old Alice said, smacking her lips. "You'll look grand riding him. For a while at least." She gave that cackling laugh again. "All right, kid," she continued, stepping off of the porch and into Mark's view. She walked over to Louis, then looked up at Mark. "Unwrap yourself from that blanket and get down from that horse."

Joe saw a horrified expression rush over Alice's dirty and wrinkled face and heard her draw in a quick breath as she looked closer at Mark. Apparently he hadn't told her what Mark was sick with. He knew she was looking at the scabs on Mark's face and knew instantly what had caused them. Maybe those very scabs would be an advantage to them. She just might tell them to ride out.

But from the speculative look in her eyes, Joe knew that wasn't going to happen.

"How long have you had the pox, kid?" she asked, her pale brown eyes almost twice their size in sudden fear.

"Almost a week," Mark replied, letting the blanket fall.

"That ain't so bad," she said, regaining some of her composure and pressing her mouth into a thin line. "You're almost well now."

"Lordy mercy," Louis said in dismay when he saw all of the guns that Mark was wearing. "He's his own blamed walkin' army. Drop all the guns, boy. Who in the devil were you goin' to fight?" He laughed gleefully.

Joe Howard, feeling about as useful as a cardboard fan in a wind storm, stood and listened and watched what was going on. He felt even more helpless and a little naked when Louis, still laughing, jerked the Colt .45 from the holster and stuck it in his waistband. Mark dropped all of his guns and dismounted.

"Do you want me to tie them up, Aunt Alice?" Louis asked, a maniacal grin on his thin face. He glanced sideways at his aunt.

"Yeah, you might as well," Old Alice said resolutely, pulling the hammer back on her S&W. She nodded her stringy-haired head and rolled her mouth in against her gums.

"Just who in the devil are you all?" Joe asked, disgust and anger at himself boiling up in his stomach for not being more careful. He'd never hit a woman in his life but he would gladly make an exception in Alice Manning's case. This old gal, who he'd thought had a soft streak when he'd told her about Mark being sick was turning out to be as hard as nails and hadn't used her conscience, if she had one, in a long time. "What do you plan on doing with us?" Foreboding sent cold chills up and down his entire body and a sick knowledge began building up in his stomach. "Why are you going to tie us up?"

"Well, I've already told you my name," Old Alice

answered, nodding and batting her eyes. "This is Louis Smith, my nephew. Ain't he cute?" She jerked her head toward Louis as he walked over to the house and took four lengths of thin rope from a wooden box under the porch. "We're going to take that horse and mule and those horses in the corral down to Candelaria and sell them to Cruz."

The name hit Joe in the stomach like a kick from Smoke. But he managed to stay reasonably calm and say nothing about the fact that he knew Vega. He just hoped that Mark wouldn't blurt out anything that would get them into any more trouble than they were already in.

It made sense to Joe now why Vega and his cut-throat friends hadn't found him, Mark, and Chedos. Vega must have known, that the way they were going would put them right smack in Alice Manning's filthy lap!

Vega still believed that Mark Humphrey was Darius Worthing. Mark would be one less responsibility for Vega. Alice Manning could take care of him, Joe, and Chedos.

But how would she know that Vega thought Mark was Darius Worthing? Joe certainly wasn't going to tell her and neither would Mark.

It was obvious that he and Mark were going to be left there. If Old Alice knew that Cruz Vega thought that Mark Humphrey was Darius Worthing she might change her mind and take Mark along and try to get to Tyler Worthing first. But Joe knew that as soon as Worthing saw Mark, no matter who he was with, he wouldn't give any money to anyone.

"Are you going to kill us?" Mark ventured in a shaky voice, his face turning white.

"I haven't decided yet," Alice replied, cocking her head to one side. "But I will say this: by the time we get back from Candelaria, you'll be gone. One way or the other."

Joe felt his heart actually stop beating in his chest, his blood ran cold and he wanted to vomit. If these two crazy people weren't going to kill him and Mark right out, how did she expect them to be gone "one way or the other" by the time they returned from Candelaria?

But wait a minute, he told himself and suddenly felt a little better about his present situation. He and Mark weren't going to die any way! Even if they were tied up and put someplace, and Alice Manning and Louis Smith left right away, Buford Chedos would come down from the mesa and untie them. They could catch up with the two and get their horse and mule back. He really had nothing to worry about. Or did he? Things were seeming too simple again.

Just as Louis Smith was returning from the porch with the rope, the front screen door flew open, slamming back against the wall, and a girl who could have been no older than fifteen came hurrying out.

"Ma, do we have to tie this one up?" she asked, looking at Mark. She was as clean as the woman she called "ma" was dirty. Butter-colored hair cascaded down her back in soft waves. Big, blue eyes were alive in excitement and a pink blush covered her round face with a dimple at each corner of her bow-shaped mouth. A crisp and clean, long, dark blue dress fitted her slender figure well. Not like the dirty rag that covered Alice.

"Ma, do we really have to tie this one up?" the girl asked again, her blue eyes still riveted on Mark. "He's just about the cutest thing I ever did see. Can't we keep him around for a while? Why couldn't he just go with us? Please!"

Joe threw a quick look over at Mark and if their predicament hadn't been so precarious, he would've laughed right out loud. The boy's mouth was hanging open and he'd never live to see another day when his eyes would be almost falling from their sockets.

"Now, Desda, you say that every time a young male happens to come this way," Alice Manning reminded in a patronizing voice. She pulled her mouth into a thin line, a tired frown on her wrinkled face.

Old Alice had just said two words that caught Joe's attention like a fish catching a worm on a dangling hook. Apparently this wasn't the first time that some unsuspecting fools had ridden by this house, out in the middle of nowhere, and had been relieved of their animals. He wondered if Cruz Vega was the recipient of all the horses that this thieving family stole?

There was one thing for sure though! Joe Howard knew that there was no way on God's earth that he was going to be separated from Serge too long. The only way that would happen was if one of them was dead! And since he was the one having his hands tied behind his back, it was easy to figure out who was likely to end up that way.

Joe really didn't plan on dying right then and Serge looked too good for anything to happen to him. If Alice Manning, her fickle daughter, and laughing nephew were in any kind of horse business, each of them knew that they had latched onto one worthwhile piece of horseflesh.

"But, Ma, he's so cute," Desda pleaded, drawing out each word and sidling over to Mark. She dropped her head, then coyly raised her fluttering eyes up and smiled at him. The dimples in her cheeks deepened enough to hold a good rain. She flipped the big sombrero from Mark's head and tousled his hair. Apparently she wasn't bothered by the scabs on his face. All the while, Mark stood there, gaping down at the girl like he was under some kind of spell. Joe wanted to lash out and kick him.

Mark was on the verge of being tied up and left to some unknown fate and he was getting moon-eyed over some girl who was probably as much a horse thief as her mother and cousin.

"Desda, we don't have time for any such foolishness now," Old Alice said in a weary voice, rolling her eyes toward the blue sky. "If we hurry, we can have these animals in Candelaria for Cruz before he gets there. It's just about time for him to go back home. He might pay a little more for that black horse."

Mark jerked his attention away from Desda long enough to look at Joe. The Mexican bandit's name had finally sunk in on him. Joe shook his head quickly. Mark turned his attention back to Desda and put the silly grin back on his face.

Some of the pieces of the puzzle, which had been bothering Joe, fell into place so suddenly while Old Alice was talking to Desda that he couldn't believe what he was hearing. This dirty old lady had just said that she and these two kids were actually stealing horses from people passing by and taking them to the same Cruz Vega in Candelaria! He toyed with the idea of telling her that Mark was Darius Worthing. Maybe she *would* take Mark with her. Buford Chedos would hurry down from the mesa, untie him, and they could make better time in getting to Vega.

But that wouldn't work. Joe had already told Alice that the boy's name was Mark.

Joe glanced at Mark again. The enraptured expression remained on his face, and although he was still gazing ardently down at Desda, Joe knew that he'd heard Alice.

Now it made sense to Joe why the ransom note had

instructed that the money for Darius Worthing's release be taken to Candelaria. By the time the money arrived, Vega, along with the boy who he thought was Darius Worthing would be there. And, if he was getting horses from Alice Manning, he'd have a few more to add to his bunch. Joe promised himself right then, that when he got his hands on Darius Worthing, he was going to beat the living daylights out of him no matter how young or fat he might be.

"All right, Louis," Old Alice said, raising her right hand with the S&W aimed at Joe, "get him tied up. Then *you'd* better tie up the boy. Desda might not do such a good job."

"May I ask you a question since we're going to be giving you our horses?" Joe ventured, sarcasm in his voice, knowing he had nothing else to lose if they took the horses. Smith had walked around behind him and was tying one of the ropes around his wrists.

"Well, sure, lad," Old Alice answered salaciously, and smiling cheerfully, her eyes twinkling. "What do you want to know?"

Joe couldn't believe how placid she was being during all of this. She must have been doing this for a long time. But why shouldn't she be calm? She didn't have anything to worry about since she wasn't the one being tied up and didn't have a pistol aimed at her.

"Would this Cruz you're talking about just happen to be a tall, good-looking Mexican bandit named Cruz Vega?" His question wiped the smile from her face and she blinked her eyes a couple of times. But the gun in her hand never wavered. Her arm was rock steady.

"Not that it's any of your business," she snapped, her face going stone serious, "but, yes. He is the same one. Why do you ask? How did you know that his last name is Vega? How did you know what he looks like? Do you know him?" Her questions were coming so fast that some of the words were running together.

Joe nodded slowly and a plan began taking shape in his mind. "Yeah, he and his bunch . . ."

Suddenly the warning bell, that usually stayed in the far recesses of his mind and rang only quietly when something was wrong went off loudly right behind his eyes and he snapped his mouth shut on the rest of what he was going to say. He glanced at Mark, a warning in his eyes.

"What were you going to say?" Louis prompted, jerking the rope tighter around Joe's wrist.

"I was just going to say," Joe began, shrugging his shoulders but making a mental note to get Smith for what he was doing, "that Vega and his bunch have a bad reputation through all this country. I'd sure hate to meet up with him if he's as mean as I've heard."

"There's nothing wrong with Cruz Vega," Desda interrupted, anger in her voice and in her flashing eyes when she tore them away from Mark and threw Joe a castigating glare. "We've done business with him for three years and he . . ."

"Shut up, girl," Old Alice shouted, swinging her exasperated attention from Joe to her daughter. "Someday your mouth will bring you ruin."

A sullen pout brought Desda's mouth together and a pink hue rushed all the way up into her hair. "I was just going to say that he always gives me pretty things. They're prettier than the cheap stuff that Louis gives Quita, Cruz's sister." She caught the side of the full skirt and twirled a half circle. She must have wanted Joe and Mark to know that the blue dress had been a gift from Vega.

Even though he and Mark were the unwitting victims of this nutty woman and her just-as-nutty relatives, and Joe should have had his mind on more important things like how to escape, he allowed himself time to wonder if the red dress that Quita was wearing the other day had been a gift from Louis Smith. If it was, it showed that the sawed-off outlaw had good taste in clothes. Desda and Smith's appearance led Joe to believe that the girl must do their washing and ironing.

"I told you to shut up," Alice Manning shouted, her brown eyes blazing. She took a threatening step toward the girl but stopped when she remembered that she was holding the pistol on Mark. "These two will think you're a kept woman, and Lord knows I've tried to raise you decent. Get into the house and put our things together. As soon as Louis ties up the lad, we can leave. We'll be in Candelaria at least by tomorrow night."

Joe wanted to laugh at Old Alice's remark about raising Desda to be decent. That was pretty good coming from a horse thief!

Desda dropped her head in embarrassment, threw Mark a fleeting glance then turned and hurried into the house. Joe grinned when he noticed that she pulled the screen door shut behind her with a hard slam. Alice Manning jumped at the unexpected sound and mouthed something under her breath. She closed her eyes and gritted her gums.

Louis had used the other thin section of rope and had tied Mark's hands behind his back. "Do you want me to take them to the same place?" he asked, giving the knot a hard jerk. When Mark tried to pull away, Louis gave the rope another hard yank.

"No," Alice answered, drawing out the word, shaking her head slowly and narrowing her eyes thoughtfully.

"Let's give these two something special, something with a view."

Ribald laughter burst from Louis Smith's smirking mouth and he slapped his slender hands against his legs. "I know just what you mean," he said and nodded, excitement dancing in his blue eyes. "But you'll have to come along with me to guard this one," he jerked his thumb at Joe, "while I tie him up."

6

Joe Howard hoped to God that Buford Chedos was watching all of this from the mesa. Suddenly a horrifying thought struck Joe with such intensity that his knees almost buckled under him and his heart began pounding like a hammer in his chest.

What if Buford Chedos was in cahoots with Alice Manning's scheme? Chedos's horse and mule weren't of the ordinary quality. He'd been on speaking terms with Cruz Vega and it just dawned on Joe that Chedos seemed to know exactly where they were heading when they came this way. Had the horse and mule been a gift from Vega?

Joe hoped he was wrong in what he was thinking about Chedos. The old prospector was all they had to depend on right then to get them out of this mess. If Joe was right, they were in deep trouble.

The four had just turned to leave the yard when the door banged open and Desda came hurrying across the porch. She'd changed into dark brown pants and a light green shirt. She'd pulled her hair back and tied it with a matching green ribbon.

Mark turned around when he heard the door open and close and his mouth popped wide open when he saw how the clothes clung to Desda's young body like a second skin. She ran up to Mark, threw her arms around his neck and placed a resounding kiss on his startled mouth.

"I hope we meet again," she said wistfully, smiling wanly up at him. "If we do, we can pick up from here." She kissed him again and stepped back. Mark Humphrey could've died a happy young man right then.

"Yeah," Louis Smith mimicked, jerking again on the rope binding Joe's hands behind him, "we can pick up from here."

"Oh, we'll meet again," Joe promised, leaning his head sideways to be sure that Smith heard him, assurance in his cold voice and level-eyed glare. "You can bet on it. But it damn sure won't be with a kiss." His brows arched over his eyes.

"Oooh, I'm scared," Louis said in a high-pitched voice and laughed as an exaggerated shiver shook his thin frame.

"You'd better be," Mark cautioned, looking contemptuously at Louis, batting his eyes rapidly. "Because if he doesn't get you, I will and the only thing I'll kiss about you is your dead ass."

"If ya'll are through jabbering," Old Alice taunted jeeringly, "let's get a move on. Time's wasting. Desda, have the horses ready when we get back. Add those two to the bunch and put some food together."

Louis Smith pulled the pistol from his holster and jabbed it against Joe's back.

Joe and Mark were prodded away from the house,

past the corral, and up a hill dotted with scrub brush and cactus about a hundred yards from the corral. Walking would have been hard enough even if they weren't tied. But since they were, they couldn't use their arms for balancing and taking steps was almost impossible on the loose sand and pebbles.

Mark fell once and landed against a cactus. Old Alice surprised Joe when she pulled the stickers out of Mark's pants leg. Joe stumbled several times and Smith got a lot of pleasure in urging him on with a jab of the pistol barrel against his back.

When I get my hands on this kid, Joe promised himself, anger rushing over him and up into his mouth in a taste like bitter bile, I'm going to make him wish he'd never seen a pistol!

After a great deal of slipping, sliding, pushing, and shoving the four people, with Alice Manning leading the way, reached the top of the hill.

Joe chanced a quick glance toward the mesa where he'd left Buford Chedos in what seemed like a lifetime ago. Although he couldn't see Chedos, he hoped that the old man was seeing what was going on and wouldn't wait too long to help them after the horse thieves left.

A fiendish gleam was shining in Alice Manning's green eyes as she stopped at a spot about ten feet from where the three men stood.

Joe's heart slammed against his ribs and he felt cold all over even though the setting sun was still emitting warm rays, at the eerie sounds he heard coming from the place that Alice Manning was looking at. He'd never heard that many at one time, but he'd heard one only a few hours ago, or was it minutes, to know that there were more than two rattlesnakes in the pit at her feet!

Joe shifted his eyes quickly away from the pit when he saw three metal rods about half an inch in diameter, with grooves along the sides on the ground a couple of feet away. Old Alice's words "you'll be gone one way or the other" echoed in Joe's ears and he suddenly knew what she meant!

There were no telltale signs except the metal rods that others had been tied here, but that didn't mean that some lives hadn't been lost here. The victims could've been bitten by the snakes, died and the bodies carried away by wolves, mountain lions, and even bears. These mountains were full of all kinds of animals.

Joe never imagined in his longest day or in his wildest dreams that such hideous thoughts would ever cross his mind. He felt sick at his stomach again. If he didn't get control of himself, he'd vomit. He needed all of his wits about him in order to think of what to do.

Being bitten by rattlesnakes would be bad enough. But being tied to a rod and unable to do anything about the bite would be even worse! Joe wouldn't allow himself to think about ending up as a meal for the animals that would soon be roaming around as night fell.

What if the snakebite didn't take effect immediately? What if he only went into partial unconsciousness and the animals came and began tearing at his body?

Darius Worthing, you fat bastard! I'm going to get you for this! Joe's breath began coming in short gasps and small, black dots swam before his eyes. He hoped he wouldn't pass out.

Joe's vendetta against Darius Worthing was pushed away by the previous morbid thoughts and he knew what his fate would be as Louis Smith grabbed him roughly by the arms and shoved him down on the ground. Forcing Joe to sit with his feet at the edge of the pit, Louis drove one of the iron rods down into the ground with the other rod and using an extra piece of rope from his hip pocket, looped it over the knots at

Joe's wrists and then tied it to the metal rod at the last groove.

Joe, still believing that Buford Chedos would come and rescue him and Mark as soon as Alice Manning and Louis Smith left, put up no resistance against Smith. But that didn't hold true for Mark Humphrey. As soon as he heard the snakes and saw Smith tying Joe to the stake, he tried making a run for it.

"You're not going to tie me up like that!" Mark yelled. There was no color at all in his face. His brown eyes were wide in terror.

Alice Manning could move a lot faster than Joe would've guessed. She caught Mark by the arm, swung him around, and tapped him on the side of the head with the pistol barrel. Mark hit the ground facedown like a poleaxed steer and for a heart-stopping second, Joe thought he was dead. That would add murder to the list in Joe's head against Alice Manning and Louis Smith.

Murder. Horse stealing. Kidnapping. But wait. He couldn't add kidnapping to the list. They were just going to leave him and Mark tied here and let the snakes and other animals take care of them.

But Joe was reassured that Mark wasn't dead when he saw his chest rise and fall as Smith dragged him by the feet back to the edge of the pit. A trickle of blood ran down the side of Mark's face. Alice Manning propped Mark up while Louis tied his hands and feet to the metal rod. Mark regained full consciousness when he heard the rattling noise from the snakes.

"Smith, I'll kill you when I get my hands on you!" Mark threatened through clenched teeth. Fear was evident in his eyes as he switched them frantically between Smith and the snake pit.

"I think it's time to go," Alice Manning said, pulling her hat down tighter on her rumpled head. "Desda should have everything ready. We'll take those horses to Cruz and he'll give us a lot of money for them. We can take it easy for a while."

Joe just wished that the two people would shut up, hurry, and leave. Joe added another item on the long list against Darius Worthing, his father, and Louis Smith when Smith picked up a handful of pebbles and tossed them over the side of the pit.

It didn't take long for the air to be permeated with the loud buzzing sound. The single rattler that Joe had locked eyeballs with earlier hadn't been nearly this loud. He knew there had to be at least a dozen sending out their song of warning and death.

Joe could hear Alice Manning and Louis Smith laughing as they walked down the hill. They were probably enjoying the fact that they'd gotten two more animals for Cruz Vega without any trouble at all.

I hope Serge throws Smith and the young horse thief breaks his neck, Joe thought grimly. He had seen the way Smith had looked at Serge and was sure that he'd ride him at least as far as Candelaria.

If Desda had everything ready as Old Alice had ordered, maybe they'd leave as soon as they reached the house and Buford Chedos would hurry down from the mesa and cut him and Mark loose before the snakes got more agitated and restless and decided to come out of the pit. Joe let himself hope that both horse thieves would fall down the hill and break their necks! If that should happen, would Desda help them? She seemed to like Mark but she had also defended Cruz Vega because he gave her "nice things."

No. Joe changed his mind. Breaking their necks would be too good for them. And besides, it would rob him of his chance at them. Whatever he planned to do to the two, they had it coming and a lot more.

The top of the hill was too far from the house for Joe to hear the horses leave, but after a reasonable amount of time, or reasonable enough to Joe anyway, especially after at least twenty minutes had passed, he began wondering what was taking Buford Chedos so long to get there.

From the top of the mesa Chedos should have been able to see everything that had taken place. Actually, he should have started down from the mesa the minute he saw Alice Manning and Louis Smith leave the hill. He should have been at least halfway up the north side of the hill by now.

Joe strained his ears for any sound that would tell him that help was on the way. The sun, now a red orange ball, was slipping faster down behind the misty, blue mountains, throwing long shadows across the land. If Buford Chedos didn't hurry up and get to them, the snakes would come crawling out and his and Mark's feet would be the first things they'd see. Shivers ran all over Joe's body and it wasn't from the cold wind that had changed from the warm breeze.

"If I'd known that it was going to take that old man this long to get up here and help us," Joe said regretfully, anger, tinged with a little fear in his voice, "I wouldn't have let that skinny kid tie us up."

Real fear widened Mark's brown eyes and his mouth was so dry that he had to swallow hard before any words would come out.

"If he doesn't hurry and get here," Mark finally said, "it'll be too late. Look." He nodded toward the pit.

A movement at the rim of the pit caught Joe's eye and sweat began pouring from every pore in his body. A flat, reddish brown head with two slit eyes undulated up over the edge of the pit. The flicking, black, split tongue told Joe that his time was running out.

"If we live through this," Joe said in a strained voice, "I'm going to kill Alice Manning."

The snake crawled over the edge of the pit and Joe Howard had never felt so helpless in his entire life. Even when Louis Smith had had him covered in the yard earlier hadn't been this hard on him.

Joe had assured himself earlier that day that he still had a lot of time left in life. Apparently that wasn't about to come true because the snake was coming closer to his feet.

The only question was, who would it strike first? How soon after the bite would death come? But then, death had many forms. If the poison didn't kill him, the other animals would.

"I guess the twenty dollars that Darius Worthing paid you to take his place on that stage doesn't look so good now, huh?" Joe said reflectively, pulling to no avail against the rope at his feet.

"I don't know who I want to get my hands on first," Mark said, a cold expression in his brown eyes. "Darius Worthing or Louis Smith."

"I'll make you a deal," Joe said, a feeble grin pulling at his mouth. "You can take twenty dollars worth of fat out of Darius Worthing's hide. Just leave Louis Smith for me."

"Why do you want Louis Smith?" Mark asked, spacing out his words and arching his brows. "Darius Worthing's the one who got us into this."

"Worthing is the one who got *you* into this," Joe pointed out slowly. "But Louis Smith stole my horse. A horse that I've had for a long time. I'm going to rip the hide from his skinny body and beat him to death with it!"

Joe's mouth curled up in a sneer. "I'll even let you

deal with Miss Hot Lips. I think, if things were different, she'd really take a shine to you."

Mark Humphrey must have heard something funny in what Joe said, because he threw back his head and laughed.

"I doubt that," Mark argued, shaking his head slowly. He coughed and cleared his throat. "From what she said about Cruz Vega buying things for her, she wouldn't trade that for anything."

"You might make an honest woman out of her," Joe continued, mostly to make conversation and take his mind off the noise in the pit not too far from his feet and the reptile that was coming closer and closer. Maybe time would begin passing faster and Buford Chedos would soon get there and get them out of a situation that shouldn't be happening to a stray dog.

"It would probably take more than me and more time than I would want to spend to make an honest woman out of her," Mark replied, shaking his head. His chin began quivering. "I just want out of this mess."

Time was definitely running out for Joe Howard and Mark Humphrey! One more snake had crawled out of the pit and even though it hadn't coiled, and a snake didn't have to coil to strike, it was giving off a warning buzz like its cousin. And its flashing, black tongue was just as busy. The leaves and grass rustled as it slithered along.

For some reason though, Joe wasn't as worried about the snakes now as he was about the mountain lions, wolves, and bear. If he and Mark sat still, the snakes would probably go back down into the pit for the warmth of their kin. From all indications, tonight was going to be as cold as last night. It was too bad that Alice Manning and Louis Smith couldn't have been humane enough to put them in a cave like the one they'd shared with Buford Chedos last night.

But if the two had done that, Joe and Mark's bodies wouldn't have been disposed of quick enough. Old Alice and Smith wouldn't be around though when Joe and Mark would "be gone one way or the other." They'd be on their way to Cruz Vega in Candelaria.

The wind had picked up more and a bone-rattling chill was spreading over Joe's entire body. He couldn't stop the shivering that consumed him. He tried to make himself feel better by thinking that it was from the cold instead of fear.

Joe had strained and struggled against the rope around his hands and feet but the only thing he had accomplished was a deep, bloody cut on his right wrist.

Joe had promised himself that when he got his hands on Louis Smith, and that was appearing highly unlikely now, since he was the one tied to a metal rod driven hard into the ground, that he was going to kill him at first sight. No questions asked! Draw the .45 from the holster, take aim, and pull the trigger. It would be as simple as that!

Joe had never killed a woman. He'd never even struck a woman. But was Alice Manning a woman? The fact that she wore a dress was the only evidence that she was of the female species. If he was loose right then and saw Alice Manning, he wouldn't think twice about letting her have it right in the middle of her toothless face with the back of his hand. He imagined some of the dirt flying off when he hit her.

Mark Humphrey had tried as hard as Joe to wiggle the stake loose behind him. But he hadn't been any more successful than Joe and he hadn't said anything in the past ten minutes. Joe glanced over at him and felt sorry for the boy. Mark's blotched face was desolate and he looked as helpless as Joe felt.

"Do you know what I wish right now?" Mark asked listlessly, turning to face Joe, expelling a long breath.

"No," Joe said softly, shaking his head. "What?"

"I wish that Darius Worthing was standing right there," Mark replied and nodded to the spot between his feet and the snake pit. "I'd kick his fat ass so hard that it would take a week to get my foot out. It wouldn't bother me in the least to see him fall over into that pit. But he's so fat that a snake bite probably wouldn't even hurt him."

Joe couldn't help chuckling low in his throat at the mental picture that popped into his mind of the fat kid toppling over into the pit with Mark's boot firmly implanted in his backside. But the image didn't last long when a coyote's yelping filled the air.

Joe cursed himself for putting so much trust in Buford Chedos. He shouldn't have believed that the old man would hurry and come help them. Chedos had probably ridden down from the mesa as soon as Mark had left and joined up with the horse thieves when they came down from the hill. All four of them were probably laughing at him and Mark right then. Chedos had his precious mule back and Alice Manning had another horse for Cruz Vega.

Joe also cursed himself for not taking a swing at Louis Smith and his crazy aunt when he'd had a couple of chances. He would never be caught that lax again if he ever got out of this situation.

Joe scoffed at the silly thought. Here he sat, tied hand and feet to a metal rod, the possible meal for some animals in the mountains after he'd died from a rattlesnake bite, consoling himself thinking about a next time!

"Do you know what I wish?" Joe asked, licking his

dry lips and pulling against the rope at his feet. Mark didn't say anything to prompt him but there was a question in his eyes. "I wish that Colonel Eric McRaney was sitting here to tell me again how simple this job was going to be."

In desperation, he gave one more sharp pull on the rope around his wrist but stopped when he felt more wetness on his wrist and something trickling down his hand.

Joe's ears perked up suddenly when he heard a shuffling sound in the dry grass and weeds behind him. He couldn't tell if a man or animal was making the noise. Chill bumps raced up and down his back and his heart was pounding so hard he could see the front of his shirt moving up and down with the beat.

He couldn't think of a worse way to die than being mauled to death by a cougar! Maybe if it was somebody, they'd just go ahead, shoot him and Mark and put them out of their misery.

He'd given up hoping that Buford Chedos was coming to help them. He didn't think that an Indian was coming up behind them. Indians didn't like to fight after dark. But there would be no fight this time. All the Indian would have to do was put an arrow in them or use a knife and take what he wanted.

"I guess ye'ns thought I wasn't never goin' to get here, huh?" The welcome question came from Buford Chedos's raspy voice! Joe felt bad now about having doubts about the old prospector and promised himself that he would apologize to him later. But right now, he was more interested in the old man cutting them free.

"What in the devil have you been doing?" Joe asked, glaring up at the old man, irritation replacing gratitude. He was angry again that it had taken Chedos so long to get there. A snake could have bitten him and

Mark. A cougar or bear could've clawed them to pieces and began having them as the main course in a meal. But he was so glad to see him that he wanted to hug him, dirt and all. "What took you so danged long to get here? Those snakes could have gotten us."

"Snakes?" Chedos asked innocently. "What snakes?"

"The snakes in that pit," Joe answered, his voice crawling up in disbelief as he nodded toward the pit.

Buford chuckled and squatted behind Joe. He took a long bladed knife from his pocket and cut the rope around Joe's wrist. While Joe got the circulation going in his arms and wiped the blood from his hands, Chedos cut Mark free and, bracing his hands on his knee, stood up.

"These here old bones of mine jest don't want to work the way they used to," Chedos said with a grunt.

Mark took Chedos's knife, bent forward, and cut the rope away from his feet, then pitched the knife over to Joe.

Chedos pulled Mark to his feet and jerked around toward the snake pit when the hissing became louder. "Ye wasn't kiddin' 'bout them snakes, was ye?" he said, standing still and staring at Joe.

"No, I wasn't kidding," Joe answered, cutting his bound feet loose, shaking his head and swallowing hard. He stood up and handed the knife to Chedos. The three men didn't waste any time hanging around on top of the hill to see what had caused the extra amount of noise.

"I guess ye'ns would like to know why I was delayed," Chedos said more than asked as they started down the hill. Joe stopped walking long enough to give Chedos a belligerent look.

"Yes, I would like to know what took you so long," Joe replied caustically, nodding his head in a quick jerk. "You should've already been here and cut us free. Those there people are taking all of the horses that were in the corral, plus Serge and old Smoke to Candelaria to sell to Cruz Vega."

Joe stopped for a breath before continuing and enjoyed Buford Chedos's surprised look.

"Did ye say Cruz Vega?" Chedos asked, his brows arching over wide eyes, then drawing his brows together in a tight frown.

"Yep," Joe answered, nodding slowly.

"Well, he ain't followin' us," Chedos said, shaking his head.

"If Vega gets to Alice Manning and her family before we do," Joe said as they began walking down the hill, "and recognizes that mule, you could be in trouble. He'll know you've helped us. I don't know if he'll remember seeing Serge in the village. But if he does, he'll probably kill Louis Smith if he thinks he helped Mark Humphrey get away. I wouldn't mind that so much if I didn't want to get my hands on Smith first. I wish that we had just one extra horse."

Joe was rambling on so much about what they needed to do that some of his words ran together and some of them didn't even make sense. He didn't notice the tolerant grin on the old man's bearded face.

"There ain't no need fer an extra horse," Chedos said, a knowing gleam in his eyes when Joe finally hushed and he was able to say something.

"Why?" Joe asked, a skeptical frown between his brows. It should be plain to Chedos that he and Mark didn't have any horses. Chedos was the only one who still had a horse and it would be impossible for the three men to ride one horse. There was no chance that he and Mark could catch up with the horse thieves on foot.

Too much time would be wasted if Buford Chedos went after them alone. The old man couldn't take the three people anyway. Even if he was able to do it, he would have to come all the way back for Joe and Mark and then the three of them would have to ride all that way again.

Unless they could suddenly sprout wings and fly, Vega and his men were the only way that they could get horses. But Chedos said that Vega and his men weren't following them.

"Well, that has a little to do with why I'm so late in gettin' to ye," Chedos said and rolled his mouth in against his teeth in a sucking sound. "Three young Apache Indian boys came along. I persuaded 'em that they didn't need two of their horses as much as I did. By the time they get untied, we'll be well on our way south. Leavin' 'em one horse to get back to their camp was the least I could do." He looked solemnly at Joe. "Don't ye think?"

Joe closed his eyes, lowered his head, and turned it slowly toward Chedos. The old man had just contradicted the very things he'd thought about him. He couldn't believe the childlike look of pleasure glowing on Chedos's face. For once in his young life, Joe Howard, army scout was at a loss for words.

The Indian boys must have come up on the north side of the mesa. Of course, there wouldn't have been much noise if Chedos had surprised them but there was something he had to know.

"Just how did you get away from three Apache boys?" Joe asked incredulously. "A horse is the last thing that an Apache will give up. They don't mind running a horse to death, but they don't mind eating one either." Joe shook his head in disbelief and frowned deeply at Chedos. "You said that they were tied up. How in the devil did you manage that?"

"It was simple," Chedos answered glibly, shrugging

his shoulders. "I held my shotgun on all three of 'em. I had one tie up two, then I tied him up. I'm s'prised ye didn't figure that out yer own self."

Joe let his shoulders drop in frustration, shook his head dismally, and didn't say anything else. There was nothing left to say. Not right then anyway. Chedos had simplified a situation just like Colonel Eric McRaney would have. The two men must be related.

The descent down the opposite side of the hill to where the two Indian horses were tied to a cedar bush didn't take very long. If those two horses were the better of the three, Joe hated to think what the third one looked like.

Both animals were small boned, the ribs could be counted and one was lop-eared. Joe knew that beggars couldn't be choosy and they would have to make do with what they had. But he hoped they would be a lot better on their skinny legs than they appeared.

"Can those horses walk?" Joe asked, expelling a deep breath and shaking his head in wonder.

"Oh, sure." Chedos's nod and spoken assurance was quick. "An Indian won't ride a horse that ain't fast."

With a lot of doubt and uncertainty, especially on Joe's part, he and Mark swung up on the back of the Indian horses that would have been bare except for the thin blankets. He knew that he and Mark wouldn't have a very pleasant ride until they caught up with Alice Manning and that rope-happy nephew and the daughter with the fickle eye.

They had to ride past the house to follow the trail which the three horse thieves took no trouble to hide. Joe was glad and surprised to see the blanket still on the ground that Mark had wrapped around him. Joe wondered why it hadn't been taken as he dismounted and motioned for Mark to get down.

Taking a knife from his pocket, Joe split the blanket and gave half to Mark. He took it, put it on top of the other blanket and remounted. Joe was just about to swing up on the horse when a wild thought struck him.

"You start on," he said, starting back toward the house. "I'll catch up." He hoped to find some kind of usable weapon in the house. The only guns they had right then was the one pistol and shotgun and knife that Buford Chedos carried.

As fast as he could, he rummaged through the neatly kept house, but didn't find anything. It would dawn on him later that the floors were swept, the beds were made, and all of the dishes were in place in the kitchen.

But the only thing on his mind right then, as he hurried from the house and got back on the Indian horse was how disappointed he was at not finding any guns.

The Indian horses had more speed than Joe had expected and he had to grip his knees tighter at the animal's side to hold on as the horse raced out of the yard. With the unexpected speed, Joe was soon able to catch up with Mark and Chedos.

The dying rays of sunset were a prelude to night claiming the land and Joe suspected that Alice Manning and her kin would probably stop somewhere for the night. The three would have nothing to worry about since they were certain that Joe and Mark would present no problem to them because they were securely tied at the rattlesnake pit. Or some animal could have already taken them away. Joe shivered as he remembered Alice saying "you'll be gone one way or the other." Now he knew what she meant.

Joe knew that he, Mark, and Buford had to find them before they met Cruz Vega. If they couldn't and Vega recognized Serge and particularly the mule, since he knew Chedos and Mark weren't with Alice, and believing that Mark was Darius Worthing and worth a thousand dollars to him, he would probably intensify his search for Mark, and Joe. Joe would really be at a disadvantage against Vega since their only defense were Chedos's weapons and that wouldn't be enough against Vega's well-armed bunch.

Joe wondered why Vega hadn't caught up with them if he already knew where Alice Manning lived and since he'd been getting horses from her. Maybe she'd kept her residence a secret in order to keep Vega from just coming and stealing the horses from her. But it was possible that they always met in Candelaria.

No, that couldn't be it, Joe argued with himself, shaking his head rapidly. If Vega really wanted to know where Old Alice lived, he would have had one of his men follow her. There had to be another reason. Joe really didn't care what it was just as long as he got to her before Vega did and took Serge and the mule.

But Joe was encouraged with another thought. Vega wasn't in a hurry to get to Alice Manning if they'd been meeting in Candelaria all this time. Vega's main concern right then was getting to Tyler Worthing before Joe did.

Joe didn't have any way of knowing how fast the horse thieves would be traveling since they weren't in any hurry. They knew that Joe and Mark were probably snake bit and wolf bait by now and wouldn't be any threat to them. But he knew he had to find them before dark and while their trail was still easy to follow. They hadn't made much attempt to hide their trail and the three men were making good time.

The two Indian horses had more stamina and speed than Joe had first suspected and it wouldn't take long for them to catch up with the others. No matter how long it had seemed to Joe that they had been tied at the snake pit, no more than half an hour had passed before Buford Chedos had cut them free.

The cooling night air was suddenly filled with the mouth-watering aroma of frying bacon and fresh coffee. That meant that someone was very near and cooking. The smell assaulted Joe's taste buds and he realized that they hadn't eaten anything since breakfast early that morning. If Mark and Chedos were like him, they were on the brink of starvation. His stomach began rumbling and he hoped the noise wouldn't give them away until he was ready for the horse thieves to know they were there.

Joe was suddenly hit with another realization that it could be one of three groups of people who had built that fire. He wanted to think that someone or anyone was just making night camp. But the chances of that happening was about as likely as him becoming governor of Texas next week.

With the way Joe's luck had been running, it would be either Cruz Vega and his men or Alice Manning and her thieving family.

God, please, if it has to be anybody, let it be old Alice Manning, Joe prayed silently. They could probably handle the three easier than Cruz Vega and his bunch.

Once again, Joe's supplication was answered.

Alice Manning, probably thinking that all of the world was theirs, had made no effort to hide the fire. It, with the three people sitting around it, was about fifty feet from where the horses had been tethered under a grove of oak trees. Why had they stopped so soon?

Joe didn't think that Desda would present much of a threat to them and would let Buford Chedos take care of her. He knew that he and Mark could get the drop on Alice Manning and Louis Smith. He wasn't too worried about making any noise. If the horse thieves heard them, they'd only think it was some animal or maybe Cruz Vega making an early call.

They dismounted and, trying to make as little noise as possible, eased toward the campsite.

"Buford, give Mark your shotgun. Let me have your pistol and you get behind the girl. She shouldn't be any problem. Mark, you'll stand a better chance against that dirty, old woman. I'll take Smith."

Joe was a little surprised when neither Mark nor Chedos argued with him about what he wanted them to do. Joe hadn't thought that Buford Chedos would give up his guns so easily. He knew that he wouldn't have done it. But maybe common sense told the old man he had no choice.

They paused behind the boulder then started toward the fire after Chedos handed Joe and Mark his guns. Joe halted in his steps and allowed himself a grin.

He had been in Colonel Eric McRaney's company too long. He was again acutely aware of how much he was beginning to sound like him. He had just made overpowering three people who had gotten the drop on him and Mark earlier sound as simple as making a pot of coffee.

Louis Smith would probably blow Joe's brains out if he got the chance and Alice Manning wouldn't hesitate a second in shooting him if she thought she was going to lose those horses.

Alice Manning was sitting on a yellow blanket spread out on the ground on the right side of the crackling fire that was in a circle of rocks. She was leaning back against a tree trunk. Joe couldn't see her S&W anywhere. But then he hadn't seen it back at the house either so that didn't mean she didn't have it close to her. The old, toothless bat could have it hidden in a fold of her dirty dress.

Desda Manning was sitting on a blue, blanket-covered log and leaning back against the tree. She looked like a princess in contrast to her dirty mother. Her long hair hung down around her shoulders, framing her face. She looked despondent, her right leg tucked under her and a cup of coffee in her hands.

Louis Smith was leaning back against a saddle on the left side of the fire, his legs stretched out before him and crossed at the ankles. Joe could see a pistol in the holster at Smith's right side and his Colt .45 was still in Smith's waistband. All three of them looked like they didn't have a care in the world. And really they didn't.

"I wonder how those two are doin' at the snake pit?" Louis asked, mirth in his voice as he reached out and filled his coffee cup.

"Well," Alice said with a crackling laugh, "either the snakes has got them by now or the coyotes have. Either way, they're gone. By the time we get back from Candelaria, it'll be hard to know that they was ever around."

Old Alice wiggled her rear end for a more comfortable position on the blanket and Joe could see a pleased smile on her dirty face. "Hand me 'nuther piece of that meat, Louis." She took it, crammed it into her toothless mouth and began gumming away on it. "Desda, do you want anything?" Old Alice wiped her mouth on the back of her hand, and then her hand on her dress.

"No," Desda replied softly and shook her head wistfully.

Joe's anger boiled up in his stomach again and he felt knots standing out in his jaws. If he hadn't had a plan in mind for Louis Smith, he would have shot him where he sat, sipping his cup of coffee and wouldn't have felt bad about doing it.

With a quick nod at Mark and Chedos, Joe motioned for Mark to step past him so he could get around behind Alice Manning at the same time that he came up behind Smith. All Chedos had to do to come up behind Desda was take a few steps to his right. Joe turned to his left and began circling to get behind Smith. Joe waited until Mark was directly behind Old Alice. Louis wouldn't be able to see him because the light from the fire was in his eyes. If Smith had been standing, he would have seen both men behind the women. Mark could see Joe from where he was. He had Chedos's shotgun ready in his hand, aimed directly at Alice Manning. He looked across the fire at Joe for his signal.

Moving as close as he could without making too much noise, and glad that he'd never gotten into the habit of wearing spurs, Joe eased up behind Smith and pressed the pistol against the back of his neck.

"Smith, if you want to see Cruz Vega again," Joe warned in a cold voice, thumbing the hammer back on the .44, "ease that pistol from the holster with your left hand and pitch it to the ground at your feet. Alice," Joe raised his voice to carry across the dancing flames, "I know you have an S&W close to you. If you don't want Mark to blow your head off with a shotgun, throw the pistol toward the fire."

Joe saw the young horse thief stiffen at his unexpected voice and directions while Alice Manning sat perfectly still, a shocked look on her face.

"Smith, take my pistol from your belt by the handle with just your thumb and finger," Joe continued and got a lot of pleasure in getting the drop on Louis Smith, "and hand it back here to me."

Even though Joe could see Smith's hands, he pressed the pistol tighter against his neck when Smith paused before doing as he was told.

"You'd better do what he says," Mark encouraged

from across the camp fire. "It wouldn't bother me at all to blow a hole in this old woman for having us tied at that snake pit."

"He's right," Joe concurred flatly, hearing Serge nicker. The horse must have either smelled him or recognized his voice. Joe got mad all over again at the thought that this person, with a sneering grin on his thin face, had stolen his horse to sell to Cruz Vega.

"If you don't hand my pistol back here," Joe urged, jabbing the .44 harder against Smith's neck, "I'm going to blow a hole in you big enough to pull a rattlesnake through." Joe thought it was an appropriate threat. He shivered at the thought.

Joe's threat must have made a believer out of Louis Smith or maybe it was Smith's realization that Joe wasn't alone and that he and his partners were armed.

"Do what he says, Louis," Old Alice advised in a tight voice, "or this kid just might do somethin' crazy. He's got a shotgun against my back and I think he'd use it."

Joe glanced across the fire in time to see Alice Manning ease her hand down by her side, pick up the S&W and pitch it to the edge of the circle of rocks around the fire. Reaching around, he took his pistol from Smith's extended hand, lowered the hammer on Buford Chedos's .44 and pitched it across to him. He paused long enough to check the load in the Colt .45 before stepping around Smith to pick up Alice Manning's discarded pistol.

Smith's courage had an upswing as soon as Joe bent down. Smith jumped up and made a quick low dash at him. He caught Joe around the knees, driving him forward to land on his stomach. Both men hit the ground only a few inches from the fire. They were so close in fact, that Joe could feel the heat from the flames on his face.

Joe hadn't expected Smith's sudden attack which knocked the pistol from his hand and he lay stunned for a second. Knowing that if Smith was ruthless enough to tie him and Mark to stakes at a snake pit, he wouldn't be above trying to beat him to the gun and if he got his hands on it, he'd shoot him without even batting an eye.

But Joe had a plan in mind for Louis Smith and couldn't allow him to get the upper hand. Bracing his left leg hard against the ground, Joe rolled over on his back, loosening his knees in Smith's grip, leaving Smith on his hands and knees.

Drawing up his legs, Joe planted both feet on the startled horse thief's shoulder and shoved back as hard as he could.

Louis Smith, whether it was from pain or surprise or a combination of both, let out a yell as he went flying backward across the small area. He landed against the trunk of a pin-oak tree and the air swooshed out of his gaping mouth. He hit the tree with such force that he bounced away from it and would have fallen sideways if Joe hadn't been a little quicker getting to his feet. Joe snatched up his .45, put it in the holster, bent down, grabbed a handful of Smith's gray shirt and hauled him to his feet. They stood almost nose to nose.

"The only reason that I don't shoot you right now," Joe told the wide-eyed man who was glaring at him, "is that I need you to show me where Cruz Vega's place is in Candelaria. I don't care what you and your thieving family do after you show me where they'll be. You all can go to hell as far as I'm concerned. I have my horse back and Buford Chedos has his mule."

Smith held Joe's steady gaze for an undetermined amount of time. Joe let go of the front of Smith's shirt but pulled the pistol from the holster and leveled it at him. Smith must have convinced himself that Joe really wouldn't shoot him if he needed his help in finding Cruz Vega. A slow, cunning smile eased across his face that was beginning to show a slight growth of beard.

"Do you mean to tell me, that if I show you how to get to Vega's place," Smith said, squinting a look at Joe, while rubbing his chest, "that you'll let us, and the horses go?" A skeptical frown pulled his brows together.

"That's right," Joe said, nodding slowly, trying to swallow the bitter-tasting words. He felt like he'd just made a deal with the devil.

"What if I refuse?" Smith asked, arching a brow. "You can't make me tell you anything and I'm not afraid of you."

The army scout's face went solemn. He dropped his gaze down to the ground, turned over some leaves and twigs with his foot, and had an idea when he saw a centipede scurrying away. Joe slowly raised his eyes to meet Smith's.

"Oh, you might not be afraid of me," Joe said drolly, making a sucking sound rolling his lips in against his teeth, "but night is coming on and there are all kinds of crawly things on the ground. You wouldn't stand much of a chance against them if you're tied to a tree and no one's around to help you. What if a rattlesnake comes at you?"

All of the color drained from Smith's face and he swallowed hard. He batted his eyes, but never took his gaze from Joe.

"Aunt Alice, are you going to let him get away with this?" Smith called out, desperation and fear rampant in his voice. "Do somethin'!"

"Well, Louis, there don't seem to be a whole heck of a lot that I can do," Alice Manning answered, a hint of laughter in her voice. "This boy has a shotgun and the man jerking you around gave a pistol to that old codger."

"What old codger?" Smith asked, a wild and puzzled look on his face as he turned toward his aunt. It was then that he saw Buford Chedos standing behind Desda, who had been quiet all of this time. Smith's mouth fell open in surprise. "Where did he come from?"

"He was waiting up on the mesa to help us," Joe said, grinning at Smith. "There was no way that those snakes would have gotten us." He couldn't stop the shivers that went all over him as he remembered how close the snakes had actually come to him and Mark.

"Just who are ye callin' an old codger?" Buford Chedos demanded in a gruff and insulted voice. "Iffen that snot-nosed kid don't tell Joe what he wants to know," Chedos paused and stepped around in front of Desda Manning and over in front of Old Alice so he could look directly down at her, "ye're goin' to be the one supplyin' the answers. And I know jest the thing to make ye talk."

Chedos bent down and pulled the long bladed knife from his right boot. "I saw what the Yaqui Indians did to a white woman one time." He squinted his eyes in thoughtful and diabolical recall and ran his thumb carefully back and forth across the tip of the wide blade that glittered in the firelight.

"It wasn't a very purty sight," he continued, shaking his grizzled head and pressing his mouth into a thin, grim line. Joe wanted to laugh when Chedos took a threatening step toward the dirty old hag.

"They staked her out," Chedos went on, spreading his arms, "as naked as the day she was born into this world. Purty little piece of fluff, she was." Chedos stopped his gruesome tale long enough to squat before Alice Manning and let his words soak in before continuing. "Then they began makin' little bitty cuts all over her body. I didn't know a woman could scream that loud."

The old prospector's voice was soft and low, as if he was telling a child a story.

Joe wanted to vomit as he listened to Chedos's halting words describe the horror but he also wanted to laugh at the sick look on Alice Manning's pale, dirty face. There was no color at all in it now. She looked like a ghost.

"They had a jug of honey with 'um," Chedos went on with pathos in his voice and his eyes boring into hers. "They poured that honey into every one of them cuts and then stood back and waited until the ants began eatin'. That really raised a racket from her."

Chedos squinted his eyes shut and shook his head rapidly. "We'uns ain't got no honey. But I got a bag of sugar. Ants like sugar 'most as much as they do honey."

Chedos struggled to his feet and grinned down at the frightened and almost-petrified woman staring up at him.

"Louis, for God's sake," Old Alice wailed and clasped her hands in her lap, "tell him what he wants to know before this crazy old man starts cutting. It's your fault that we're in this mess in the first place!" She glared at her nephew, contempt in her eyes.

"My fault?" Smith repeated, doing a double take and staring at her. "Why is it my fault? You've been around him as long as I have."

Alice Manning expelled a disgruntled breath and started trying to get up from the ground even though Chedos still had the knife in his hand. "You should've looked around better to see if they had any friends waiting somewhere."

If looks could have killed, Louis Smith would've

joined the ranks of corpses from the deadly expression in his aunt's eyes.

"We would've been rattlesnake meat if we hadn't had a friend waiting," Joe said, taking his gaze from Smith just long enough to look over at the old woman who had regained a little of her composure when Chedos stepped back and allowed her to get to her feet.

"If you don't tell or show us where Cruz Vega's place is," Joe went on, "you're going to be a dead man if he ever catches up with you." Joe enjoyed the fearful expression shooting across Smith's face.

"Why would he want to kill me?" Smith asked in stuttering words and falling for Joe's trick. "We've been doin' business with him for a long time."

"Because when he sees you all riding with us," Joe explained in clipped words, "he'll either think one of two things: First is that you were trying to get Mark Humphrey for the thousand dollars reward."

Joe wanted to laugh when Smith's mouth dropped open at the mention of so much money he'd allowed to slip between his fingers. He threw a quick glance over to his aunt. She returned the look with a smirk.

"Why is he worth a thousand dollars to Cruz?" Desda Manning asked. Up until now, the girl hadn't said anything except to answer her mother when she'd asked if she'd wanted anything to eat. She had only sat, looked, and listened.

"Cruz Vega kidnapped Mark in Fort Davis," Joe began explaining. "He thinks he's Darius Worthing, the son of a rich man from Pecos. He wants a thousand dollars in ransom for him. If he should ride up right now and see all of us together, the only one he's going to make sure is alive is him." Joe jerked his head toward Mark.

"But you said Vega thinks he's," Louis glanced at

Mark, "someone else. If he ain't who Vega thinks he is, why would Vega still want him?"

Joe wondered where Louis had been when brains were passed out.

"If someone kidnaps you," Joe began, expelling a disgruntled breath, "wouldn't you try convincing them that you were someone else if there was a chance that you could end up getting killed in case the ransom wasn't going to be paid?"

"Yeah," Louis agreed, looking down at the fire. "You've got a point."

"The other thing is," Joe continued, arching his brows. "Vega knows Chedos," he nodded toward the old man. "If he sees my horse and Buford Chedos's two good-looking animals with you, he's going to wonder how you got them, and if you've been stealing horses and selling them to him, he's going to be really mad if he thinks you were trying to keep them for yourself."

Joe had to allow himself a smile in order not to laugh at the confused boy standing before him. Joe didn't really need Smith to tell him where Cruz Vega would be heading. He already knew that. He could just find him a lot sooner with his help. He only hoped that he could find Tyler Worthing before Cruz Vega did.

"I think it would be to your advantage," Mark Humphrey advised. He'd been quiet all of this time, still standing behind Alice Manning. "I don't know how long you've been doing business with Vega. But I was around him for only two days and he doesn't seem like the kind of man who would like to be double-crossed."

"I never said anything about double-crossing him," Smith yelled, glancing from Mark, over to Chedos, and finally back to Joe. "He wouldn't even know that I had such an idea."

"Oh, yes, he would," Joe said, emphasizing each

word sharply, nodding and letting his voice climb slowly with each threatening word.

"Why?" Smith asked, having trouble getting the word out of his dry mouth. He blinked his eyes quickly a couple of times.

"Because," Joe answered, leaning forward a little and peering closely at the boy almost cowering before him. "I'm going to find Cruz Vega, with or without your help. I'll tell him that you could've been at his place a lot sooner with more horses but you decided to wait."

Smith expelled a deep breath and leaned dejectedly back on the same tree that he'd fallen against only a short time ago. Joe knew he'd made up his mind when he swallowed hard and licked his mouth as he nodded.

"Okay. Okay. You've got a deal," Smith agreed as he expelled the breath. "We'll show you. But, you promised that you'd let us and the horses go when we get to Candelaria."

"I know what I said," Joe replied. "I'll keep my promise."

7

"Does that mean I'll get to ride along with you?" Desda Manning asked, getting up from the log where she'd been sitting quietly. She hurried over to Mark and fluttered her lashes up at him. When she took hold of his arm and pressed her face against his shoulder, the poor boy almost passed out.

"I thought you had your eyes on Cruz Vega," Joe reminded, arching his brows, unsure whether to feel sorry for Mark or laugh at him. The boy was looking down at Desda like a sun-struck cat.

It was a good thing that Buford Chedos had put the fear of God into Old Alice and she'd discarded her pistol. Mark Humphrey probably wasn't even aware that he was holding a gun in his hands.

"I don't see anything wrong with it, if she wants to ride along with me," Mark interrupted, tearing his eyes from the girl's upturned face long enough to give Joe an annoyed glare. "I'll be responsible for her."

Boy, you've got a lot to learn about women, Joe thought rancorously to himself. Desda knew now that Mark was worth at least a thousand dollars to Cruz Vega. He could almost see the dollar signs in her eyes. She was probably thinking that he really belonged to a family who was wealthy enough to pay that kind of money for his return. Either way, she would come out on the winning end if Vega got the money first, or if she stayed with Mark and they beat Vega to Tyler Worthing who would really have a thousand dollars on him.

Joe realized that standing there and arguing with Mark Humphrey whether or not Desda Manning could ride along with him was getting them nowhere fast. Cruz Vega and his men could ride up on them at any minute.

Vega probably knew by now that one of his men had been killed, and no doubt by Joe and had guessed that Buford Chedos was with him and Mark. He probably also knew that the way they were going would put them right in Alice Manning's lap.

Unless Vega came down with smallpox, he wouldn't have anything to worry about, would know that he would be getting at least one more horse and mule, and could head straight to Tyler Worthing in Candelaria.

"All right," Joe said, turning away from Mark and lowering the pistol but still keeping it aimed at Louis Smith. "We should leave early in the morning to beat Vega to Candelaria. Or, we can leave right now, ride all night and be sure to beat Vega to Worthing. If you promise you won't try to get away, I won't have to gag and tie you and your aunt up and leave you out here."

Joe saw a motion from the corner of his eye and turned just in time to see Mark Humphrey making a dash away from Desda and toward Smith.

"If you'll give me a few minutes with this lowdown horse thief," Mark raged, his eyes blazing, "I'll make him tell you what you want to know." He must have had his attention on Desda when Joe was persuading Smith to help him. He pitched the shotgun over to Chedos.

"I already told him that I'd help," Smith snapped, glaring at Mark.

But before Joe knew what was happening or Louis Smith could say anything else, Mark reached out, grabbed a fistful of Smith's shirt, pulled him close and smashed his fist squarely in the center of Smith's shocked face. Blood began running from Smith's thin nose and trickling from a cut on his upper lip when his bottom teeth had cut into it.

"That'll be enough," Joe shouted, surprise widening his eyes as he caught Mark's arm and pulled him away from Smith. "He won't be able to talk with a busted mouth."

Joe had no idea that Mark Humphrey would even be the type actually to react to violence. For the past few days, he'd been so quiet, almost docile. But then he'd been sick. Maybe that old adage was true: still water always runs deep.

"Keep him away from me," Smith said, wiping the blood from his mouth on the back of his hand, fear in his voice. He stared at Mark who was still standing spraddle-legged, his fist doubled up and ready to come at him again. "I think my nose is broken."

Joe, glancing from Smith to Mark smiled and wished that Mark had cut loose on Smith sooner.

"No, I don't think it's broken," Joe scoffed, holstering the .45. "Maybe just a little rearranged."

Louis Smith must have thought that Joe was just going to sit down by the dying embers of the fire and wait for tomorrow to come, then start out for Candelaria. But that wasn't going to be the case.

"To make sure that you *are* going to be here in the

morning to show me where Vega will be," Joe said, narrowing his eyes as he looked at Smith, "I think it's best that I *do* tie you up. It's only fair, you know. You were hoping that Mark and I would be gone when you all returned from Candelaria, one way or the other, when you tied us up at that snake pit. I want to keep you in one place so nothing will happen to you."

Joe didn't know if it was the level tone in his voice or the threatening glare in his eyes. Whatever it was made a believer out of Smith. He didn't resist when Joe took a long, thin rope from his saddlebag, led him over to a small juniper tree, and let him get into a comfortable sitting position on the ground.

Joe tied one end of the rope around Smith's left wrist, wound the rope around the tree and the other end around his right wrist. Then he tied both ends of the rope together. There was no possible way that Smith would be able to untie the rope and get away.

"I thought you said that we were going to leave right away," Mark reminded Joe when he stood back and took a deep breath.

"No," Joe answered, turning his head and looking toward the west. The sun was too far down behind the mountains and the night air was getting much colder. It would be too dark in only a matter of minutes for them to make any distance.

Inky, velvet darkness would enshroud the land and the twinking, diamondlike stars and the pale, yellow moon just breaking the horizon in the east would be their only light since the fire was almost out. It would be too risky for them to leave tonight.

"It's best that we stay here for the night and start out early in the morning," Joe said, shaking his head. "We already have a fire built. All it needs is more wood and we have accommodations for the night."

"Do you want me to build up the fire?" Mark asked. While he waited for Joe's answer, he rummaged through Smith's saddlebags, found the Mexican's gun belt, wrapped it around his waist, and pushed the long-barreled pistol down into the holster.

"Yeah," Joe finally said, grinning when Mark had to put the belt in the last notch and the end of the belt into his pocket.

"What are ye goin' to do with them?" Buford asked, jerking his jagged-nailed thumb over his shoulder at Alice Manning and then at Desda.

"Oh, I don't think Mrs. Manning would leave her cute nephew," Joe said sarcastically, nodding at Smith. "There won't be any need to post a guard."

"I wouldn't bet my last dollar on that if I was you, lad," Alice Manning said, a caustic challenge in her voice.

"Well, if my mother leaves," Desda said in a determined yet whiney-edged voice, "I'm going with her."

Desda Manning apparently didn't know where her loyalties lay. First she wanted to ride along beside Mark. She knew he was worth some money. Now, she wanted to go with her mother. Old Alice and she would know where Vega was and if they could escape and leave before morning, she could get to Vega sooner and he could still buy her "nice things." He might already have something for her.

Joe wondered what kind of play she'd make for him if he waved some money before her.

At that very second Joe wished that he was back in Fort Davis, at either the Desert Rose Saloon shooting the breeze with Queenie Jeanie and Betty Young over a cold beer or eating sourdough biscuits and gravy at Billy Leon's Cafe with Polly Bullock. He really wouldn't even have minded sitting on the front porch at the fort and "discussing" things with Colonel Eric McRaney. He'd enjoy hearing the colonel telling him how simple his next job was going to be.

If he could be at any of the three places, he wouldn't be standing there listening to two querulous women telling him what they would or wouldn't do. In either case, he knew that he'd heard all he wanted from both of them. Their voices were beginning to grate on his nerves.

"Neither of you are going anywhere tonight," he said through clenched teeth, feeling a knot working in his jaws. "Just shut up! Mark, it looks like we'll have to use a guard after all. Do you feel like taking the first watch?"

Mark, dropping an arm full of limbs by the fire, with uncertainty, nodded.

"Are you going to tie us up like you did poor Louis?" Old Alice asked pitifully, lowering her head, then cutting her eyes cunningly back up at Joe.

"I really should," Joe replied sharply, taking a threatening step toward her, a glare in his eyes. She stepped back and he liked it when her face lost a little color, although it was hard actually to tell under all of the dirt.

"What do you mean, 'poor Louis'?" Joe asked, narrowing his eyes. "At least he isn't tied with his feet almost in a rattlesnake's mouth. You are probably counting on the three of us falling asleep." He nodded at Mark and Chedos. "Then you will try to get away since you know exactly where Vega will be. You wouldn't lose any time in getting to him if you think he'd give you a share of the thousand dollar ransom for the Worthing kid." He couldn't bring himself to use the fat kid's first name. That was just too much. "I just hope we get to Worthing first."

Joe had wished that so many times during the past few days that he was getting tired of thinking and hearing it. He'd be glad when this entire sorry mess was over. If he hadn't wanted to see the look on Tyler Worthing's wide face so bad when the big man saw Mark Humphrey and learned what his son had done to him, he would ride away right now and let the chips fall where they would.

Mark Humphrey wasn't being held hostage any longer, his face would be almost clear by morning and Joe had his horse back. But he knew in his own conscience that he'd see it through. Colonel Eric McRaney had sent him out on a job and he'd never left anything unfinished, no matter how unpleasant it might be.

This is definitely going to be my last job, Joe promised himself decisively. Or if not my last, he reconsidered for a second, I'm certainly going to take some time off by myself. I haven't been fishing in a long time. That would be nice.

Since night had dropped its blanket of darkness over the land, the temperature had dropped fast and the cold wind forced the six people to get closer to the bigger fire that Mark had built and wrap up in their blankets. They could have broken camp and tried to find a cave. But Louis Smith was already tied to a tree and if Joe untied him to move the camp, the little horse-thieving weasel was probably slippery enough to escape.

There was probably a suitable cave nearby but it was too late to move all the people and animals. Even if he, Mark, and Chedos went out and looked for some kind of shelter, any number of things could happen.

Chedos must have read Joe's thoughts because he crossed over to him by the oak tree. "What are the chances of that big fire bein' seen tonight?" he asked, pulling a long, black-wool coat he'd taken from his saddlebags closer about him. "It gets purty dadblamed cold out here at night. These old bones of mine ain't used to campin' out in the open. Too bad we'uns ain't back at the cave."

Joe couldn't stop the shiver that raced all over his body. He would have to get the sheepskin coat out of the bedroll before long.

"The chance is fifty fifty, I guess," Joe replied, shrugging his shoulders. "A big fire will come in handy, though. Not only to keep us warm, but to keep the horses safe. Maybe we should bring them in a little closer. Spread out like that, they're a prime meal for a mountain lion or wolf. And I heard that there are some Indians around here." He wiggled his brows up and down.

"That's a good idea," Chedos agreed grinning and nodding. "I don't know what that boy was thinkin' 'bout when he spaced 'um out like that. I'll gather up more wood if ye want to bring 'um in." He started walking off but turned around and looked at Joe. "That includes old Smoke. I'd hate fer anythin' to happen to that old gray mule-ass bag of bones."

Spreading the horses out would have been an excellent idea if Smith had more people with him. If something happened and the horses got loose he would have succeeded in keeping only one. If they had been close on the same tether, he could have kept maybe three.

Joe, Mark, and Chedos could probably hold on to at least six and with the way Joe's luck had been running on this particular job, something was bound to happen!

Joe whistled to Serge and was relieved, and surprised to see that his saddlebags and bedroll were still tied behind the saddle. Smith must have thought that Vega would pay more for the black horse if he was fully equipped.

Joe rubbed between the horse's ears and Serge nodded his head up and down and nickered low in his throat. Joe was so glad to see the horse and know that he'd be riding him tomorrow that he'd forgive forever any mistake the big horse might make.

Even though Joe had folded the blanket four times and hadn't ridden Smoke that far, his backside still smarted no matter how fat the old mule ass, as Chedos liked calling him had been.

Joe took his bedroll from behind the saddle, gathered up Serge's reins, then picked up the other horses' reins and led them closer to the fire. He had to pull a little harder on Smoke's reins to get the animal moving. The cantankerous mule wanted to stay where he was.

Chedos had dumped an armful of limbs on the ground and was adding short sticks to the fire. Joe dropped his bedroll, untied it, took out the sheepskin coat, and put it on. The immediate warmth rushed over him and he suddenly discovered that he'd been shivering.

Taking his and Chedos's ropes from the saddles, he tied them together, then ran the rope through the reins, giving the horses enough room to space out a little, but not as much as before, then tied each end of the rope to a tree only a few yards from the fire. By the time he'd finished, Chedos had another roaring fire going and had made a fresh pot of coffee.

Joe took the tin cup of steaming black brew from Chedos and dropped down on a log a few feet away from the glowing fire. Mark Humphrey was sitting a few feet away from Alice Manning, the rifle he'd taken from the cabin across his lap but aimed directly at her. Chedos poured coffee into another cup and carried it to him. Despite what Mark had said about not liking coffee, he took a long swallow.

Joe took a sip and looked up to see Desda Manning

coming hesitantly toward him. She had taken a long, blue wool coat from a grip on the ground beside her and put it on. In the glow of the fire, Joe saw a nervous smile on her lips and couldn't begin to guess what was on her mind. With the way she'd been changing her mind, it could be almost anything. Joe would have guessed though that she would've stayed close to Mark and was more than a little puzzled at what she was doing.

"May I talk to you, Mr. Howard?" she asked, standing before him, gripping her hands tightly.

"Sure," Joe said, after he'd swallowed the coffee. "Sit down." The log was long enough for both of them and he patted a place beside him. "What do you want to talk about?"

Desda dropped primly down beside him and made a big production of smoothing the legs of her black pants before she crossed her legs and expelled a deep breath. She licked her lips before speaking.

"I'm not sure what will happen after we meet with Cruz tomorrow," she began slowly. "I guess you've figured out by now that we, and I include myself in this, tie people up, take their horses, and sell them to Cruz Vega."

Joe didn't say anything. He only nodded, took another sip of coffee and waited for her to continue. He just hoped that she wasn't going to try and con or bribe him into doing something to get her out of her situation. She was as deeply involved in the family "business" as Old Alice and Louis.

"I know it's wrong," she went on, dropping her gaze to her lap, then raising it demurely up at him. Here it comes, Joe told himself.

"After your business is over with the man who's paying the ransom to Cruz for his son," she continued, "I want to go with you to El Paso or back to Fort Davis and try to start a new life." She fluttered her lashes at Joe. Her actions were comical and sickening at the same time. Joe didn't know whether to laugh or vomit. He wondered if she used this line on Mark while he had been busy with the horses?

This was a complete turn of events and Joe hadn't expected it. Why was she talking to him? Why wasn't she still trying to sweet-talk Mark? He'd been quick, not too long ago to agree to let her ride along with him to Candelaria.

"Why do you want to come with me?" Joe finally asked, wrapping his cold hands around the hot cup. "Not only is what you're doing wrong, it's also illegal. Knowing what you, your mother, and cousin have been doing, I won't have any choice but to turn you over to the nearest sheriff. There should be one in Candelaria. Stealing horses *is* a crime, you know. Horse thieves usually hang and, you could be tried for murder."

"I haven't killed anyone!" she snapped, forgetting that she was trying to appeal to his sympathy.

"You knew that your mother and cousin were tying people up and leaving them at a rattlesnake pit to either die from bites or whatever kind of animal would come by." Joe's voice was cold and hard.

"But I didn't tie anyone up," Desda insisted, wringing her hands in her lap.

"You've been with your family every time they've taken horses to Vega," Joe pointed out. He was beginning to enjoy this. Too bad it wasn't Alice Manning asking him for help. He wouldn't mind bashing her in her toothless mouth. "You all could hang for what you've done. You wouldn't be the first woman to hang."

Joe did feel a little sorry for the girl when she took a shuddering breath and her chin began quivering. Apparently she hadn't heard him telling Louis Smith that he would let all of them go if Smith would show him where Cruz Vega lived in Candelaria.

Joe knew immediately, especially from her quick intake of breath to regain her composure, that Desda's plan hadn't gone as she'd wanted. In a disappointed huff, she jumped up from the log and hurried around the fire to Mark. Joe knew that she was playing two ends against the middle and guessed that Vega would be in the middle. Whatever she'd just told Mark must have pleased him because a wide smile raced across his face and he nodded down at her.

"Would it be okay if Aunt Alice brings me a cup of coffee?" Louis asked pitifully, breaking into Joe's amused thoughts. "I could sure use it. It's really cold out here."

Joe could almost see the self-pity dripping from Smith's mouth as he turned his head and gave him an imploring look.

"Smith, I might have been born at night, but it wasn't last night," Joe said flatly and standing up. "Letting your aunt bring you a cup of coffee would be like letting a dog guard a soup bone. Mr. Chedos will be happy to bring you a cup of coffee. I'll even let him spread an extra blanket over you." Contempt was in Joe's every word. He didn't offer to take Smith coffee because he was afraid he'd tie into him. "Now, isn't that nice of me, considering what you did to Mark and me at the snake pit?" If Joe hadn't needed the little horse thief to hurry them in finding Cruz Vega, he wouldn't have thought twice about shooting him where he sat even though he was tied to a tree.

In the fire's glow, Joe could tell from Smith's agitated expression that his plan had failed. Joe grinned slightly as he glanced across the fire at Alice Manning. She'd heard Louis ask that she bring him coffee and Joe wondered what kind of trick she would have used to free him.

Did she have some other weapons hidden on her? It hadn't occurred to Joe to even search her. He almost vomited at the thought.

"Mark, I've changed my mind," Joe called out, seeing a cunning gleam in Old Alice's eyes. "I'll take the first watch." He poured another cup of coffee, then sitting down with his back to the tree, "Chedos, you take the second. Mark, that will leave the third one to you."

"That's okay with me," Mark said, standing up to spread a blanket on the leaf-covered ground.

"Mark, Chedos, whatever you do," Joe cautioned, draining the cup, then pouring out the dregs, "don't take your eyes off of that old woman." He shifted his glance between each of them for their assuring nod, settled down, and watched Mark and Chedos get comfortable, and finally go to sleep. Desda, Old Alice, and Louis settled down in their blankets, went to sleep, leaving Joe awake to listen to the crackling fire and watch the dancing flames.

Joe had to fight to stay awake for two hours and his eyes closed instantly after he got up, threw more wood on the fire, then nudged Chedos awake for his turn at watching, and sat back down on the ground.

The next morning dawned cold, misty, and gloomy. Dreary, gray and rain-laden clouds obscured the mountain peaks in the distance. If nothing changed, and Joe hoped it would, rain would be falling on them before noon. That was all the six people needed.

Joe pushed himself up from the ground and was sure that every bone in his cold, stiff body would break before he was able to stand up straight. He was positive that this time was definitely going to be his last job for Colonel Eric McRaney. There had to be a much better and easier way to make a living than sleeping out in the open like an animal and chasing after people. His body couldn't take sleeping on the hard ground, instead of a soft bed much longer. The cold, night air didn't help much either.

The crackling fire and aroma of coffee told Joe that Buford Chedos was already up and probably packed to go. But Joe got a surprise when he finally convinced his body that it wouldn't crumble into a dozen little pieces when he finally stood up and walked over to the fire.

Mark Humphrey and Desda Manning were the ones making breakfast. The old prospector was still wrapped in his blankets and snoring. Joe would probably have been awake sooner if the old man had been sleeping closer to him. Alice Manning was still in the same place as she was last night. Only now she was huddled down in several blankets.

Joe shifted his sleepy-eyed gaze over to Louis Smith, still tied to the tree. The only thing different about the short horse thief was he now had two blankets draped over his thin shoulders. He grinned up at Joe as Desda untied him and handed him a cup of coffee.

"Are you surprised to see that I'm still here?" Smith asked mildly, struggling to stand up, flexing his arms and fingers to get the circulation going. There was a look deep in his blue eyes that Joe didn't like. He couldn't tell if it was a threat or if Smith was just needling him. Whichever it was caused Joe to want to shoot him.

"No," Joe answered simply, pushing his hair back out of his face and replacing his hat. His hands were itching to grab Louis and shake the leering grin from his stubbled face. "I knew you'd be here one way or the other."

Joe arched his brows, hoping that Smith would remember that those were the same words that his aunt had used yesterday. Joe wanted to laugh and did allow a small grin to pull at the corner of his mouth when the snide smile left Smith's face.

"Mark, he can stay untied," Joe called out, pouring coffee into a cup, pulling Mark's attention away from Desda. The two were sitting so close to each other on the log, that it was hard to tell whether or not they were glued together. "Be sure and keep an eye on him all the time."

Boy, you'd better watch it, Joe thought wearily.

"If he moves just one tiny muscle," Joe continued, walking over to Chedos and nudging him in the side with the toe of his boot, "shoot him in the foot."

A shocked stillness raced over Smith's face and his eyes bulged in obvious fear.

Chedos grumbled in his sleep. Joe nudged him a little harder and he finally opened his eyes and stood up. He pushed his matted hair out of his whiskered face, clamped his hat down on his grizzled head, and poured coffee into a cup then took a piece of bread and salt pork from Desda.

"What do *I* have to do to get fed 'round here?" Alice Manning asked in a whine. Desda, drawing in a long breath, put a piece of meat between some bread and took it over to her. The old woman didn't say anything to her daughter.

Maybe the girl isn't as guilty as her mother and cousin in stealing the horses, Joe thought. She just might be the victim of circumstances and was really trying to get away from her mother. But hadn't there been other chances for her to escape?

Joe didn't know anything about her education but there had to be something that a girl as pretty as Desda Manning could do. Things that weren't necessarily illegal or immoral.

Jeanie Orms and Betty Young owned the Desert Rose Saloon and Polly Bullock managed the Billy Leon Cafe. Most all of the shops in Fort Davis employed young women and a young woman was even a typesetter at the newspaper.

Joe decided to give some more thought to Desda's situation as they rode toward Candelaria.

It didn't take much time for the six people to finish the breakfast of flat bread, coffee, and fried salt pork then put the things away. They would be able to make more time since Joe was riding Serge again and Mark had a horse to ride.

Joe, not wanting to put any more money into Louis Smith's pocket or contribute to Cruz Vega's collection of horses, removed the leather bridle from the two Indian horses and swatted them across the rump. They didn't waste any time in leaving the camp.

"Why in the devil did you do that?" Louis asked, hostility in his eyes. A hard knot worked in his jaw and an angry frown pulled between his brows. "Cruz Vega would've paid me for those horses, no matter how bad they looked." He whirled around in the saddle to face Joe after he'd watched money on the hoof, as it were, galloping away and disappearing down into a gully.

"I'm not going to help you make money on stolen horses," Joe snapped, giving words to his previous thoughts. He just hoped that Smith wouldn't think to ask him where the horses had come from. He wanted to reach across and slug Smith. He wondered how Smith would react if he knew that Chedos had stolen the two horses? Joe didn't understand why the old man had taken two horses instead of just one. Maybe it was to put the Indians at a disadvantage with only one horse for the three of them to ride.

"By rights," Joe continued, a dark frown pulling

between his brows, "I should turn all of these horses loose. But I gave you my word and I'm going to let you keep what you have. But, don't press your luck."

Joe looked at Smith long and hard. Smith didn't argue with him. He knew from Joe's cold attitude toward him that he didn't like him and it wouldn't take but an ounce of provocation for him to shoot him.

"All right, everybody," Joe called out, swinging up onto the comfortable, contoured saddle on Serge's back, "let's move out. We probably have a long way to go unless Mr. Smith knows a shortcut."

If Vega had a home in Candelaria, and if Smith showed him exactly where it was, and if Joe could stop him before he met Tyler Worthing, that would simplify things to some degree. Joe knew he was going to have his hands full trying to convince Worthing that his spoiled son had, in some way been responsible for all of this.

"God, I wish I was in Fort Davis," Joe muttered in a low voice.

Joe believed that they could reach Candelaria by early evening if nothing got in the way. By this time tomorrow, everything should be over. Tyler Worthing would still have his money. Cruz Vega would have some extra horses and Joe could be on his way back to Fort Davis. The clouds were lifting and the sun just might shine.

When I get back to the fort, Joe promised himself with a scoff, I'd better take some time off, get away from McRaney and rest. This is beginning to sound too easy, especially since I just thought that Cruz Vega would be satisfied to ride away from a thousand dollars with his horses. Any number of things could and probably would happen before and after they reached Candelaria.

The rested travelers and horses, plus one mule covered a lot of ground by noon. The sky had become more overcast and thunder, sounding like a drum in a circus parade rumbled across the mountains.

"Looks like we'uns is gonna get it," Buford Chedos predicted, squinting up at the ominous, gray sky.

Another clap of thunder, directly overhead added credence to Chedos's words.

"I think you're right," Joe said, looking around for some cover from the impending rain as small droplets began falling at random intervals, to be quickly absorbed by the dry ground. He knew they could handle a sprinkle or much-needed shower. But a full-fledged downpour would present a real problem. The dry land was in prime condition for a flash flood. The six people, plus the horses, could drown. Joe didn't care if the ten stolen horses got loose. They could probably make do on their own. Of course, Cruz Vega would have a fit if he lost the animals. But, he wouldn't know they were coming.

Thunder boomed again, just as raindrops began falling harder and faster. Joe shot a quick glance at Louis Smith and didn't like the calculating look on his face. Joe knew that Smith was thinking that he'd have trouble keeping an eye on him in the storm and the rain would be to his advantage.

Joe was riding a little back of Smith's left. He realized now that he'd made a mistake in not having Mark riding at Smith's right. Instead Mark and Desda were about ten paces behind Joe. Buford Chedos, slumped in the saddle and probably dozing, was in front of Mark and Desda and to Alice Manning's left.

Smith and Old Alice each had five horses on a tether lead rope.

To make matters worse, a long, jagged bolt of yellow lightning danced across the boiling clouds. Another slender finger of fire penetrated a cloud, to slam into an oak tree, no more than ten yards from the people and animals, splitting it down one side. The splintered limb crashed to the ground to the right side of the horses that Smith was leading.

Without warning, the five horses bolted, almost jerking Smith from the saddle. The five horses would never be seen again.

Taking advantage of the elements, Smith slammed his heels into his buckskin mare's sides and bent low over the saddle horn.

Joe, anticipating such a move, because he would have done the same thing if he'd been in Smith's position, reined Serge hard to the right as the buckskin took off at a fast gallop just as the clouds opened to dump a torrent of warm rain on everything.

"Smith! Stop!" Joe shouted, batting his eyes as the rain pelted him in the face.

Louis Smith glanced back over his shoulder, a satisfied grin splashing across his face.

"Mark, watch them," Joe yelled out, hoping he was heard over the thunderous noise. He urged Serge forward to come up on Smith's left side. The driving rain hampered Joe's vision. He reached out, caught hold of Smith's arm and jerked. Smith left the saddle, pulled free from Joe's wet hand and landed on his back on the ground.

Joe jerked the Colt .45 from the holster and started to aim it at Smith. But his hand was wet, just like the pistol handle. The .45 slipped from his fingers to land in the increasing amount of mud only a few inches from Louis Smith's feet.

"Get the pistol, Louis!" Alice Manning screamed over the booming thunder and driving rain. "Shoot him!"

Joe leaped from the right side of the saddle. Louis

scrambled up on his hands and knees and made a dive for the pistol.

Joe had the misfortune of slipping on a wet rock and losing his balance, giving Smith time to pick up the pistol and aim it at him.

Joe felt the hot orb of metal tear into his left wrist only a second after he heard and saw his own Colt .45 belch out a yellow flame.

"Drop the gun, Smith," Mark Humphrey ordered. "I know Joe wants you alive, but if you don't drop it, I swear I'll blow your head off."

Conviction edged Mark's nervous command. His hands were steady as he held the rifle and aimed it at Smith.

Joe gripped his bloody wrist and struggled to his feet, at the same time watching Smith drop the pistol back into the mud. Mark picked it up.

"How bad 'er ye hit, boy?" Buford asked, his eyes wide in concern as he dismounted, dashed the rain from his face and hurried to Joe.

"I think the bullet went all the way through," Joe replied, unbuttoning and pushing back his wet shirt sleeve that had a pink stain on it. The bullet had gone through the fleshy part of his arm and he held it out to let the pouring rain wash away some of the blood.

"I'll pour sum whiskey on it fer ye," Buford offered, "and tie it up with a rag."

"Let's get under that rock overhang," Joe suggested, nodding toward an outcropping about forty feet long, ten feet deep, and twenty yards away. He hoped Chedos's rag would be clean but he had his doubts.

"It's too bad Louis didn't kill you," Alice Manning said, swinging her sorrel mare over to the rocks.

"Old Alice," Joe said contemptuously, rain streaming from the dip in his hat brim, "shut up!"

"Don't you talk to my mother like that," Desda snapped. Her loyalty had changed again.

"I'm not in the mood to listen to either of you," Joe said, dividing a glance between Desda and Old Alice. "If you both don't hush, I'm going to slap a gag in your mouth and tie your hands behind you so you can't take it out."

Humphrey had marched Smith under the outcropping and had already tied his hands behind him.

Buford Chedos took a half-filled bottle of amber-colored liquid from his saddlebag, held it over Joe's extended arm and poured the stinging whiskey into the raw flesh. Joe pulled in a quick breath through clenched teeth and squeezed his eyes shut.

Chedos rummaged through his saddlebags again and pulled out a gleaming white piece of cloth. That was the very last thing Joe thought Chedos would have. It was in complete contrast to the dirty clothes he wore.

"The hole in yer arm looks worse'n 'is," Buford said, tearing the cloth into two long strips. He drenched one of the strips in whiskey, then wrapped it around Joe's arm. He wrapped and tied the dry strip of cloth around the other one.

"We might as well stay here until the rain slacks off," Joe said grimly, a jabbing bolt of pain shooting from his wrist all the way up to his shoulder. "I don't want any more surprises."

Joe wondered how Sheriff Sam Dusay would have handled this situation as he glanced at Louis Smith and Alice Manning. Rage pulled a knot in his stomach when he saw a pleased smile on their faces.

"I'll see iffen I can scratch up 'nuff wood fer sum coffee," Chedos offered, putting the whiskey bottle back into his saddlebags. He went to the end of the overhang and soon returned with enough limbs and twigs to get a large enough fire going to make a pot of coffee.

The six people, with Mark sitting close to Smith, sat or stood under the dry shelter of the overhang, sipping quietly on the coffee as the much-needed rain continued down in torrents. Joe volunteered Desda to hold a cup of coffee for Smith to drink. He wasn't going to chance untying the little horse thief as long as it was raining so hard.

Unsure how long the rain would last, the remaining five horses, the five that Alice Manning had been leading, and the ones the six people were riding and old Smoke, were unsaddled and tethered at one end of the overhang.

The rain smelled fresh and clean and had a hypnotic sound hitting the ground and rocks. Joe was so overcome with the lulling effect that his eyes began closing and he had to jerk his head rapidly several times to wake up.

The rain continued falling heavily the rest of the day with only an occasional letup. It soon became apparent that they would lose another day and night because of it and began making ready to spend the night under the overhang.

Joe didn't think that Desda Manning would try to escape when she indicated that she had to be excused for a private moment. But Old Alice did present a problem.

Buford Chedos wouldn't be any match for her if her running speed was as quick as her movements pulling a gun on Joe yesterday. Mark Humphrey was embarrassed to the point of turning purple when Joe told him to accompany her when she boldly told Joe that she had to go pee.

"You don't have to stand right over her," Joe argued, wanting to laugh, "but don't let her out of your sight. If she gets away, I'll shoot you in the leg."

"Me?" Mark said, arching his brows. "Why?"

"Just for the heck of it," Joe answered with a weary smile. *Darius Worthing,* Joe told himself, pulling in a deep breath, *I promise, you will wish you'd never seen Mark Humphrey when I get through with you.*

Time dragged by. The rain continued falling although it was a steady, slow drizzle now. Joe's arm felt like it was on fire but he knew that Buford Chedos had done all that could be done for him. The bullet had gone all the way through and the whiskey would kill any infection. He'd just have to wait it out.

Joe thanked God that it wasn't his right arm! He'd need it if he had to shoot Cruz Vega or beat the holy crap out of Louis Smith!

Darkness came sooner with the rain and when it became evident that they would indeed be spending the night under the overhang, Mark and Buford searched around, although they returned soaking wet, for enough wood to build a bigger fire in order to make bread and coffee and fry some salt pork.

The six canteens were opened and braced upright with rocks, ready to be filled.

"I wonder if anything will ever happen," Joe said pensively to Buford as they munched on bread and meat, "when rain won't be good to drink?" He shook his head sadly.

"What's wrong with ye, boy?" Buford asked, a shocked frown drawing deep lines between his brows. "Nuthin' won't never happen to mess up that sky. God made it and He don't aim fer nuthin' to spoil it."

Joe lapsed into quiet thought. What Buford said made sense. But there was also an arguing side. Not that Joe Howard would ever argue that God hadn't made the sky. But, He'd also made people and so far, they hadn't done a very good job of keeping things the way they should be. As far as Joe was concerned anyway.

"I know yer goin' to argue agin' what I said." Buford's voice interrupted Joe's thoughts. "So let me hear it 'fore ye bust a gut."

Joe drained his cup and tossed out the dregs. "I know it says, in the Bible that man was created in God's image and that people should care about each other." Joe reached out and filled the coffee cup.

"But if people actually cared," he continued, after taking a swallow of coffee, "there wouldn't have been wars since the beginning of time or families killing each other. You've heard about Cain and Abel?" Buford nodded. "There've been all kinds of revolutions in the world. Even before the Civil War. The Indians have been called savages for wanting to hold on to their homes or way of life."

"Hold on, boy," Buford interrupted, holding up his gnarled hand. "Yer gettin' way too deep fer me."

"Yeah," Louis Smith said, taking a sip of coffee from the cup Desda was holding for him. "Talk about somethin' else."

"Okay," Joe said, sliding his mouth into a smirk. "We'll talk about something that should interest you. How about stealing horses?"

Smith threw Joe a cold look and leaned back against the rock wall.

The rain finally stopped and the gray clouds began breaking up in chunks to reveal the sun going down behind the mountains amid wavering streaks of gold, purple, and silver.

"Wouldn't you just know it," Joe grumbled, getting up and walking to the end of the overhang. "The rain would stop when it's too late to go. We'll spend the night here and leave early in the morning."

Joe, disgust all over his tired face, walked back and sat down between Mark and Chedos. Desda and Old Alice were sitting just under the overhang. Water was running down in a steady stream from some runoff above and Desda was washing her hair. Joe turned slightly to his left and looked at Mark. The boy was totally enraptured watching her.

Joe hoped that Alice Manning would at least hold her grimy face under the water and wash it. But, she didn't.

Louis Smith sat quietly, a sulking glower on his stubbled face, about two feet from the end of the overhang, sipping a cup of coffee.

"Buford," Joe said, trying to flex his left hand but stopping when the pain was too much, "do you have any more of those potatoes? Those were good the other night."

"I might have a few left," Chedos replied, pulling his feet under him, then pushing himself to a standing position. "They did taste good, didn't they?"

They hadn't eaten since early that morning, and although no one had complained about having only coffee in what seemed like a long time ago, it didn't take long for the potatoes fried in pork grease, flat bread, and coffee to disappear. Even Louis Smith, untied, ate with gusto.

The pain in Joe's arm was almost forgotten when the first taste hit his mouth,

"We're going to keep a fire going tonight, aren't we?" Mark asked, squatting down close to Joe.

"Yeah," Joe answered, jerking a look up at Mark when he heard the uneasy tone in his voice. "Are you scared?"

"Ah, no," Mark hedged, looking down at the ground. "Well, maybe a little." He took a deep breath. "Let Buford have the first watch. You or I should be awake all the time. I'll take the last watch."

Joe didn't think anything would happen tonight since he was positive that Cruz Vega was heading toward Candelaria. Joe wondered how much time the rain had cost Vega? But he knew that, for some reason Mark was scared and no amount of words would reassure him. Mark Humphrey had been through a lot and if standing guard would make him feel better, what the heck.

The night passed as Joe had suspected. He was in and out of sleep when Buford touched him on the shoulder when it was his turn to stand guard. Mark came awake instantly when Joe woke him for his turn.

Joe was the second one awake the next morning. The sun was a red marble pushing its way over the edge of the mountains. White, cotton-ball clouds meandered leisurely along in a pale blue sky.

Joe's arm ached and his fingers and thumb were swollen. He untied the soiled cloth and his heart skipped a beat when he looked at his inflamed wrist.

Tasting bitter bile coming up in his throat, Joe glanced over at Louis Smith. He was sleeping soundly even though his hands were tied behind him. But, he suddenly thought, he was as much to blame as Smith for the hole in his arm. He should have been more careful when he'd pulled the wet pistol from the holster.

The aroma of freshly brewed coffee wafted across to Buford Chedos. The old prospector rolled over, rubbed the sleep from his eyes with the heels of his hands, and stood up.

"It ain't gonna rot off," Chedos encouraged, squatting down beside Joe, a cup of coffee in his hand. "It jest looks like it will."

"I hope you're right," Joe said morosely, taking a sandwich of meat and bread from Desda.

"Jest be thankful it weren't yer gun hand," Chedos said, clapping Joe on the shoulder then walking around the end of the overhang.

Everyone, including Louis Smith, was in a hurry to leave for Candelaria. Each knew that someone was going to die today. That someone wouldn't be Desda or Alice Manning or Louis Smith. Even though Smith had shot Joe, he was still going to let the little thief and the remaining horses go after they reached Candelaria and Smith showed him where Cruz Vega usually lived.

Joe's conscience began gnawing at him. How could he really allow someone like Louis Smith to ride away scot-free when he knew perfectly well that he and his aunt had stolen horses and had caused the death of no telling how many innocent people?

But a sudden thought satisfied Joe's conscience. Just because he'd told Smith that he could ride away after he'd done what he'd promised didn't mean that Joe couldn't tell a sheriff what they had done.

8

The six people, with Joe Howard and Louis Smith leading the way and Mark Humphrey leading the five horses, rode southwest until the sun was directly overhead before stopping for a noon meal. Most of the clouds had cleared away and it would have been a pleasant day for doing absolutely nothing, except maybe going fishing.

They had made a few stops mostly to rest the horses if they were lucky enough to find a stream or river. But now everybody was tired and hungry and the rest would do them good.

Buford and Desda made coffee and bread and fried the last of Buford's potatoes. Mark kept a close eye on Louis and Alice. Joe changed the bandage on his wrist and let a long sigh escape through his teeth when he saw there wasn't as much red around the wound. The tightness had also lessened and he could flex his fingers more easily.

Maybe his hand would be useful by the time they reached Candelaria.

Buford tore two more strips from another white cloth, dunked one in whiskey, wrapped it around Joe's wrist and tied the dry one around it.

"I'm going to buy you a new bottle of whatever you like to drink," Joe promised, grinning up at Chedos.

"Well, iffen yer buyin'," Chedos said, rubbing his chin with a curved forefinger, "I might try some of that champagney stuff."

"You've got a deal," Joe said, nodding. He buttoned his shirtsleeve and took a cup of hot coffee from Desda.

"When we get to Candelaria," Joe said, sitting down by Smith on the ground, "all I want you to do is show me Vega's house. After you do that, you can do whatever and go wherever you want."

Joe couldn't be sure but he thought he saw Louis Smith relax at his statement, as if he'd been reprieved from a long sentence.

"You mean you're really not going to turn us over to the sheriff?" Smith asked in a stammer, a shocked frown pulling between his brows. "Even after I shot you?"

"Why would I do that?" Joe asked, holding Smith's level gaze. "I said you could go. You did what you could." Joe let a full smile ease over his face. "If I don't let you go, it will only mean that I have to be around you that much longer. If I happen to find Vega first, there won't be any reason for me to even tell him that I've seen you."

"I don't suppose you'll untie me?" Louis asked, lowering his head, a devilish smile in his eyes.

"Not right now," Joe replied, grinning at Smith. "But I will just before we reach Candelaria."

That seemed to satisfy the little horse thief. "You have a deal," Smith agreed with a disappointed grin. Not that there was much he could do about it since he was the one who was tied up.

When everybody and everything had been fed and watered and the utensils put back into the grub sack, they mounted up and started toward a meeting place with either Tyler Worthing or Cruz Vega.

Joe hoped to God that he found Worthing first. If that happened, they wouldn't have to wait around for Vega. He, Mark, Buford Chedos, and Worthing could start out for El Paso to find Darius Worthing.

Joe could hardly wait to see the look on the fat kid's face when he saw his father and Mark Humphrey at the same time. *I wouldn't miss this for the world,* Joe told himself caustically. *It's going to make this bullet hole in my arm worthwhile.*

Candelaria wasn't all that big and it didn't take long for Louis Smith to point out where Cruz Vega was as they stopped on a small rise on the outskirts of town.

"Being a bandit does have its advantages," Joe said in awed and hesitant words. The white, sprawling, adobe house with a red cobblestone roof was probably the showplace of town. A courtyard, with a black, wrought-iron gate was filled with flowers and trees that hadn't lost their blooms.

Joe couldn't believe that Desda Manning wanted to pass all of that up to go with Mark Humphrey. He turned around in the saddle and looked at her. She must have known what he was thinking because her face turned red as she dropped her gaze from his.

"Okay," Joe said, grinning slyly at Smith, "you've done your part," after Smith had pointed out the exact house. "What you do is entirely up to you. Just don't get in my way." He untied Smith's hands.

"I don't want any part of this," Smith said, shaking his head and looking over at Mark Humphrey. "I guess we're lucky that we beat Vega here. None of the servants have arrived yet. I just want to sell those horses to Vega and then all of us to be on our way back home."

"I'm going with Mark," Desda called out from behind Joe and Smith.

Joe swung around in the saddle and stared at Mark. The boy's thin face was much clearer now and he had that sun-struck look again.

"In that case," Joe said, riding back to the young people and looking at Desda, "you'll have to stay in town a little while longer." He saw an argument building up on Mark's face. "You've got to go with me to the meeting place. Tyler Worthing has to see you. He needs to know, from you that Vega mistook you for his son and that his kid was going straight to El Paso on the train. He won't take my word for it since he showed me a picture of Darius."

Joe heard laughter burst from Buford Chedos and looked over at him. The old man slapped his hands down against his legs and laughed again, his eyes almost lost in the wrinkles around them.

"I wouldn't miss this fer the world," Chedos chortled. "If ye're ready, I want to go with ye." He kneed Thimble in the side and pulled her around to stop beside Joe.

"What about me?" Alice Manning asked in a tense voice, a worried expression on her face. Joe wouldn't have thought it possible, but the old, dirty woman looked like a lost soul sitting there on her horse.

"Like I said," Joe replied grimly, pulling his hat down low on his forehead, open dislike in his eyes, "I'm going to keep my word to your nephew. I would really like nothing better than to blow you right out of the saddle for what you did to Mark and me. You're the sorriest excuse for a woman and mother that I've ever seen." He shook his head contemptuously. "But I want to think that I'm a little above shooting a woman."

Joe turned around in the saddle and took one more look down at Vega's showplace house. It sickened him to think that it had been built with stolen money.

Satisfying himself that no one was there, since there were no signs of human or horse, he picked up the reins and took a long, deep breath. He knew he'd just traded one problem for another. The one he was riding into was just as apt to get him killed as the one he was riding away from.

"Well, sitting here and talking about it won't get it done any sooner," he said resolutely, kneeing Serge in the side. He wasn't surprised when Alice, Desda, and Smith didn't ride out with him, Mark, and Chedos. "Just don't tell Vega that you've seen us," he called out over his shoulder. Joe wouldn't have laid money on the odds that they wouldn't do it.

Joe, Mark, and Chedos rode through Candelaria and toward the west. The note had said due south from Fort Davis and a cabin in the river. That shouldn't be too hard to find.

Joe's stomach began pulling into knots as they turned south, crossed a narrow, wooden bridge and then toward the river. His gut instinct told him that something, which would cause a dramatic change in Tyler Worthing's life was about to happen, one way or the other.

But what if Worthing had beat him to the drop place, found another note, and had already left for Fort Davis? What if Worthing had already started out and had met Vega and his men?

That thought had been in the back of Joe's mind ever since he'd left the fort. It came roaring to the front of his head as they turned onto a narrow trail that angled up to a low bluff above the river. They were able to see east and west for a couple of miles. He didn't worry about the north since that was where they had just come from.

Joe wondered if Vega and his men would come through town first or swing around to the west and come directly to the cabin? Would Vega know that Louis Smith had some horses for him? The only way that could happen was if they were to meet in Candelaria at a specific time.

Joe's heart began beating faster when he saw a low, adobe cabin on a small island in the center of the river. Just like the ransom note had described. Did the cabin belong to Cruz Vega? But that couldn't be. It was in the middle of the river and couldn't be owned by anyone. But someone had to build it. Joe wondered what it was for.

Going down the bluff to the river would be easy on the horses and Joe kneed Serge in that direction with Mark and Chedos close behind him. He had a clear view of the east, front, and west side of the cabin and breathed a sigh of relief when he saw Tyler Worthing's bay mare tied to one of the porch supports.

There were no other hoofprints leading out of the water and up to the cabin other than the one set belonging to the bay. Joe knew they had beat Vega to Worthing. His skin began crawling as he imagined the look on the big man's wide face when he saw Mark Humphrey instead of his spoiled, fat son.

Joe didn't have to wait as long as he thought he would to see that look. The big man must have been watching like a hawk out the window to the right side of the door which suddenly flew open.

Joe wondered how long Tyler Worthing had been at

the cabin. He must have pushed the bay for all it was worth and ridden through the rain to get here this fast!

Worthing's huge body filled the doorway and expectation was alive in his eyes. He used only a fraction of a second to tear his gaze from Joe to look at Mark Humphrey and Buford Chedos who were following close behind the army scout.

"Did you find my son?" Worthing asked in such a hurry that one word ran into another. It was hard to tell where one ended and the other began. "Did you find Darius?" His eyes bored intently into Joe's and he was breathing hard.

If the immediate situation hadn't been so serious, since they all could end up getting killed at any minute, and if Tyler Worthing hadn't been put through so much hell by his son during the past week, Joe would have had a little fun out of the pompous man who was still as well dressed as he'd been when Joe had first met him at Fort Davis.

A dark blue broadcloth, specially-made suit fitted his massive body. His clean shaven and ruddy face was emphasized by a dazzling, white shirt and dark blue tie. Only his black boots showed any soil and they were water spots from his ride into the water to the cabin. Joe wouldn't have been surprised to learn that the big man had gotten up early to dress for the occasion.

Joe and the others dismounted. Joe walked up to the door and looked long and hard at Tyler Worthing before speaking. Shifting his weight from one foot to the other, Joe pulled in a deep breath and slowly expelled it. "Mr. Worthing," he finally said, squinting his eyes, "I have some good news and bad news for you."

"Well, get on with it!" Worthing bellowed, gripping his ham-sized fists at his side. "Don't stand there all day trying to play some game with me. Either you did or didn't find Darius. Which is it? Who are they?"

"Well, I didn't exactly find him," Joe answered, almost scared to death that Worthing, in his present state of mind would take a swing at him. He knew one blow from a fist that size would take a man's head right from his shoulders, or make eating solid food impossible for a long time. "But I know where he is."

"How in the devil could you know where he is if you didn't find him?" Worthing asked in a murderous voice. His blue gray eyes were blazing fire and Joe could almost swear he saw smoke coming from the man's ears.

"Your son is in El Paso," Joe answered quickly, hoping to calm the big man down. If he didn't, Worthing would probably have a stroke right where he stood. A thick blood vein was already pounding between his eyes and a purple hue was edging up his throat and face.

Worthing stared at Joe for a second, blinked his eyes a couple of times, turned abruptly, and stomped inside the cabin. He sat down in one of four chairs at a small table in the center of the room. He stared down at the table for a long time, or it seemed long since time was of the essence. Cruz Vega and his men could be coming at that very minute! Joe was surprised that they hadn't already arrived.

But it really didn't matter so much now. Joe had beaten Vega to Worthing and the big man still had his money and his son was safe. But that didn't mean that Vega still wouldn't try to take the money anyway. The Mexican hadn't ridden all this way for nothing. A thousand dollars would be a hard thing to give up. He was still believing that Mark Humphrey was Darius Worthing and it would take a lot of convincing, or maybe even a bullet to make him change his mind.

Plus the fact, Vega probably knew or suspected that

Alice Manning and her family would have some horses for him. Joe allowed himself time to wonder about the five horses that had gotten away during the storm.

Mark Humphrey had followed the men into the cabin and was standing at the far right of the door. Buford Chedos was leaning against the wall to the left of the door. The only sound the four men could hear was the water splashing gently on the bank outside the cabin.

"If you didn't find him," Worthing finally asked skeptically, raising his head, "how do you know he's in El Paso? How did he get there? That's where he was supposed to meet me with a report on the stage line. I was going to surprise him in Fort Davis on his birthday. That's why I was in town." He narrowed his eyes and shifted his gaze from Joe over to Mark and back to Joe.

Joe thought the big man was going to cry and felt both sorry and embarrassed for him. He hated to have to tell him what his son had done. He wondered if the boy was being mean to his father or was just lazy?

"For some reason," Joe began in a quiet voice after swallowing hard, "your son paid Mark Humphrey," he motioned to the boy standing behind him, "twenty dollars to take his place on that stage. Mark was supposed to make notes along the way and give them to him when the stage arrived in El Paso." He let his voice trail off on the last words and looked at Worthing.

A look of total disbelief drained all of the color from Tyler Worthing's face, leaving it ashen and his mouth wide open and gaping.

"Is that true, boy?" Worthing demanded, slapping his hands down on the table and pushing himself up. His mouth was pressed into a hard line. His eyes were still blazing. He glared at Mark and the boy could probably feel his life ebbing away.

"Yes, sir," Mark replied in a quick and squeaky

voice, moving a little further to his right and well out of Worthing's reach. He hoped that the mountain of a man, almost breathing fire wouldn't think that he'd instigated his son's conspiracy.

"Did he tell you why he wanted to do such a stupid thing?" Worthing roared, the words bouncing off the four adobe walls.

Joe had never seen so much rage in one man. I'd hate like the devil to be in that kid's shoes when his father sees him. Men like Tyler Worthing didn't like to be made fools of.

"Well, sir," Mark began nervously, taking a long breath and arching his brows, "he said he didn't see any reason why he should waste his time riding a dusty stage all the way from Pecos, down to Fort Davis, and then on out to El Paso just to see what kind of accommodations were available for stage travelers when he could pay me to do it for him. I was supposed to meet him at the Desert Valley Hotel at the end of the week with all of the notes. He hadn't counted on being kidnapped. He just wanted a nice train ride." Mark shrugged his shoulders, indicating that his narrative was over.

"Did you make any notes?" Worthing asked, a different kind of expression cutting across his face.

"I've got them in my head," Mark answered, relaxing a little when it became apparent that Worthing wasn't going to rearrange his body. "I didn't get a chance to write them down. Cruz Vega and his men came along and I was already coming down with smallpox."

Mark's illness didn't have any affect on Worthing.

"One thing has been puzzling me all of this time," Joe said, looking from Mark over to Worthing and back to Mark. "You've got to admit that there's a great deal of difference between you and Darius Worthing. Whoever planned the kidnapping didn't see you get on the stage in town or him get on the train. How did you make the switch without being seen?"

That question had been trying to make its way to the front of Joe's mind ever since they'd left Cruz Vega's village. He was about to learn who had conspired with Cruz Vega to kidnap Tyler Worthing's son! His stomach knotted up and he held his breath as he waited for Mark's answer, which would clear up the mystery.

"Darius bought a stage ticket for El Paso," Mark began, taking a deep breath and slowly meeting Worthing's angry gaze. "I was waiting outside of town with a horse and took his place on the stage. He was going to ride over to the railroad and catch the train to El Paso."

Joe now knew who had set up Darius Worthing to be kidnapped. He wondered what the stage manager's cut would be in the ransom money? In a way he was glad that Tyler Worthing was already at the cabin. This way, nobody would get any money. He was glad, too, that he hadn't had to wait for him. But it would have been better if he could've intercepted him somewhere before they reached the cabin. That way, he wouldn't have to worry about Cruz Vega walking through the door at any minute!

"When I get my hands on that boy," Worthing growled through tightly clenched teeth as he stood there breathing hard, "he's going to wish he had never seen a stage! He's going to remember this birthday for a long time. I can't believe he'd do this to me. I've always given him everything he's ever wanted. This is how he repays me!"

Worthing clamped his mouth so tightly shut that twin knots stood out in his jaw, moving the thick sideburns in and out. There was enough fire in his blazing eyes to heat the cabin.

Joe had no idea how anyone would punish a fifteen-year-old boy as big as Darius Worthing except maybe take away some of his eating privileges. To miss a few meals might not hurt the boy. In fact, it might do him some good.

"If we don't leave soon," Joe pointed out, resting his hand on the .45's handle, "Cruz Vega will be here. I'm surprised that he hasn't already gotten here. He'll be wanting his money."

"Why should that matter now?" Worthing asked, frowning at Joe. "I still have my money." He patted the left side of his coat where an inside coat pocket would be. "This boy isn't my son and Darius is safe, for the time being anyway, in El Paso."

Tyler Worthing looked at Joe Howard as if he'd been explaining something to a young child or a very stupid person.

"Cruz Vega doesn't know that Mark isn't your son," Joe said, shaking his head, "although Mark tried to tell him." A grin pulled at his mouth when Worthing said that his son was safe, momentarily in El Paso. "All he has on his mind right now is that a thousand dollars is waiting for him right here in this cabin."

"Ye two had better decide purty quick who's gonna tell 'em," Buford Chedos called out, his voice rising up from outside the cabin. Joe hadn't even noticed when Chedos left the cabin. "Here they come!"

"At last!" Tyler Worthing said in a hard voice. Joe threw a quick look at the big man. A cold gleam was in his narrowed eyes and his face was a mask of hate. Joe couldn't take the time to ask Worthing what his words meant as he turned and rushed over to the window. Along the bank across the river and about a hundred yards away were seven riders coming at a slow but steady pace. Joe wondered if Vega, who was sitting tall on the white horse, had recruited someone along the way to take the place of the man he'd killed at the cave or if someone from the village had joined him. Joe half expected to see Louis Smith in the bunch.

Maybe bloodshed could be avoided if Joe could talk to Vega. If he could convince him that Mark Humphrey wasn't Darius Worthing, everything would be all right. That was about as likely to happen as it being cold in his part of Texas in July. His simplistic idea sounded like McRaney's.

Obviously, Buford Chedos wasn't as sure as Joe was about how things would come out. He jumped back into the cabin, or jumped as fast as a man of his age and physical ability could, slammed the door shut, and moved over to Joe at the window.

Joe, Mark, and Chedos could pick the Mexicans off before they could cross the river. But if Vega would only listen to reason, no one would have to get killed.

"Vega will know that ye and me are here when he sees yer horse and old Smoke," Chedos whispered almost in Joe's ear. "Do ye think he'll storm the cabin er want to talk?"

"I hope he'll want to talk," Joe replied, amused that Buford was standing so close to him. He felt sweat oozing from every pore in his body. His mouth was cottonball dry.

Cruz Vega pulled his white horse to an abrupt stop. He turned around in the saddle and said something to his men. He knew that Joe and Chedos were in the cabin when he saw Serge and Smoke. Vega jerked a rifle from a scabbard and aimed it at the cabin. When he yelled out "Hey, gringo" instead of "Señor Worthing" Joe was sure Vega knew he was inside.

"All I want is the money," Vega said in his velvety smooth voice. "Tell Señor Worthing to throw it out the window, along with all of your guns. We will leave the guns at the foot of the bridge in town. I will give you five minutes to make up your mind." Vega's accented voice was controlled and confident. Joe didn't know why. All of the cards were stacked against the Mexican bandit. Worthing still had his money, and as far as Vega was concerned, his son.

A thick silence hung over the cabin. The four men exchanged looks.

"Now, that's what I call a lot of gall," Worthing said gruffly and wagging his huge head, closing and opening his heavy-lidded eyes slowly.

"Cruz Vega didn't ride all this way for a few stolen horses," Joe said candidly. "He knows there's a thousand dollars waiting for him in here." Joe noticed that the angry look was back in Worthing's eyes as he turned back to the window. His stomach pulled into a knot and his heart began pounding harder. Counting Vega, there had been seven men on top of the bluff. Now there were only three! In the time that it had taken Joe to turn away from the window, speak to Worthing and the four men exchange looks, then turn back to the window, four Mexicans, with enough ammunition in cross belts, and gun belts to start a small war, had managed to get to the cabin!

There was only one door in the cabin. The window in the front by the door and one at either end of the cabin were the only means of escape. Joe knew they couldn't be taken by surprise. He was a little encouraged by that thought. He just hoped that the Mexicans wouldn't think about setting fire to the cabin.

Joe motioned for Mark to guard the right window and Buford Chedos to take the one at the end of the cabin. He didn't count on much help from Worthing. He probably didn't even have a gun.

Joe was and wasn't surprised that Tyler Worthing

hadn't brought along a bodyguard as he and Sheriff Sam Dusay had suggested. Maybe he'd kept telling himself that his size and position in life were deterrent enough against any assassins.

But then, David had killed Goliath!

"Hey, gringo," Vega's taunting voice called out, "your time is almost up. What are you going to do? Isn't your stinking life worth more to you than a thousand dollars?"

Before Joe could stop Worthing, or was even aware of his intent, he bolted away from the table, hurried over to the door, and jerked it open.

"You're not getting my money," Worthing yelled, gripping the side of the door in white-knuckled hands. "My son isn't here. He's in El Paso. I don't even know this boy."

Joe made a flying dive at Worthing and grabbed him around the knees just as a bullet whizzed past his head and slammed into the back wall. The two men hit the floor with a grunt from Joe as Worthing almost landed on him when the big man fell backward in surprise.

"If you don't want to get killed," Joe snapped, rolling away from Worthing, "stay down."

Apparently Worthing thought that everything would be over when he told Vega that Darius was in El Paso and that he didn't know Mark Humphrey. Even Joe Howard wouldn't have believed it unless he had seen a picture of Darius Worthing.

Worthing must have also thought that everything would be settled with words instead of bullets and that Vega would just turn and ride away without making any further attempt to get the money. But that wasn't the way greed worked.

Mark dropped to the floor below the window, slammed a shell in the rifle and sprang up. Chedos, flattened against the wall, stuck the shotgun barrel out the window and, moving his head around enough to aim, got off a blast at the two Mexicans creeping up to the window. He missed.

Bullets began hitting the wall by the window immediately where Chedos was standing and sent fragments of adobe into the old man's face. His crusty beard was probably the only thing that kept him from being cut.

Mark pushed the sombrero off and aimed the rifle at one of the Mexicans trying to reach the cabin from the protection of a small bush in the river. He squeezed the trigger and the Mexican dropped in his tracks, holding the front of his tan shirt, a look on his brown face like someone had poured hot water on him.

"Oh, my God," Joe heard Mark say in a sick voice. Joe knew that the boy had just killed his first man. He remembered back to the time he'd been in Mark's shoes, and the cause had seemed right, and knew that Mark was on the verge of vomiting.

Joe, in his prone position on the floor, reached out with his right foot to kick the door shut just as Cruz Vega's rifle belched out a streak of yellow fire.

Joe heard Worthing gasp in obvious pain and looked around to see the big man grasping the calf of his right leg where a red stain was already showing on the dark blue pants.

"How bad are you hit?" Joe asked, rolling to his knees and inching toward Worthing.

"The bullet will have to be dug out," Worthing said between clenched teeth, rolling over on his back and pulling up his pant leg. "You can do it after you kill that murdering bastard."

Joe nodded, raised up into a squatting position, and shuffled back to the window, too preoccupied for Worthing's statement to register on him. He removed his hat and raised up just enough to peep over the windowsill. Cruz Vega had returned the rifle to the scabbard.

Joe knew that if Cruz Vega wasn't able to give orders, his men would probably leave since one of them had already been killed. He didn't want to kill Vega. He just wanted to be told how the stage manager and he had planned Darius Worthing's kidnapping. Without Vega's statement, there would be nothing against the stage manager.

"Mark," Joe said, never taking his eyes from Vega, "throw me your rifle."

"What are you going to do?" Worthing asked, catching hold of a chair to pull himself up to sit against the far wall. He pulled a white handkerchief from his coat pocket and pressed it against his leg.

"I'm going to try and save your money and find out who planned with Vega to kidnap your son," Joe answered, glancing from Worthing to Mark. He still had a sick expression on his pale face and looked like he was going to pass out.

Joe caught the rifle on the fly. He wanted to wing Vega and would have a better chance of doing it with the rifle than the .45.

"I need to talk to Vega," Joe said, over his shoulder. "There's no need for anymore of us to die. If I can get him in the shoulder, maybe the others will leave when they see him go down."

It sounded so simple. Joe almost looked around for McRaney.

"Ye gotta be jokin'," Chedos scoffed, a frown pulling between his brows as he brushed the adobe splinters from his beard. "Would *ye* ride away with all that money up fer grabs?" He lowered his head, raised his gaze, and shook his head doubtfully at Joe.

Joe, knowing that Chedos had a good point, stood

up and stepped back from the window just far enough so he wouldn't be seen but would still be able to see Vega and put the rifle up to his shoulder.

Cruz Vega, a confident expression on his brown face, had turned around in the saddle and was reaching to take something out of the saddlebag. That was the perfect shot for Joe. An unexpected hit in the right shoulder would probably knock Vega out of the saddle, his men would get scared, and ride away. Joe would get the information he needed, they would take Vega into town, turn him over to the sheriff, and everything would be over. And, they all would live in a palace.

Joe told himself and smiled, that he must be on Colonel McRaney's wavelength. Everything was sounding so simple that something was bound to go wrong.

Just as Joe's finger began squeezing against the trigger, Cruz Vega turned around in the saddle. In his left hand was a stick of dynamite with a long fuse!

Joe couldn't help wondering why in the world Vega would want to blow up the cabin with everyone, and the money in it? Maybe he was running out of patience and thought that mangled money was better than no money at all. Vega bent over a little in the saddle and everything began happening in slow motion.

Joe's rifle exploded, spitting out a streak of yellow flame. The bullet tore into the center of Cruz Vega's brown face just as he struck and put a match to the end of the fuse. Vega's head snapped back. The black sombrero fell off, landing at the edge of the river. Some involuntary reflexes slapped his hands up to what, until a few seconds ago, had been a lean and handsome face.

Then things began happening a lot faster. The dynamite had been flung to Vega's left, instead of toward the cabin. It landed in a tall cedar tree, blowing it into a thousand pieces.

The impact of the blast threw the white stallion and what was left of Vega sideways. Vega landed, with a splash, facedown in the river beside the terrified horse.

Joe watched in horrified disbelief as the horse floundered, stumbled and finally, miraculously struggled to his feet and staggered away. Vega's mutilated body bobbed up and down in the rippling water, which was now turning red.

Joe wanted to vomit as he shifted his stunned gaze from Vega to the splintered tree. If he hadn't shot Vega when he did, the cabin could just as easily have been that tree.

Everything was quiet until the sound of retreating horses' hooves broke the stillness. Joe moved quickly over to the east window and should have felt better about seeing three Mexicans riding away from the cabin back toward Candelaria. They hadn't taken the time or didn't care enough to go around to the other side of the cabin to get their dead companion or what was left of their leader. So much for loyalty.

Joe slammed another shell into the chamber, opened the door that was splintered with bullet holes, and stepped outside. The other two Mexicans, still sitting on their horses on the bluff, probably in a state of shock, raised their hands over their heads without hesitation. Joe had been correct in guessing, that with their leader dead, some of the men wouldn't know what to do. He wondered why they hadn't run with the others?

Joe regretted that Vega had been killed instead of just wounded. But if he hadn't killed the Mexican, he would've had time to throw the dynamite and those in the cabin would've been the dead ones.

"*Avanzar*," Joe shouted and motioned for the two men to come forward. The Mexicans kneed their mounts in the sides and with their hands still high over their heads, rode past Vega's body without looking down at him and crossed the river to the cabin. They pulled the horses to a stop a few feet from Joe but made no attempt to dismount.

"Were you in on a plot to kidnap a boy in Fort Davis?" Joe asked bluntly in English, glancing from one obviously frightened man to the other.

"*No habla inglés, señor,*" one of the men said, shaking his head nervously. Joe knew he'd get no information from either of them even if they taught English in a school.

It really didn't matter anyway. With Cruz Vega dead, there was nothing he could do about the kidnapping. The stage manager in Pecos would go free. He would actually be the only one involved in the plot not to be really affected by it except that he was still alive but wouldn't get anything for his trouble.

Joe Howard's job was over. He'd kept Cruz Vega from getting the thousand dollars that was still safe in Tyler Worthing's coat pocket. The big man's fat kid was safe in El Paso and Joe was free to go back to Fort Davis and wait until McRaney found another "easy" job for him.

"*Vamos!*" Joe shouted in disgust, waving his hand away from him. The two Mexicans lost no time in riding around to the back of the cabin and crossing the river into Mexico. They, too, left the dead man where Mark's bullet had dropped him.

Joe wondered why the other three had gone back to Candelaria? Then he remembered that Louis Smith was still in town with the stolen horses. But they were none of his business now, since he'd told Smith and old Alice that they could keep the horses in exchange for Smith's help. He dismissed them from his mind.

But Mark Humphrey hadn't. "What will happen to

Desda and the others?" he asked, a frown pulling between his brows.

"Desda is waiting for you," Joe replied through clenched teeth. "I don't give a tinker's rip what happens to that old lady and Smith. I've done what Colonel McRaney told me to."

Anger and disgust boiled up in Joe like water in a pot over a roaring fire and he turned around and looked at Tyler Worthing. "Two men were killed here today because of your son." Worthing was sitting in a chair at the table. Buford Chedos had cut the pants leg up the outside and had dug the bullet out while Joe had been talking to the Mexicans. Worthing didn't bat an eye. Joe glanced back to Mark.

"If I were to see Alice Manning and Louis Smith right now," Joe said, knots working in his jaws, "I'd still want to kill them for tying us up at that snake pit! Have you forgotten that you were there? Have you forgotten that you just killed a man?"

"No," Mark said, shaking his head in short jerks, frowning deeply at Joe. "I'll never forget that. But it was either him or me. Just like it was with you and Vega. Besides, Desda didn't really have anything to do with tying us up."

"She didn't do anything to stop it either," Joe argued, his temper rising. It hadn't taken Mark long to forget about being tied up and left to die only three days ago by that girl's family!

"Look," Joe continued, his patience wearing thin, "you can go back and see her if you want to. But I don't want any part of them. I just want to get out of here." He expelled a deep breath and shifted his weight from one foot to the other. He was ashamed of himself for losing his temper with Mark. But his arm was aching like the devil and Tyler Worthing falling on it hadn't helped at all.

"I thought ye wanted to go to El Paso with Tyler Worthing," Buford Chedos reminded, moving away from the wall. "I thought ye wanted to see that Worthing kid." A sly look gleamed in Chedos's blue eyes.

"Why do you want to see my son?" Worthing asked, a hard knot bunching up in his jaw. A furious scowl pulled his thick brows together over his glaring eyes. He forgot about the pain in his leg when Chedos mentioned his son.

"I just wanted to see how he'd look," Joe began, a grin pulling at his mouth as he began relaxing, "when you walk in before Mark has time to get to him with the information about the stage line for him to give to you. Wonder how he'll react when you tell him about the kidnapping? How will he feel about you being shot?"

Joe suddenly realized why he had jumped down Mark's throat. Everything was beginning to catch up with him. He'd just killed a man who could have blown them ski high. The man he was supposed to be helping had been shot in the leg and he really hadn't found Darius Worthing although he knew that he was safe in El Paso. And, last but certainly not least, he'd been shot, not to mention being tied to a rattlesnake pit. He could still see the advancing rattlesnakes. That image would stay with him for a long time.

"This *is* going to be quite interesting," Worthing said, sucking his lips in against his teeth in sudden pain when he put his foot on the floor to stand up.

Mark suddenly forgot about Desda Manning when the other men began talking about Darius Worthing. It was the fat kid's fault and, although he hated to admit it, some of the fault was his that he was here and he wanted to hear what kind of explanation Worthing would give his father. He also wanted to see how Worthing would react when he learned he'd been the object of a kidnapping. He wanted to see the look on Darius's face when he walked in with Tyler Worthing. He could always come back to Desda.

"This *is* going to be something to hear and see, isn't it?" Tyler Worthing stated more than asked, looking down at the floor for a second before raising his gaze to meet Joe's. "Darius owes all of us an explanation and, by God, he's going to give us one! He almost cost me a thousand dollars. His selfishness almost got you two killed." He looked from Joe to Mark. "He got you shot." He looked back at Joe. "And, he got me shot." He reached down and gently touched his leg. He stopped talking and Joe could see a plan taking shape in the big man's brain. A sly and somewhat smug look replaced the fading frown.

Joe didn't know what the big man was planning but he knew that he didn't want to be in the boy's place when Worthing caught up with him. But he knew he wanted to be there when it happened.

"He could've been kidnapped, or killed, you know," Joe said grimly.

"I know that," Worthing admitted, expelling a deep sigh, raising his head to look at Joe. He nodded thoughtfully while the smugness vanished. "But he doesn't know that and should be taught a lesson. This is the first time I've ever asked him to do something important for me as far as business goes. He assured me he could do it and that I didn't have anything to worry about. All the time he was trying to deceive me. I know this is going to sound greedy but it could have meant more money for us if his report was good and if I had decided to buy the stage line."

Anger replaced Worthing's thoughtful look and his

mouth pressed into a thick line. His plan was forming again.

"Since I still have all of my money," Worthing said, tapping his coat and narrowing his eyes, "and you wouldn't take any money before, I think I owe you a trip to El Paso, and not on the stage. I've changed my mind about buying the Overland Stage Line. While I was riding down here, I figured out that it would be a waste of money. Since the train runs through most of this country, there's not much need for a stage anymore. We'll go by train. Would you two like to go along?" He divided his look between Chedos and Mark. "You'll be my guests."

Joe couldn't believe what he was hearing. Tyler Worthing was offering to pay their way to go with him to El Paso to see and hear his son explain the stupid thing he'd done! Joe would've paid his own way to go along since he'd calmed down. But now the big man was offering to take all three of them and that was even better.

"I wouldn't miss it," Chedos said, nodding. "What about him?" He jerked his thumb toward Vega's bloody remains at the edge of the river.

"I guess he needs to be buried," Joe replied dryly. "But I'm not going to do it. I might have killed him but I'm not going to waste my time burying him. My arm is killing me."

Joe Howard never thought he'd live to hear himself saying what he just did. But this trip had taken a lot out of him, especially the rattlesnakes. He'd been shot before. But he'd never been that close to snakes. It would be a long time before the rattling sound left his ears and he didn't want to look at anymore dead bodies today.

Buford Chedos, seeing that Joe was serious about not burying Cruz Vega, hitched up his pants and started toward the door. He stopped, his hand on the doorjamb, turned around and looked at Mark. Worthing would probably just as soon let Vega lie where he'd fallen in the river.

"Let's don't forget the one I shot," Mark reminded, following Chedos to the door. "He needs to be buried also."

"Ye're right, so let's hurry and get 'em in the ground 'fore the buzzards start circlin' overhead," Chedos said, squinting up his eyes and jerking his head as he shivered.

"A buzzard-pecked body isn't a very pretty sight," Joe said, watching Mark intently. He got the same sickening look from Mark as Chedos got from Alice Manning when he'd described what Yaqui Indians had done to a white woman.

Without saying anything, although he did give Joe a puzzled look, Mark followed Chedos outside.

"Why do you think Darius did such a terrible thing?" Worthing asked dismally, sitting down on the edge of the table and propping his leg on the chair. His broad shoulders slumped if the weight of the broadcloth coat was too much for him to hold up. The smugness had left his face and his eyes were downcast. "I'm his father!"

"I don't know," Joe replied, licking his lips and shaking his head. He felt sorry for Worthing and knew he wanted to be there when his question was answered.

A silence hung over the cabin. Joe didn't know what to say to Worthing. Actually there was nothing he could say. The problem was between him and his fat son. His official part in all of this was over. That had ended when he'd blown a hole in Cruz Vega's face.

Suddenly something began trying to make it to the front of Joe's brain. Something that Worthing had said. But so much had happened that Joe couldn't catch it. Maybe it would come to him later.

The uncomfortable silence was finally broken when Chedos and Mark came back into the cabin.

"Do you want to leave for El Paso now?" Joe asked Worthing. He saw the big man take and expel a long, decisive breath.

"Yeah," Worthing answered, swallowed, and stood up. "There should be a train through here this afternoon. What are you going to do until then?"

"I've got to send a telegram to Colonel McRaney and let him know that everything's okay," Joe answered, starting toward the door. "By the time I get back, he should have some more easy jobs lined up for me." He remembered promising himself some time off. It still sounded like a good idea and going to El Paso as Worthing's guest would take care of it.

"What are ye really gonna do about the woman and Smith?" Chedos asked. Joe stopped, his hand on the door, an indifferent expression on his tired face.

"It's like I said before," Joe replied simply. "I'm not going to do anything about them. But that's no reason that the sheriff in Candelaria shouldn't be able to do something about them. They belong in jail. They might not have actually shot anybody. But they tied people to stakes so snakes or animals could get them. That's the same as murder."

Joe looked down at the deep cuts on his wrists as a reminder and hard evidence of what had happened to him and Mark.

But he admitted to himself that he was more interested in hearing Darius Worthing's explanation to his father than he was in seeing Alice Manning and Louis Smith punished for stealing horses. They'd be caught sooner or later anyway. And if he just happened to see a sheriff in town, it could be sooner.

"Mark, what did Desda tell you last night?" Joe

asked, an idea taking shape in his mind. He really didn't believe that Desda was as deeply involved in the "family business" as Alice and Louis Smith were and maybe since Cruz Vega was dead she would turn things around for herself. Everybody deserved a second chance, if they were willing to make it work. It was too late for Louis Smith and his aunt. They would probably end up being hanged one day.

"Well, now that's a little personal," Mark objected, a frown and blush covering his face at the same time. "But," he hurried on at the intense glare in Joe's eyes, "she said that she wasn't as bad as you thought and she wanted to go wherever I went."

That was pretty much the same thing she'd told Joe at the camp fire two nights ago. So, maybe she was looking for a way out. He allowed himself time to wonder what she'd do if Cruz was still alive and if she'd be influenced by all of the "pretty things" he could give her? But that couldn't happen now. Cruz Vega was dead.

"Okay," Joe said, making a sucking sound rolling his lips in against his teeth, "when we get to town, I'll send McRaney a telegram and tell him about Louis Smith and Alice Manning. He can take care of them. Mark, find Desda. Ask her if she wants to go to El Paso with you. Do you have enough money for her train fare?"

Mark's face, with most of the scabs gone, brightened when he nodded.

"I'd be more than happy to pay the young lady's fare," Worthing offered and smiling, reached toward his inside coat pocket. "I think I owe you that much."

Worthing pulled out the same cream-colored, leather wallet that Joe had seen before and opened it. It seemed to him that Worthing couldn't wait to give away some of his money.

"No, that's all right," Mark refused, shaking his

head. "You paying my fare is enough. It's as much my fault as it is your son's that I'm here. I didn't have to take his money. I didn't have to go along with his plan. I still have most of the money he paid me. It might make a big difference in Desda's life if she gets away from her family."

The four men walked outside and stood silently by their horses.

"Do ye think the old lady and Smith er still in town?" Chedos finally asked, hauling himself up on Thimble. He sat down on the saddle with a grunt. "Suma these days, I jest ain't gonna make it."

"They're not in town if the three Mexicans found them," Joe said passively, swinging up on Serge. "Alice Manning and Smith know by now that Vega is dead and have started back home. Mark, did Desda say she'd meet you anywhere in town?"

"Well, yes," Mark said slowly and ducking his head in embarrassment. "I'm supposed to meet her at the Leaning Oak Hotel when all this is over."

Joe Howard stared at Mark for a second then threw back his head and laughed until his eyes smarted. The two young people had really put one over on him.

"Buford, do you and Old Alice have a thing going?" Joe asked, after he'd coughed and cleared his throat. "Are you in a hurry to get back to town and see her?"

"Good Lord, no!" Chedos answered, doing a double take, disgust in his voice as he swung Thimble around and caught up the mule's reins. "That woman's too mean and dirty fer me. Even on my worst day, I'm cleaner than she is. Come on, Smoke, you worthless old mule ass."

Joe, Mark, and Worthing laughed at the old prospector.

9

When the four men reached Candelaria, Worthing bought four train tickets to El Paso and Mark, still insistent about Desda Manning, bought one ticket. Joe sent a telegram to Colonel McRaney. He didn't go into direct details about Darius Worthing's plot or anything else that had happened. He wanted to see the expression on McRaney's face when he told him. He just hoped that no one had the misfortune of passing Alice Manning's house until McRaney had time to know about her and Louis Smith.

True to Desda's words, she was waiting for Mark at the Leaning Oak Hotel when Joe and Mark dismounted. Mark was embarrassed and turned a brilliant red when Desda came running from the hotel and hugged him.

"Three of Cruz's men told us he was dead," Desda said, looking Joe straight in the eye and still holding onto Mark's arm. "They took the five horses. Cruz had paid Louis for them before he left for the river."

For some reason Joe had thought Desda would still be in some state of shock knowing that Vega was dead. After all, she'd known him for a long time. But she didn't seem the least bit upset. She must be really good at hiding her feelings or she had actually decided to change.

"I guess Mark told you that I'm really going with him to El Paso," she continued, looking up and smiled at the now sun-struck boy.

Joe only nodded. It wasn't his place to criticize or form judgments.

"Ma gave me part of the money," Desda went on, a slightly desolate expression on her face. "She didn't seem very upset that I wasn't going back with her and Louis."

Joe thought he saw the girl's chin quiver. He hoped that a rattlesnake would get the dirty old hag for what she'd done to her daughter.

After a long pause, she asked: "Are you going to tell the sheriff? Am I a horse thief because I took some of the money and for the things that happened before?"

"Well," Joe said slowly and thoughtfully, looking around through narrowed eyes, "I don't see anybody around with a lot of horses and I don't see anybody around wearing a badge. So, how can I tell about something that I don't see?"

Joe was shocked, but felt a warmness wash over him when Desda impulsively rushed at him, threw her arms around his neck, and kissed his stubbled cheek.

"Thank you," Desda said in a soft voice and blinked her eyes.

"We have a little time to kill before the train comes," Joe said, swallowing hard and taking a deep breath. He adjusted his hat self-consciously as Tyler Worthing and Buford Chedos walked up. "Why don't we get a couple of rooms at the hotel, take a bath, clean up, and have a good meal? It's a long way to El Paso. Train food can't be very good." An image of Darius Worthing, sitting at a table in the train dining room, swaying with the motion and trying to put food into his mouth, flashed in Joe's mind. Knowing that Worthing probably wasn't in any mood to hear anything funny about his son, Joe struggled to keep his face straight.

They all agreed, even Buford Chedos, in going to the hotel, although he didn't mention taking a bath.

The hotel dining room wasn't very crowded at three in the afternoon and the five people were seated at a round table in the center of the large room. The only ones actually recognizable after a bath and change of clothes were Desda Manning and Tyler Worthing.

Desda had changed into a dark blue velvet dress that must have been made specially for her because it fitted too well to be store bought. Joe wondered if it had been a gift from Cruz Vega? Her butter-colored hair was piled up on her head in curls. She must have packed the dress.

Despite his wounded leg and slight limp, Worthing looked perfectly healthy in a blue shirt and blue-gabardine suit.

Buford Chedos would never pass for a member of the gentry with his slouched and bent-kneed walk, but neither did he look like a dirty bum now. His scraggly beard and dirty hair had been washed and trimmed. The gray in his beard and hair was actually silver. His baggy and tattered clothes had been replaced by a brown wool suit over a yellow shirt. Joe noticed though that he still wore the same scuffed boots.

"Well, I ain't givin' up ever'thin'," Chedos explained in a piqued voice, stroking his beard that was now about an inch shorter.

Joe hated to think what the water looked like after the old prospector had bathed in it. He hoped, as a shiver scurried up and down his back that the water had been poured out before someone else used it.

"I think you look very nice, Mr. Chedos," Desda complimented, fluttering her long lashes and sitting down in the chair that Mark pulled out for her at the table.

"Ye don't look so bad yerself," Chedos said, beaming at her.

Mark Humphrey looked completely different from when Joe had seen him four days ago. All of the scabs were gone from his carefully shaven face and only light pink dots were any evidence that he'd had smallpox. He wore new jeans and a dark green shirt. His light brown hair had been washed and trimmed. He'd probably bought new clothes to impress Desda.

Joe Howard hadn't bothered with a haircut, but had shaved after a long, soaking, hot bath. His left arm looked much better and should heal faster on the trip to El Paso since he wouldn't have to be using his hands in anything more strenuous than feeding himself.

His clean, white shirt and black pants felt good after wearing the same clothes for so long. He had to admit that the five of them would make a very distinctive group when they got on the train for El Paso later that afternoon.

As they ate, Joe kept looking across the table at Tyler Worthing, trying to remember what the big man had said that had gotten stuck in the quagmire of his brain. He couldn't understand why something was bothering him now. Tyler Worthing still had his money and his son was safe. Or he would be until his father arrived in El Paso. Joe, Mark, Desda, and Chedos were going to El Paso as Tyler Worthing's guests. Everything should be perfect. So, why was Joe still wondering about the kidnapping? It had been settled.

Joe hoped that whatever was bothering him would surface before they reached El Paso.

As the train cut through the mountains, across barren desert and over creeks, streams, and rivers, Joe agreed with Darius Worthing that a train ride beat the heck out of riding a stage. The seats were more comfortable and the food more varied. Tyler Worthing, who could have afforded a compartment, chose to sit with Joe and Chedos. Desda and Mark were inseparable.

Joe began noticing an increasing nervousness about Worthing as the train steamed toward El Paso. He wondered if the big man was worried about his forthcoming confrontation with his son or if it had something to do with what he'd heard Worthing say at the cabin after he'd killed Cruz Vega?

A midday sun, softened by a cool autumn breeze, filtered through the gray-tinged white clouds. It was a nice day. Not a day for family dissension. But that was bound to happen when the two Worthings met.

Joe didn't know who was the most nervous about seeing Darius Worthing; he or Tyler Worthing as they waited for the horses to be led from the boxed car at the end of the train. Buford Chedos had even brought old Smoke.

Joe felt knots in his stomach. He had planned on doing so many things to the insufferably spoiled fifteen-year-old, fat brat that he wasn't sure which one would give him the most pleasure. He enjoyed the idea most of tying the kid to a stake out in the middle of nowhere and, knowing how much Darius liked eating, to sit down before him at a table with everything imaginable on it and eat without offering the boy a single bite. He could almost see Darius salivating.

Joe had wondered about the odd name for over a week now and he had to know about it. Maybe Worthing and his wife had gotten it from some Greek or Latin story.

"Mr. Worthing," Joe began, grinning skeptically up at him, "may I ask you a question?" He dusted cinders from his coat.

"Sure," Worthing answered absently, looking up and down the tracks.

"Where in the devil did you get the name Darius?" Joe was set to hear something about a philosopher, or astrologer, or prophet.

"It was my father's name," Worthing replied simply.

"Oh," Joe said, shifting his weight from one foot to the other. He didn't think it would be a very good idea to ask anymore about it because he could see two bulges working hard in Tyler Worthing's jaws and his huge hands were gripped into fists at his side.

"Where do you think he'll be?" Joe asked, watching the big man intently. It was easy to see that a battle was raging inside him.

Worthing looked sideways at Joe for an instant then turned his full gaze on him. "Mr. Howard," Worthing began, sarcasm in his voice as he arched his brows and took a long, dejected breath, "if you were a boy that size, where in the devil would you be?" His voice dropped down in disgust and shook his head.

Joe blinked his eyes a couple of times and hoped to God he wouldn't laugh. Ridicule was the last thing Tyler Worthing needed right then. But, no matter how hard he tried, Joe couldn't control himself. Good-natured laughter, or so he hoped Worthing would think, burst from his mouth. Worthing turned red and glared at Joe. Joe was sure that the big man was going to rearrange his face.

But, he felt a little better when he saw a small grin pulling at Worthing's mouth.

By now, all of the horses, and mule had been unloaded and since the train station wasn't that far from the center of town, they decided to walk, after being on the train for so long and get the kinks out of their legs. Tyler Worthing led the short distance and stopped in front of the Desert Valley Hotel and Restaurant. "We'll check in later," he said.

Apparently Desda Manning wasn't as anxious as the men were to see what would happen between the Worthings. She said something to Mark, he blushed and nodded. She turned around, smiled at Joe then hurried into the hotel.

"Well, it's almost twelve," Worthing said resolutely, replacing the gold watch in his vest pocket. "We might as well go on in the restaurant. If Darius isn't there, he will be soon. He likes to eat early while there's still enough food." He took a deep breath, squared his massive shoulders and stepped up on the plank sidewalk.

Joe stepped around Worthing and opened the frosted, half-glass door. The aroma of food made Joe aware that he and the others hadn't really had a good meal since they'd left Candelaria. The food on the train had been good but it lacked something. But, from the stiff look on Worthing's red-hued face, Joe knew that food was the last thing on his mind.

The four men entered the spacious and well-appointed dining room. Joe looked around and even though the picture that Worthing had shown him had been taken almost a year ago, there was no mistaking the fat boy sitting at a table in the far right corner within easy distance of the kitchen. Darius Worthing was in his element with a red-and-white checked napkin tucked over his shirt collar and draped over his rotund stomach. Before him, on the checked-cloth covered table was probably everything the kitchen had to offer!

A plate of fried chicken. A bowl of mashed potatoes. A smaller bowl of yellow butter. Gravy. Greens. Corn on the cob. Biscuits. Chocolate cake. Last but not least, a pot of coffee and a tall glass of milk. His fat hands looked like eggbeaters as he shoveled the food into his already-full mouth. He was so engrossed in stuffing his face that he wasn't aware of anything or anyone around him. His head of curly brown hair swung from side to side as he chewed the mouthful only a couple of times before swallowing, apparently trying to decide what to put into his mouth next.

Joe caught hold of Worthing's thick arm and stopped him from going any farther into the dining room. Worthing looked down at Joe's hand and frowned disapprovingly. The army scout was probably the first one who'd touched him like that in a long time.

"Do you really want to get the kid?" Joe asked, mischief twinkling in his eyes as he disregarded Worthing's glare. Since it was he and Mark who had suffered a lot of pain and were almost killed because of Worthing's inconsiderate son, he thought he should have first crack at Darius.

"Sure," Worthing replied and nodded.

When Joe finished telling Worthing his plan, he was shocked and surprised when Worthing nodded again and laughed.

Tyler Worthing, Joe Howard, and Buford Chedos moved further into the sparsely filled restaurant in single file. Mark Humphrey, according to Joe's plan went back outside, just out of Darius's view, just in case he should look up from the food on the table. Mark would still be able to see what was going on.

The three men walked toward Darius Worthing's

table. The boy was enjoying his food so much that he wasn't even aware of them until his father called his name.

"Darius, are you enjoying your meal?" Tyler Worthing's voice was complacent although Joe caught an edge in it.

The boy almost choked on a mouthful of potatoes when he looked up to see his father smiling fondly down at him. He started to return the smile but it froze on his stuffed face when he realized that his father had arrived in El Paso before Mark Humphrey.

Joe saw drops of sweat popping out on Darius's round face and knew he was going to have a nervous fit because he didn't have any notes for his father.

"Oh, yes," Darius sputtered, swallowing the wad of food in his mouth. "The food is very good here." He licked his lips and some potatoes stuck to the corner of his mouth.

"How was the stage ride?" Worthing asked, pulling out a chair to Darius's right so Darius would have to turn his head fully in that direction to look at him. Worthing would still be able to see Mark, who was still standing outside at the edge of the window. "I hope you made enough notes about the route. A new stage run in that part of Texas will put a lot of money in our pockets. You can buy that custom-built carriage. Do you have the notes with you? I can read them while you eat."

If Joe hadn't known better, he would've sworn that a sweating, fat, brown-haired angel was sitting there, a fork in one hand and a knife in the other, from the innocent look on Darius Worthing's face.

"Well, I . . ." Darius began, picking up the coffee cup in his bulky hand that Joe noticed was shaking so much that some coffee sloshed out. Joe wondered, expectation pulling a knot in his stomach, how the kid was going to talk his way out of this? The terrified expression on Darius's fat, sweat-shining face had been worth the train ride from Candelaria to El Paso.

Joe wasn't disappointed when Tyler Worthing began shaking his head slowly from side to side and the smile vanished from the boy's face. Joe knew that Worthing didn't have the patience to sit there, playing games with Darius and listening to his son lie to him. And, Worthing knew that whatever Darius would tell him would be a lie because Mark Humphrey was standing outside without any notes.

The plan to lead Darius on had sounded good to Joe but he would probably have hurried things along if he knew that someone was lying to, or was going to lie to him. The big man held up his hand and motioned for Mark to come in.

Darius Worthing's face turned red and then as white as the checks in the tablecloth and his blue eyes widened more than they would ever have cause to again when he realized that his father already knew what he had done. Joe knew the guilty look on the boy's pale face was almost worth being tied to the stake at the snake pit at Alice Manning's house.

Mark Humphrey came stomping into the restaurant, anger blazing in his eyes. "Do you know that you almost got me killed?" he asked through clenched teeth. "I was kidnapped by a Mexican bandit. Joe Howard was sent by your father to find you after he found out that it was supposed to be you who was kidnapped. He helped me escape from a Mexican village!"

"You couldn't have been hurt too much then," Darius pointed out, taking a sip of coffee to regain a few degrees of his composure.

"No, we weren't hurt too much," Joe interrupted, taking a step toward the glutinous tub of guts. "We were just tied to stakes at a rattlesnake pit by a crazy old woman and her nephew." He held out his wrist so Darius could see the red mark around it left by the thin rope.

Joe felt good when the color drained from Darius's face again. "If Buford Chedos," he motioned, jabbing a thumb over his shoulder at the old prospector who was leaning against a chair, "hadn't been hiding up on a mesa and come down to cut us loose, the snakes, or other animals would have gotten us and *we would* have died."

"Did you say kidnapped?" Darius asked, batting his eyes as the word finally sank in, his hands falling to the table, the fork and knife clutched tightly in them. He batted his eyes and swallowed hard. "Thank God, I wasn't on that stage. I would've been kidnapped." He paused to take another sip of coffee to moisten his dry mouth. "Who kidnapped you?" He glanced back at Mark.

Something began working in the back of Joe's mind when he saw Darius throw a skeptical look at his father.

"Cruz Vega," Mark snapped, drawing Darius's now-frowning look back to him.

"Cruz Vega," Tyler Worthing said in a cold voice. Something happened in the big man and he flopped back in the chair, a wild expression replacing his placid smile. "I got that murdering bastard at last."

A hundred bells began ringing inside Joe's head at the same time as Worthing's last phrase popped into place. That's what he had been trying to remember for the past three days!

"What do you mean, 'you finally got Vega'?" Joe asked, a deep, angry frown pulling between his eyes as he stared down at Worthing. Something told him that he wouldn't like Worthing's explanation.

"Cruz Vega killed my wife last year," Worthing said

dryly, taking and expelling a deep breath, "when he held up a stagecoach not too far from San Angelo. I've wanted him dead ever since."

Joe felt sick in his stomach and he wanted to kill Tyler Worthing for what he'd tricked him into doing. Worthing had wanted Vega dead for killing his wife. Joe couldn't fault him for that. He was just angry that Worthing had relied on his pride and a little bit of egotism to, in Worthing's words, get Vega. Cold chills ran up and down Joe's back as a bitter taste burned up into his throat and mouth from his stomach. Was that the taste of hate, disgust, or embarrassment?

Joe remembered thinking that maybe, just maybe, Tyler Worthing might have had something to do with his son's kidnapping when he'd met him at Fort Davis almost a lifetime ago. He should have listened to his own misgivings. But would it have solved anything? Probably not.

"How and who did you plot with?" Joe asked around a hard lump in his throat. "Weren't you even a little afraid that he'd be killed?" He jerked a nod at Darius.

"No," Worthing answered calmly, shaking his head and taking hold of his coat lapels. "Rayfus Claxton, the stage manager in Pecos,"—Joe had already figured out that the stage manager in Pecos would be involved in the kidnapping,—"knew Vega. I told him to get in touch with Vega, tell him that a very rich man's son was going to be on a stage that would arrive in Fort Davis on a particular day. I even told Claxton to mention that I might be there on, or a few days after Darius was."

Joe stood listening to Worthing recount his plot and he couldn't believe it. He knew Worthing had more to say and maybe the rest of his sick explanation would make it clear.

"I knew Vega wouldn't kill Darius if he thought a lot of money was involved," Worthing continued, shifting his bulk in the chair. "It's too bad about that old man on the stage." There was no feeling in his voice.

"How much money?" Darius asked, tight-lipped disbelief on his pudgy face. He'd forgotten about all of the food on the table before him.

"A thousand dollars," Worthing replied, a smugness replacing the wild look in his eyes. "I knew the sheriff wouldn't go after Vega if there was a chance he'd end up in Mexico. I'd heard how good you were at scouting for wagon trains," Worthing looked cunningly up at Joe, "and I knew you'd end up killing Vega for me one way or another, either before or after reaching Candelaria."

"In other words," Joe said in tight-lipped anger, clutching the back of the wooden chair so he wouldn't yank the .45 from its holster and blow Tyler Worthing out of his chair as he wanted to, "you set up your son, and me, just so I'd kill Vega for you."

Joe stared down in disgust at Tyler Worthing. He couldn't believe how calm Worthing was about the entire matter.

"I've never seen anyone play a part as well as you have," Joe said, taking and expelling a deep breath. "You actually had me convinced that you were really worried about your son." Joe shook his head in absolute dismay. Tyler Worthing looked as if he'd been telling a story to a group of people or holding court.

"Didn't it occur to ye that the boy might'a put up a fight?" Buford Chedos asked, a deep frown adding another wrinkle to his grizzled brow. "He coulda got hurt, ye know." Chedos shifted his disgusted look from Worthing, over to Joe and then back to Worthing.

A stillness settled over Worthing's face before a smirk took its place, then turned into a smile.

"A fight?" Tyler Worthing scoffed incredulously. He looked at Chedos as if he'd just been asked the world's stupidest question. "Look at him." He turned toward his son, a repulsive snarl on his thick mouth. "How could he put up any kind of fight, for God's sake? His only defense would be falling or trampling on someone if they got between him and something to eat."

Darius Worthing blinked his eyes as wounded disbelief parted his lips and he stared at his father. "You don't have to be so mean," he said in a choked voice and swallowed hard.

Joe was sure he saw the boy's double chin quiver and he felt sorry for him. No one, especially a child, deserved this kind of humiliation.

"Did you really plan on buying the Overland Stage Line?" Mark asked, patting Darius's thick shoulder as he pulled out a chair beside him and sat down, his wide-eyed gaze riveted on Tyler Worthing. Pity had softened the glare in Mark's eyes.

"Of course not," Worthing snapped contemptuously, curling his lips. "That was just an excuse to get Darius on the stage and trap Cruz Vega."

"What would've happened if Darius, or as it turned out to be Mark, hadn't been kidnapped?" Joe asked, still having a hard time controlling himself. He wanted to shoot Tyler Worthing in the worst possible way. The man didn't deserve to live. Joe appreciated his loss in the death of his wife and sympathized with him up to a point. But that was no excuse for him to plot against his son to get revenge on Cruz Vega.

Tyler Worthing reminded Joe of a lizard he'd seen once. He'd stood and watched mesmerized as it changed colors. That's what Tyler Worthing had done. He'd seemed so concerned about his son when he'd come to the fort, almost foaming at the mouth, for someone to go after the boy, knowing perfectly well that Vega wouldn't give the boy up without a fight if there was a chance he would lose a thousand dollars.

Joe understood now why Worthing hadn't insisted on going with him when he'd ridden off alone to work on his own plan.

Now, Worthing had changed into a man who seemed like he couldn't wait to get away from his pale son who was still staring at him, waiting for his answer.

"We don't have to worry about that now, do we?" Worthing stated. He narrowed his eyes as the smugness crept across his face again. "Everything worked out the way it was supposed to. Cruz Vega is dead."

Joe Howard suddenly realized that he was presented with a problem. Tyler Worthing had plotted to have his son kidnapped with the ulterior motive of getting Cruz Vega killed. Would Tyler Worthing actually have minded if his son had been killed so long as Vega was out of the way?

But, kidnapping *was* against the law, no matter what the reason and there was no way, if Joe could possibly help it, that he was going to let Worthing get away with it.

Joe had let Alice Manning and Louis Smith go but he would tell Colonel Eric McRaney and Sheriff Sam Dusay about them as soon as he returned to Fort Davis and he knew they would be arrested. But he knew he couldn't turn his back on the Worthing situation and ride away from El Paso. Worthing had plotted so that Joe would kill for him. Alice Manning just wanted him dead for his horse.

"I thought Alice Manning was a poor excuse for a parent," Joe said, glaring at Worthing, grinding his teeth so hard he thought they'd crack, and knots stood out in his jaws. "But you're a lot worse than she'll ever be!" Joe's voice rose to a shout. He backed toward the door.

"Worthing, are you wearing a gun," Joe asked in a cold voice, jerking the Colt .45 from the holster, making a decision and aiming his gun at the still smirking man.

"No," Worthing said, shock freezing his mouth open. "Why? What are you doing?"

Joe wasn't going to take any chances. "Mark, search him." Joe took a quick breath. "Then we're going to find the sheriff."

The waiter and few customers in the restaurant hadn't made any attempt to get involved. They just watched in silence, the food getting cold on their plates.

Mark Humphrey got up and walked behind Worthing's chair. He patted over Worthing's coat, looked up at Joe, and shook his head.

"You're going to regret this," Worthing warned, shaking his head slowly, his eyes snapping.

"The only thing that I'll ever regret," Joe argued in a cold voice, "is getting involved in your sick-minded scheme in the first place. If you don't have a gun in your boot, let's go."

Worthing saw deadly intent in Joe's eyes. The army scout would probably shoot him right where he sat if he didn't do as he was told. He stood up and walked out on the plank sidewalk. Joe was close behind him.

"Hey, mister," the frightened waiter called out, holding a wooden tray in front of him, "the sheriff's office is across the street and down a block."

"Thanks," Joe said over his shoulder, feeling sorry for Darius Worthing as he continued sitting at the table, staring down at the mound of cold food on his plate.

Joe wondered why Tyler Worthing hadn't put up any kind of resistance as he walked ahead of him down the sidewalk. But maybe that wasn't important to him now. The big man had accomplished his mission.

"What 'er ye gonna do after we'uns find the sheriff?" Chedos asked, hurrying along beside Joe as he pounded down the sidewalk.

"After I tell the sheriff all about this sorry mess," Joe answered, feeling less betrayed and used, knowing that Tyler Worthing would be in jail in a little while, "you and Mark can back me up, I'm going to find the nearest saloon and get a cold beer. A town this size should have at least two saloons."

Joe turned his attention away from Worthing, who was still walking ahead of them and smiled at Chedos. For some reason, and he would later wonder why, he holstered the .45.

"Mr. Howard, look out!" Darius Worthing's high-pitched warning voice was full of terror. Joe didn't take the time to turn around to look at the boy, or wonder why he'd followed them.

In the scant amount of time that Joe had turned away from Worthing and looked at Buford Chedos, the big man had bent down, reached into his right boot and brought out a small, snub-nosed pistol. When he straightened up, the pistol was aimed directly at Joe. If he killed Joe, he'd have nothing to lose. He couldn't be hanged any higher.

"Drop the gun, Worthing," Joe said, cold fear washing over him. "You know this isn't worth getting killed over." Joe felt stupid. Here he was, telling a man, who had nothing to gain, to drop his gun when his own hands were empty. An expression of fury swept over Worthing's wide face.

"I'm not going to jail!" Worthing bellowed through clenched teeth.

Joe knew he had to do something. He could almost

see Worthing's finger tightening on the trigger. With a speed that had kept him alive more times than he wanted to count, Joe was somehow able to jerk the .45 from the holster and manage to get off a shot before Worthing pulled the trigger. But then he was aiming at a much larger target.

Joe's pistol exploded. The bullet tore into the center of Tyler Worthing's pale blue shirt right where the thumb-sized pearl tie tack would have been if Worthing hadn't decided not to wear it that morning. A small, black hole marred the shirt before Worthing reached up with his left hand, as if trying to claw something out of his chest.

Worthing took two stumbling steps backward from the impact and went crashing down on the plank sidewalk with a grunt. A reflex in Worthing's right finger squeezed the trigger. The pistol belched out a flame of yellow fire as the pistol ejected the bullet, which only drove a hole in the ground at Worthing's side.

By the time that Joe and everyone within hearing distance of the two shots had reached Tyler Worthing he was dead. Blood was seeping between Worthing's fingers where he gripped the shirt. His right hand still clutched the pistol handle at his side. His blue-green eyes stared at nothing. Joe knelt down beside the lifeless body, closed Worthing's eyes, took the pistol from his right hand, and eased Worthing's bloody left hand down by his side. Joe reached out, picked up Worthing's expensive hat and placed it over the bloody hole on Worthing's chest.

When Joe finally looked up, Darius Worthing was standing beside Mark Humphrey. Darius's face was pale in shock. What other feelings he had for his father had probably been destroyed by the big man's plot. But Joe felt like he owed the fat kid something even though Tyler Worthing had drawn on him.

"I'm sorry, Darius." The boy's name didn't taste too bad in Joe's mouth. "I had to do something. I guess I owe you my life." But then a thought struck Joe. "Why did you warn me? I just killed your father!"

"Don't worry about it," Darius said flatly, taking a deep, shuddering breath. "He plotted to have me kidnapped. No matter what he thought, I could've been killed. I guess he knew what would happen to him if he was sent to jail. He was a good father until Mama died. Then he didn't seem to like anybody. He . . ."

"What in the devil's going on here?" A gruff voice demanded, interrupting Darius and a medium-built man wearing a badge rushed up to Joe as he holstered the .45.

"I'll tell you all about it, sheriff," Joe said, looking down at the bewildered lawman, "right after we've had a beer."

"I'll drink to that," Buford Chedos said, licking his lips eagerly.

"I want one, too," Mark added. He must have forgotten about Desda. She was probably waiting for him at the hotel.

"Could I come along for a beer, too?" Darius asked, looking uncertainly up at Joe, down at his dead father and finally out into the street.

"You boys are too young to drink beer," Joe said, taking hold of the boy's thick arm to lead him past the body. He pulled in a deep breath and then expelled it. His job was finally over. "Beer's bad for your health." He felt stupid saying that. All of them could have been killed and beer was nowhere around. "You can have sarsaparilla."

"Then what 'er ye gonna do?" Buford Chedos

asked, a sorrowful expression on his wrinkled face and deep in his eyes.

"Start back," Joe answered, arching his brows. "It's a long way to Fort Davis. After I tell McRaney and Dusay about all of this, I'm going fishing."

"Kin I tag along with ye?" Chedos asked, flashing a skeptical grin up at Joe.

"Yeah, I guess so," Joe said, nodding and grinning. "I've sort of gotten used to you and that old mule ass."

Saddle-up to these

THE REGULATOR *by Dale Colter*
Sam Slater, blood brother of the Apache and a cunning bounty-hunter, is out to collect the big price on the heads of the murderous Pauley gang. He'll give them a single choice: surrender and live, or go for your sixgun.

THE REGULATOR—Diablo At Daybreak
by Dale Colter
The Governor wants the blood of the Apache murderers who ravaged his daughter. He gives Sam Slater a choice: work for him, or face a noose. Now Slater must hunt down the deadly renegade Chacon...Slater's Apache brother.

THE JUDGE *by Hank Edwards*
Federal Judge Clay Torn is more than a judge—sometimes he has to be the jury *and* the executioner. Torn pits himself against the most violent and ruthless man in Kansas, a battle whose final verdict will judge one man right...and one man dead.

THE JUDGE—War Clouds
by Hank Edwards
Judge Clay Torn rides into Dakota where the Cheyenne are painting for war and the army is shining steel and loading lead. If war breaks out, someone is going to make a pile of money on a river of blood.

HarperPaperbacks *By Mail*

5 great westerns!

THE RANGER *by Dan Mason*
Texas Ranger Lex Cranshaw is after a killer whose weapon isn't a gun, but a deadly noose. Cranshaw has vowed to stop at nothing to exact justice for the victims, whose numbers are still growing...but the next number up could be his own.

Here are 5 Western adventure tales that are as big as all outdoors! You'll thrill to the action and Western-style justice: swift, exciting, and man-to-man!

Buy 4 or more and save!
When you buy 4 or more books, the postage and handling is FREE!

VISA and MasterCard holders—call 1-800-331-3761 for fastest service!

MAIL TO: **Harper Collins Publishers, P. O. Box 588, Dunmore, PA 18512-0588, Tel: (800) 331-3761**

YES, send me the Western novels I've checked:
- ☐ **The Regulator** 0-06-100100-7 . . . $3.50
- ☐ **The Regulator/Diablo At Daybreak** 0-06-100140-6 . . . $3.50
- ☐ **The Judge** 0-06-100072-8 . . . $3.50
- ☐ **The Judge/War Clouds** 0-06-100131-7 . . . $3.50
- ☐ **The Ranger** 0-06-100110-4 . . . $3.50

SUBTOTAL . . . . $_____

POSTAGE AND HANDLING* . . . . $_____

SALES TAX (NJ, NY, PA residents) . . . . $_____

Remit in US funds, do not send cash

TOTAL: $_____

Name_____

Address_____

City_____

State_____ Zip_____

Allow up to 6 weeks delivery. Prices subject to change.

*Add $1 postage/handling for up to 3 books...
FREE postage/handling if you buy 4 or more.

H0131

If you enjoyed the Zane Grey book you have just read...

GET THESE 8 GREAT

Harper Paperbacks brings you Zane Grey,

THE RAINBOW TRAIL. Shefford rides a perilous trail to a small stone house near Red Lake, where a new enemy awaits him—and an Indian girl leads him on a dangerous adventure toward Paradise Valley and his explosive destiny.

THE DUDE RANGER. Greenhorn Ernest Selby inherits a sprawling Arizona ranch that's in big trouble. Pitted against the crooked ranch manager and his ruthless band of outlaws, Selby is sure bullets will fly....

THE BORDER LEGION. Roving outlaws led by the notorious Kells kidnap an innocent young bride and hold her in their frightening grasp. Thus begins a wave of crime that could be stopped only by a member of their own vicious legion of death.

THE MAN OF THE FOREST. Milt Dale wanders alone amid the timbered ridges and dark forests of the White Mountains. One night, he stumbles upon a frightening plot that drives him from his beloved wilderness with a dire warning and an inspiring message.

THE LOST WAGON TRAIN. Tough Civil War survivor Stephen Latch will never be the same again. Emerged from the bloodshed a bitter man, a brigand with a ready gun, he joins a raging Indian chief on a mission of terrifying revenge—to massacre a pioneer train of 160 wagons. But fate has a big surprise!

WILDFIRE. Wildfire is a legend, a fiery red stallion who is captured and broken by horse trainer Lin Stone. A glorious beast, a miracle, Wildfire is also a curse—a horse who could run like the wind and who could also spill the blood of those who love him most.

HarperPaperbacks By Mail

ZANE GREY WESTERNS
the greatest chronicler of the American West!

Zane Grey is a true legend. His best selling novels have thrilled generations of readers with heart-and guts characters, hard shooting action, and high-plains panoramas. Zane Grey is the genuine article, the real spirit of the Old West.

Buy 4 or More and $ave

When you buy 4 or more books from Harper Paperbacks, the Postage and Handling is **FREE**.

SUNSET PASS. Six years ago Trueman Rock killed a man in Wagontongue. Now he's back and in trouble again. But this time it's the whole valley's trouble—killing trouble—and only Rock's blazing six-gun can stop it.

30,000 ON THE HOOF. Logan Huett, former scout for General Crook on his campaign into Apache territory, carries his innocent new bride off to a life in a lonely canyon where human and animal predators threaten his dream of raising a strong family and a magnificent herd.

MAIL TO: Harper Collins Publishers
P. O. Box 588, Dunmore, PA 18512-0588
Telephone: (800) 331-3761

Visa and MasterCard holders—call
1-800-331-3761 for fastest service!

Yes, please send me the Zane Grey Western adventures I have checked:
- ☐ The Rainbow Trail (0-06-100080-9) $3.50
- ☐ The Dude Ranger (0-06-100055-8) $3.50
- ☐ The Lost Wagon Train (0-06-100064-7).......$3.50
- ☐ Wildfire (0-06-100081-7)..................$3.50
- ☐ The Man Of The Forest (0-06-100082-5)....$3.50
- ☐ The Border Legion (0-06-100083-3) $3.50
- ☐ Sunset Pass (0-06-100084-1)..............$3.50
- ☐ 30,000 On The Hoof (0-06-100085-X).......$3.50

SUBTOTAL ....$_____

POSTAGE AND HANDLING* ....$_____

SALES TAX (NJ, NY, PA residents) ....$_____

TOTAL: $_____
(Remit in US funds, do not send cash.)

Name_____

Address_____

City_____

State_____ Zip_____ Allow up to 6 weeks delivery. Prices subject to change.

*Add $1 postage/handling for up to 3 books...
 FREE postage/handling if you buy 4 or more.

H0011
HP-001-12 11 10 9 8 7 6 5 4 3 2 1